1...LAST LIE SHE TOLD

LIES AND MISDIRECTION(BOOK 1)

K. J. MCGILLICK

THE LAST LIE SHE TOLD

ISBN-13: 978-1722307042

ISBN-10: 1722307048

DEDICATION

In memory of my grandparents Florence and William

Dedicated to my son Mark-Michael and grandchildren Rinoa
and Jude

THE LAST LIE SHE TOLD

CHAPTER ONE

Jackson

A S I GAZED OUT THE WINDOW OVER THE DOWNTOWN DENVER skyline, my mind wandered. I didn't regret having left the FBI, the decision to leave had been a good one. But in the past, I'd gotten to work on cases as they'd been assigned to me. Now, as the owner of my own security firm, I felt I had to take every case that came through the doors in order to stay afloat.

I refocused on the conference call we were having with Benjamin Hightower, an old high school buddy, whose baritone voice emanated from a triangular speaker. He'd gone into corporate business and was now CEO of a biotechnology firm, while I'd chosen law enforcement, working as a US attorney and then as an FBI agent. He was asking for my help. A vital new piece of research of cutting edge technology had been stolen from his firm.

I looked around the conference table at my employees as they took notes. Mary, a ninety-year-old investigator with white puffy hair and oversized black glasses, and Lee, an ex-Chicago cop I'd hired as a skip trace person, were engaged in the conversation.

Benjamin gave us a rundown of the crime scene. "The

pictures were nauseating, Jackson," Benjamin said. "Dennis's ankles looked like barbequed pulled pork. The blood-crusted handcuffs had dug so far into his skin I'm positive the metal met bone. The handcuffs had chunks of skin and hair embedded in the small wells; they had rubbed his wrists raw and had cut into the tendons."

Mary made a face of disgust while Benjamin paused to collect his thoughts. He sounded exhausted, but he pushed on.

"I don't understand how people stomach the savage destruction people do to each other. What the hell is wrong with people?"

"You'd be surprised how desensitized our civilization has become," Lee, the new member of my team, said. "When I worked Chicago's gang division and then homicide it felt like I was in the middle of some tribal war."

Benjamin let that sit and continued. "The crime scene photos showed three stab marks inflicted without hesitation at points that would cause the most damage. I'm not a blood splatter expert, but it looked like someone had straddled Dennis at the hips and plunged the blade from a back overhead reach into his stomach until the blade hilt fully sank into his stomach. The attacker ripped the blade upward and then tore it out. Think of the brutality it took to cut him open like that—gutted like a deer. The stab penetrated his aorta and killed him.

"But from what the report indicated, the punctures in his femoral arteries triggered the gusher-like blood spray, which was easy to visualize pulsating in rhythm with each heartbeat. Jackson, I swear, the room looked like Pollock had risen from the dead just to put his signature splatter and drip marks on the cream-colored walls," Benjamin said, taking a deep breath through his nose.

"They found Ryan passed out next to Dennis. His chest was smeared with dry blood, and his face was painted with blood in a war paint manner. He had no visible injuries but was in a coma. They transported him to the hospital.

"A long blade, like a hunting knife, was found on the floor. Part of the handle was still sticky with brown, crusted blood. The sheets were soaked with whatever blood hadn't hit the walls. The report said the room had a metallic and urine smell."

Benjamin's voice wavered, and I wouldn't be surprised if he bolted to puke. I suppose that visual of all that blood burned into your brain would haunt you forever.

"So, what makes you think this Fiona person was with them?" Lee asked as he jotted notes on his short yellow pad.

"There aren't any cameras at the motel. But when the police took statements, one witness said she'd seen a woman matching Fiona's description knock on the door ten minutes after the men entered. However, the witness appeared inebriated, so they're taking what she said with a grain of salt. There's no physical evidence placing her in the room," Benjamin said.

"What a mess," Lee said.

"But I don't understand why you need us," I said. "You need to let local law enforcement handle this mess. This is a job for them."

"I need you to find Fiona. The police are treating this case as a murder. Ryan's in the hospital with high levels of ketamine. If he wakes up, he might not remember anything, and there's no physical evidence he murdered Dennis. But I believe they feel strongly that Ryan is the main suspect in the murder. The police aren't going to look for Fiona. They're going to focus on the murder, and unless Fiona becomes a person of interest or she's dead too, she's not on their radar. Fiona is an adult, and the police said our only option was to file a missing person report, if warranted.

"Here's my dilemma, Jackson. Ryan, Fiona, and Dennis were working on a sensitive project. Someone in that department stole the entire research project and wiped the server and cloud of all data." He hesitated.

"So why not alert the FBI or local law enforcement?" Mary interjected, raising an eyebrow and leaning forward to get closer to the speaker on the table.

Benjamin cleared his throat. "We acquired the project from a lab in Berlin. Berlin found a mechanism that allows the alteration of DNA at the base level. The implications are enormous. Upon completion of the project, our price to sell it would be in the neighborhood of half a billion. It could be used for good, to cure disease, or for bad, to alter existing DNA after someone committed a crime. Whoever stole the project, wiped all the servers of the information after they completed the transfer to an external drive. On the dark web, it could be sold for billions. We wanted to sell it to one entity, so that party could fully develop it and market it. On the dark web, however, it could be sold again and again. So where is it? Either Dennis hid it, or Ryan or Fiona have it. I need you to find out which one of them has it, or where they hid it."

"So, like Mary said, why not get the FBI involved?" Lee asked, fishing for an explanation that seemed to be hidden.

After an uncomfortable silence, Benjamin said, "We obtained the information in a manner that might be frowned upon by the government. We've been working under their radar, and if I tell them what we lost, they may open an investigation into everything we've been doing, and I can't have that."

Well, that didn't sound good. The last thing we needed to

do was to get involved in something illegal. However, Benjamin had only asked us to find the project, not help him develop it, and we had no reason to believe he planned to use it for nefarious purposes despite the fact the circumstances he acquired it under were shady.

"If you're in the middle of something illegal, and a crime is being committed, you realize we can't help—"

"What's your best guess where this information is?" Mary interrupted.

I signaled for her to be quiet. I needed to determine, if we took this case, if we'd be accessories to a crime before we continued the conversation.

"I've no idea. What I'm sure of is that at some point someone transferred it to an external drive; then someone destroyed that sector of the server and the cloud data. Anyone on the team, knew how to wipe the data.

"According to the police evidence list, no external drive was recovered at the motel or when they searched Dennis's and Ryan's homes," Benjamin said, sounding anxious.

"Let me make sure I've got this right," Lee said, removing his boots from the table. "Until the day of the motel incident, you were in possession of information with a high-value price tag. That day, some unknown person or people stole it. We know one of three employees who had access to it was murdered, and another was drugged and is in a coma. The third employee, who may or may not be involved, either left or met with foul play. No evidence was recovered to suggest either of the two men were in physical possession of the external drive. No one knows where this Fiona is, why she left, or if she has the drive. To be crystal clear, you want us to track down the drive, and that will be our only objective. You don't want us to bring

Fiona back, but you think she has the drive. Is that correct?"

"Yes," Benjamin answered quickly. "If she stole it, ideally I'd like her prosecuted. But that would open a Pandora's box for me."

I had to stop this before my employees talked a prospective client out of hiring us. I gave them the "wrap it up" sign.

"Benjamin, I emailed you our engagement contract, which has a non-disclosure in it. You can wire-transfer the funds. I'll arrange for Mary and Lee to meet with you day after tomorrow," I said. "Dropbox whatever information is available, and we'll be ready. Talk later."

"So, thoughts?" I asked after I'd hung up.

"BDSM gone wrong?" Mary asked.

Naturally, Mary would go to the most salacious theory. Mary was a complex woman. Three years ago, she'd helped close a dangerous FBI case, and last year she'd earned her private investigator license. The fact she looked like the mother from *The Golden Girls* often led people to underestimate her.

Lee sipped his coffee, and his eyes met mine over the rim of his cup.

"I'm not sure we're not walking close to an obstruction of justice here. Don't the police have a right to know what might be at the root of this incident?"

Lee had a point, and because both of us had come from a law enforcement background, we knew there were lines we couldn't cross.

"Lee, let me pose it to you this way. We don't have proof the information has anything to do with the incident at the motel. Maybe two people got high, and drugs fueled a murder. Perhaps, as Mary said, a BDSM encounter went wrong.

"The police have that investigation underway. We have no

credible evidence that this Fiona chick was there, or that she had any part in that incident or has the missing information. We're being hired to track down a missing drive, not to solve a crime," I said.

My email inbox dinged, alerting me the signed documents from Benjamin were waiting for my signature. The vibe I had at this point told me to rethink this, but we needed the money. I didn't have the luxury of thinking like an employee anymore. I had to evaluate this as a businessman.

"Hey, you're the boss. You sign my paycheck, and if this is how you want to spin it, I'm in. But, if we come across information that has something to do with this murder we'll need to have another conversation," Lee said.

I understood how he felt. With his twenty-two-year background on the Chicago police force, Lee seemed to be a person who liked rules and regulation.

"Not necessarily," Mary interrupted.

Christ, here we go.

"There's no law that mandates saving a drowning person. There's no law saying you must do the cops' job for them or volunteer information to them. My opinion is the NDA should protect you. If they ask specific questions, that may be a different story, but I don't even think that could hold water toward an obstruction charge."

I wanted to ask her where she'd received her law degree, but I was too afraid of her answer.

"It's a slippery slope. Right now, there's no evidence to suggest the homicide had anything to do with the missing information. We've no idea who the players are, so let's put the murder aside and treat it like a red herring. We'll treat our case as solving a corporate espionage and a theft. Everyone is a suspect. Get with their IT and security people and start your investigation there. Now, are we all on board?" I looked from Mary to Lee.

I could read from Mary's eyes she was in on the plan. Lee rubbed his face, stretched, then nodded.

"Who's going to be in charge?" Mary asked, tapping her papers on the table.

"Lee."

There was no doubt this case demanded a seasoned investigator.

"Why?" she asked, ready to argue.

"Because he has more experience than you," I threw back, hoping to cut off any more argument.

"Maybe he has more homicide experience, but I thought you said the homicide wasn't a factor? I'm an equity partner, and I should take the lead."

She stood, bracing her hands on the table and tilting forward. God, if her white cotton hair moved, or her black owl glasses slipped down her nose, we were screwed. That was always a signal she was in the fight for the long haul.

"Hey, people, I'm good with that; let her take the lead," Lee responded as he stood and headed toward the door.

"Why? What's the catch?" Mary asked, disappointed when no argument or drama ensued.

"You get to do the paperwork and arrange the timetable. I float along and do my job."

Lee smiled and sauntered out, closing the door behind him. Smart. He didn't want Mary calling after him with a change of heart.

"Guess I fell right into that." She plunked back down in her seat, deflated.

All I could do was smile because Lee had bested Mary at

her own game.

"Get the plane tickets, and get out there to Seattle and meet with Benjamin's people. In the meantime, he's sending us personnel records and anything pertinent to the crime scene, including the lab area where they worked and the motel. Anything else you need, boss lady?"

"Nope," she said, not trying to cover her anger as she stomped from the room.

Mary was a necessary evil and my nemesis. We'd opened this office after Cillian, my old partner, and I had left the FBI. The venture had become more complicated than we'd expected. Between the move from Washington, DC, to Colorado, and the actual financial commitment we'd made, this new enterprise had proved more cumbersome than we'd predicted. Thank God Mary had offered the money left from her age discrimination suit to get us up and running. But that brought other problems. She was now an equity partner with voting rights, a nightmare we'd never considered.

Lee was a godsend. His experience in the Chicago police department brought the practical experience we needed, and it balanced Mary's need to blow things out of proportion. Lee was drama-free while Mary lived in a world of organized chaos. He and Mary seemed determined to outwit each other.

My phone buzzed with a text; the bank had received the retainer funds. A $125,000 retainer should go a long way to keep us afloat. With this in mind, I texted Mary to upgrade the seats to Seattle to first class. Usually we flew economy, but this gave us an opportunity to work in private on the plan. My email dinged. The files I'd requested were in my Dropbox, and I forwarded them to Mary and Lee to help them to get a jump on the case.

CHAPTER
TWO

Lee

IRPORTS, I HATE AIRPORTS. TOO MUCH HURRY UP AND WAIT, AND too much chaos. I like my world orderly and logical. As Mary and I rushed to our terminal, I remembered how I'd had second thoughts before accepting another law enforcement-type position, but what else was I equipped to do? At my age, how could I start in an entirely new career? The wicked things people do to each other, and the excuses they make up to justify it, disgusted me. The gang murders in Chicago had become a standard, daily expectation. After a while, I didn't see the victims as people anymore. Instead, when I arrived on the scene, my mind clocked the wounds, and the weapon used. Nothing else applied to my assessment.

I knew I had to get out. The invisible tap on the shoulder for me to resign came out of a domestic violence murder. The place was an affluent address officers had visited too many times over the past year. An attractive young woman lay dead on her bedroom floor, a victim of a prolonged beating that had continued even after death. Investigating the scene and listening to her husband rant had almost prompted me to verbalize, "So what did she expect? That he would change?" I blamed the victim for her death.

At that point, I realized I'd gone beyond jaded to callous, and it was time to leave the force. I had burned out; I was no longer able to speak for the victim. I'd lost part of my soul when my wife had died of breast cancer, and the job had eaten up the rest of it. At forty-two, I felt the emotional weariness of a seventy-year-old. I had seen too much as a cop that was impossible to forget. Sex was a faceless release of tension for me, and when a woman inched a little too close, expecting a piece of my heart, I cut her loose.

"Lee, is that OK with you?" I heard Mary say as she shoved a paper toward me.

"Look, Mary, no offense, but I should take the lead in the employee interviews. I've done this for the last ten years on hundreds of cases. It takes years to learn how to make people drop their guard. I've watched you question people, and they become defensive. You have this nonverbal accusatory way about you. In some situations, your age works for you, and in other situations, people don't take you seriously," I said with a nonchalant shrug. It was the truth; why sugarcoat it? I wasn't saying it to be difficult, just stating a fact.

"In a corporate culture, where most people have not one but two PhDs, I'll go out on a limb and say you're out of your depth," I continued. "You can't outthink them, so you'll need to rely on instinct. You're the lead. If you want to do the interviews, I have to accept it. However, Jackson hired me for my skill set, and one skill I've honed is how to get information from people."

Mary's sharp eyes bored into mine with an unwavering stare, not even a blink. The realization I didn't care and wouldn't participate in her drama caused her to lean her fluffy hair against the headrest. Her body language taut, tension radiated from her as if she wanted to unload on me, but she worked hard to hold it back.

"I'm not sure I like you. You're not much of a people person, and you could use some work on your communication technique," she said, averting her gaze.

Fair enough, a correct assessment.

"Mary, I get that, but talking is overrated. I say what I mean. That's all you have to understand for us to get along. I respect your accomplishments and the skills you bring to the table, but I'm here to do a job, give your company the best I can, and get paid. So, if my honesty offends you, get over it, or fire me, because those are your only two options."

I stretched my legs forward and reached into the seat pocket where I'd stashed a bottle of water.

"Think of this encounter with me as your good karma in life," Mary said with a head bob. Impossible. I didn't need to share my feelings with her; I wasn't that guy. "Pretty Zen, Mary," I said, acknowledging I'd heard her but attempting to cut her off from saying more.

"Lee, you have no idea. Picture me as your personal life coach, your own Tony Robbins," she said, tapping the armrest.

"Who the hell is that?"

"He is one of the greatest motivational speakers of our times. Google it."

"Think I'll pass," I replied, gazing out the window, uncaring.

Benjamin Hightower's office was an architectural wonder, combining glass, steel, and wood to make a distinct first impression. Not a place I'd find comfortable to work in but aesthetically pleasing. The offices surrounding his were encased in glass. Nowhere for anyone to hide. It appeared our client wasn't a trusting soul. Possibly his secrets caused him to add a layer of caution.

As we entered his office, he hit a button, and the glass frosted over for privacy. Good trick. He could still see out, but no one could see in.

Like his habitat, Hightower was sleek, polished, and reeked of money. His yellow tie against his crisp white shirt and gray suit set the tone of exactly what to expect from him. Efficiency and a mover and shaker. I'd already decided we couldn't trust him, because he'd admitted to being involved in a questionable, if not illegal, activity.

I was about to open my mouth when Mary began. "Good morning, Benjamin, you have a lovely facility."

Before he could position himself behind his desk, Mary walked to a conversation area with a round table, sat down, and waited for us to join her. OK, I had to admit that was a good move, take him out of his comfort zone and level the playing field.

Once we were seated and our pads were out, I again tried to open the conversation, but Mary again jumped right in with no small talk.

"All your employees are required to have a high-security clearance akin to a government standard. Why is that?" she asked, leaning forward.

He looked a bit startled. Obviously not a question he had come prepared to answer.

"Sometimes we review government projects, and that's a government requirement." He leaned back, pulled at his right cuff, and balanced his right foot on his left knee.

"I see Fiona didn't have that clearance. Why is that?" she asked.

A good question I hadn't thought to pose.

"We'd never assign a person on probation to a project that needed security clearance. Once she had been here for six months, that would've been a requirement," he answered without voice inflection, returning Mary's stare.

"So, how did she get access to this project to steal it, if she did? It's marked classified, so she must have had some level of clearance," Mary said.

Benjamin leaned forward with his elbows on the table, steepling his index fingers under his chin. "Let me be clear; I never said she stole the project. I said she was a person of interest who may be in possession of my information."

Wait, why was he being so evasive now?

"Care to elaborate?" I asked.

He continued, "Fiona had amassed many male admirers, and I believe one of them may have taken the project for her. However, I have no evidence to substantiate that conclusion. It's just a gut feeling."

"Did you rule out that the other two men, Ryan and Dennis, removed it for their personal use? Or are you saying they may have been the conduit for Fiona?" Mary tapped her ballpoint pen twice on her notepad, making an indent.

"The latter," he replied, his shoulders stiffened. "To be candid, I'm uncertain we would have extended a permanent offer to Fiona after her probation. Her work was meticulous, but she was becoming a distraction in the work environment."

This would be a good time to tease out more information. I leaned forward with my forearms balancing on my legs in a non-threatening stance. Before I could speak, Mary steamrolled over me.

"You had sex with her."

It was a statement not a question. Surely such a base-less accusation would have Hightower showing us the door. Jackson was going to be furious.

Without losing a beat, he responded, "A brief regrettable indiscretion."

She nodded in understanding. "OK, that's out of the way. I prepared a list of people we need to interview today," she said, handing him the list.

"You can use conference room 211. While you set up, Nancy, my administrative assistant, will ask their project super-visor to escort them to you." Hightower rose, and as he walked out the door, he hit the button to clear the glass of frost. We followed him.

Our walk was short, and he pushed the thick glass door to another glass-walled room. He excused himself as we settled in.

I walked to the ceiling-to-floor windows to admire the view of Seattle and to try to absorb the energy of the place. All this glass, so cold, so exposed. I turned to ask Mary how she came to her conclusions but waited when I saw her busily scribbling on her pad. As I moved to take a seat opposite her, she motioned me over to her with a tip of the head. I ambled over next to her and glanced at her pad.

She'd written, "Three cameras in the room" and marked X's for their placement. My eyes casually swept the room and landed on the well-hidden devices. Was Hightower monitoring us, his employees, or all of us? I didn't like that he was observ-ing us without our permission, and I didn't like that he'd had a fling with Fiona. I hoped this wasn't some wild goose chase to find this girl because he was a spurned lover, and she'd decided to cut and run.

From the interviews we conducted, Fiona appeared to be a charismatic woman who knew her way around a man's ego. Her academic record proved exemplary, and she was a member of Mensa. In other words, she was a genius. There were no complaints about her work. The interviews produced nothing of interest that would lead us to believe Fiona had stolen the drive. However, it troubled me that Fiona had shown way too much interest in the information's end use.

The only thing that caught Mary's interest was the one co-worker who had indicated Fiona had approached him to escort her to a venue. Once he'd arrived, he felt she'd duped him into attending. She had taken him to a BDSM dungeon that had proven to be a bad experience for him, and that was all he would say. He provided us with the address of the place and said it was a private, high-end sex club. I took satisfaction thinking that, if Hightower was watching, I hoped he was having a panic attack wondering if he should make an immediate appointment to be tested for STDs. Served him right. This piece of information was something worth investigating, though, considering the way the crime scene appeared.

By the end of the afternoon, we were no closer to determining the chain of events. The camera footage in the lab had been erased, leaving nothing to help us answer who, what, when, why, or how.

As we packed up to leave, Hightower told us Ryan was conscious and alert enough for the police to interview him.

Although he would remain a person of interest, they hadn't arrested him. There were no fingerprints on the handle of the knife, and the fact he'd been in the room was circumstantial, not direct evidence. I'd have loved fifteen minutes to question him. He'd know if Fiona had been in the motel room or not. But that would be out of the question; we'd never be allowed access to him at this point.

Although Mary and I argued about investigating the sex club, I overruled her. We told Hightower our next stop would be the university Fiona had graduated from in Los Angeles. We wanted to get a feel for her from people she'd interacted with for over two years. In the back of my mind, it niggled away at me that someone may have abducted her to get the drive she'd hidden, or had taken her for some other evil reason. With little else to go on, visiting the university was our plan, and Hightower was on board.

We settled into our booth, and I ordered a Jameson, and Mary ordered a cola. I needed to feel the burn slipping down my throat to clear my head. People committed homicides for a reason. Revenge, jealousy, anger, and greed were the top reasons. Less often mental health issues came into play. I still couldn't figure out the motive behind this murder, but I reminded myself it wasn't ours to solve.

"I'm stumped," Mary admitted, cleaning her silverware with the linen napkin. "No one stands out. If we knew why Fiona disappeared, we could probably figure out how."

"I agree. Nothing feels right about Fiona stealing the project. She had a low-security clearance, and it would have been difficult for her to access that project without help. But why run if you're not guilty? And who wiped the server? I would think you'd need a background in IT for that."

"We can sit here all night and go through what-ifs, but it will circle us around to where we are now. Let's proceed as if she's guilty and take a week to gather information about her. What else can we do? The police have searched the men's apartments and don't have probable cause to search hers, unless they accept Benjamin's missing person report. So, let's head to LA, as we planned, and see what turns up," Mary said.

"You're the boss," I replied, throwing back the rest of the whiskey.

"So, what's your story? Do you enjoy doing the skip tracing for the firm?" Mary asked, placing her silverware next to each other.

"For now." I shrugged, twirling the glass, waiting for a refill.

"Got big plans?" she asked as the waitress saw my empty glass and nodded.

"Living day to day, Mary."

"Not much of a talker," she said.

I suppose this was her way to engage me to share my feelings.

"Nope."

"Well then, I'll accept that as a challenge to crack you open like a walnut," she retorted as she moved aside for the waitress to replace my drink and take our order.

"Knock yourself out."

We plotted our next two days and finished the meal in relative silence. After Mary finished her dessert and mine, we retired for the night to prepare for an early flight to LA.

I spent the next two hours, before dozing off, researching

Benjamin Hightower and didn't like what I found. Several years back, he'd been investigated for insider trading, but no charges had been filed. And the FDA had pulled some of the clinical trials he had worked on but hadn't disclosed why. I wondered if Jackson knew what his friend had been up to?

CHAPTER THREE

Lee

L os Angeles, I hate it. Please, Governor Moonbeam, secede from being a member state. Go your own way. Do it, now.
"Mr. Stone and Ms. Collier, Dean Mathison will see you now," the secretary said as she waved us toward his office door.

"Thank you, dear," Mary said. "Your hair is so pretty and full of volume. Are those extensions that make it so sexy? I've thought of getting some myself. Bubblegum pink would be my choice."

The young lady's face went from a full smile while accepting the compliment to shock as the visual of Mary with bubblegum-pink extensions manifested in her mind. What the hell was she thinking? That fluffy cotton-white hair that reminded me of a Q-tip, streaked with pink, what a nightmare to picture. Not the best look for her. Poor receptionist may be damaged for life.

I moved Mary forward with a hand to her back. "Mary, you ladies can swap beauty tips later."

The man behind the desk, the dean of students, looked to be in his early sixties and appeared to be the school's head airhead.

He guided us toward the left by the window and offered us a seat in a small conversation area. We told him a legally sanitized version of why we were looking for Fiona O'Dell. That version emphasized the fact she hadn't arrived for work one morning, and we were treating her as a missing person.

"I am sorry, Mr. Stone; you made this trip for nothing. We are under a contract with Ms. O'Dell that prohibits me from speaking about her except to say she was a student and graduated. I can add that since she left, I have not seen nor had any contact with her." He shifted and assumed a defensive position.

Mary and I exchanged glances, which she broke to address him. Mary had an impressive ability to morph at will into different personas, a real chameleon. Today she chose her "Trust me; I'm a little old lady" persona.

"Dean Mathison, please indulge me. I can become forgetful at my age; that's why Lee is here to keep me on track." She smiled and patted my hand in a grandmotherly fashion. "We won't take up much of your time and don't want to place you in an awkward position."

His body unfolded and relaxed; he'd bought it.

"Lee, sweetheart, can you be a good boy, and fish out my note pad and pen from my purse so I can take a few notes?" she asked as her large glasses eased their way down her nose.

As requested, I rummaged through her purse, which, to my horror, was replete with makeshift weapons. I saw a pen that was pepper spray, a lipstick stun gun, and hornet repellent I assumed was for an emergency. We'd be having a serious talk later.

"Now, Dean, my understanding is an incident occurred involving Fiona that embarrassed the school. We don't need the details," Mary said with a dismissive wave.

Wait, what? When were we briefed on this; had I missed something?

"Now, now, don't be uncomfortable. I can understand your hesitancy to share the details. Would you tell us who Ms. O'Dell's last roommate was?" Mary asked with her brightest smile. "If my granddaughter were missing and had everyone worried to death that something had happened to her, I'd hope people would cooperate."

The dean sat back and pondered the conundrum she'd placed him in.

"We guard our students' privacy. The most I can say that may help you is that the news articles mentioned information about her roommate, and we tried to rectify that blunder. I would be more comfortable if you tracked her down through an independent source. Is that all?" he said, standing to signal the meeting was over.

It was clear we couldn't pry any more information from him, so we thanked him and left.

We availed ourselves of one of the many green spaces on campus. Mary found a stone bench and claimed it by placing her massive bag on it. We needed to regroup.

I paced around the bench before I lost my shit. "What the hell, Mary! A heads-up you'd found information would've been nice!" I said as she sat on the stone bench.

She looked up at me for a moment, then opened her enormous handbag, and removed a tablet. After adjusting her hideous owl glasses, she focused on the screen and waited for her search results to appear.

"Mary, did you hear me?" I asked, becoming more annoyed.

She responded by handing me the tablet. I skimmed the article as I planted my ass on the stone bench.

I hit the back arrow and found the only other article about the incident at the school involving Fiona. The school, or someone, had used clout to make the matter disappear.

"Damn. How did you know?"

"Lee, no one signs a non-disclosure unless something bad has happened. I bluffed, and he folded. The article doesn't give the roommate's name but gives the student complex name, so let's start there; there's always a blabbermouth on hand. Let me do the talking while I'm into my little-old-lady frame of mind. Now, before we go, I need to fuel up on caffeine. There has to be a Starbucks in the student center. Let's go." She packed her tablet and intertwined her arm with mine; I suppose in character with her old-lady role. With Mary, you never knew what her game entailed. We were all her puppets being moved around at her will.

The unsecured entrance to the building was too accessible, and someone needed to tighten up security. A visit to the resident assistant's office gave us the name of Fiona's last known roommate, Claire, who still had a room in the grad student apartments. After a few turns through crowded hallways and an elevator ride up to the fifth floor, we were knocking on a door. A disheveled woman of about twenty-five, who appeared to have just awoken, opened the door. After we explained we were tracking down Fiona, she leaned against the doorjamb to consider our request. Her eyes darted back and forth, and she chewed her right thumbnail for a few moments before she invited us in.

She excused herself to change, a definite sign she was willing to spend time with us.

"Lee, I changed my mind; you take this one. She gave you the twice over, and obviously wants to impress you," Mary whispered. "Make sure you call her Claire, not miss. She wants to get personal."

"Thanks for the tip, Mary," I said, having to restrain an eye roll.

Claire returned dressed in yoga pants that were too tight and a top showing too much cleavage. Christ, the girl was young enough to be my daughter.

"Claire, what can you tell us about the incident?" I asked, giving a quick eye sweep around the room.

The girl disliked Fiona, and because of that, we gained a wealth of information. "She asked for it," she said, snapping her hair into a ponytail as she leaned forward in the oversized chair.

Now that was unexpected. "How so?" I asked.

"I didn't know her endgame, but what girl in her right mind dresses like she's every guy's Catholic schoolgirl fantasy?" she asked. She leaned back as she brought her legs up onto the chair.

"Pardon?"

"You know, the whole plaid skirt and saddle shoes. Every morning I'd watch Fiona put her costume on, different skirts, same style. She'd start with the oxford white shirts with darts at the chest to make sure it was taut there, and you'd be drawn in to check out her boobs on display because she'd left one-too-many buttons unbuttoned. Then the too-short box pleated skirt so that when she bent over to adjust her slouchy socks, you'd get an eyeful of her lace panties. And don't get me started on how she polished those stupid shoes every night. Because the worst is yet to come, those stupid, stupid high-on-the-head pigtails just did me in." She took a breath to collect her thoughts

24

and calm down.

"So, she wore a variation of this outfit every day?" I clarified. This conjured a fantasy I had to wipe from my mind to avoid an embarrassing situation that threatened to develop.

"Yes, except when she went to her sex club. Then it was all leather, and 'Look at me I'm a dominatrix.' That crazy bitch even had nipple rings. I mean how, no, *why* would anyone want to put themselves through that much pain?" She looked between Mary and me for the answer to the question.

I had no clue how to answer.

"Shameful," Mary responded.

She nodded. "Right? So what did she expect advertising her goods like that?"

"Did that behavior attract a lot of male attention?" Mary asked, as if taking her into her confidence.

"Of course. Light blonde hair, schoolgirl fantasy, and leather, men tripped over their dicks chasing after her. It was a game to her. Picture the barbeque scene in *Gone with the Wind* where Scarlett sat on the porch and men tripped over themselves to be at her beck and call. That's Fiona. Every man, young and old, fell under her spell. Even old Professor Langston fell for her ruse. And what did that get him? Fired." She brought her feet back to the ground and sat forward for emphasis.

"Whoa, whoa, whoa. Are you saying Fiona had a romantic relationship with a professor?" That startled me, but it shouldn't have after learning of her relationship with Hightower.

"Nothing questionable about it. She fucked the old man's brains out. Now I can't honestly say I didn't get some joy out of the fact it happened to him the way he sat all on his moral high horse. But he was just one of the many that, even after she'd dumped their asses, still followed her around like trained puppies. And I'll add one more thing. She even tried flirting with my boyfriend, Adam. And get this, she offered a three-way. As if—"

"OK. I've got the idea, and you don't seem to approve of her lifestyle. But who would? That's a crazy situation you were living in," I said, and her down-turned lips at the corners and a bob of her head showed I'd scored points. "What can you tell us about what happened?"

"All I know is what I read online and heard from campus gossip. Someone heard Fiona screaming as they came back to their room. They went to her bedroom and found her tied up in some crazy way, naked on her stomach. I didn't see her because I'd spent the night at Adam's. The floor buzz was she had a cherry-red bottom, whip marks that ripped her skin apart and bled like crazy. Somehow, she'd worked a ball gag from her mouth, and her lips were a mess and swollen. It's rumored whoever did this sodomized her. I don't want that picture in my head again," she said, moving her feet under her butt.

Mary and I exchanged glances, and she continued the interview.

"Claire, dear, that's awful. People do horrible things to each other. There's no reasonable explanation for it. From the small news article, we read, it appeared they arrested someone. But it was impossible to figure out the outcome from the article," Mary said, patting Claire's arm.

"That's not unusual; around here they keep everything on campus. None of the sexual assaults reach the paper; the administration locks that shit down. You don't want donors squawking now, do you? Anyway, Fiona said her attacker was another student. He wore a face mask, but she said he had a distinct voice, and she recognized his accent. She said Mahir

Abajian did it.

"It was all hush-hush when his parents flew in from Manhattan, with his mother being a big shot lawyer and his father a doctor. If you want my opinion, Fiona overplayed this and bit off more than she could chew. She probably thought there would be a quick hush-money payoff, and she could be 'persuaded' to drop the charges. Wrong. His mother swooped in all badass Armenian in her red-soled Louboutins, and those twelve-hundred-dollar shoes kicked ass and took names. By the time the drama settled down, the district attorney had dropped the charges, and the school gave Mahir and Fiona both a golden parachute of early graduation. Shit, if I could get that deal, I'd pay someone to beat the hell out of me," she said, twisting her ponytail between her fingers.

That information was a lot to digest.

"Was anyone convicted?" I asked.

"Hell no. After mama bear got finished with Fiona, her ass was gone, and good riddance. She may have tried to shake the school down for money, but she got early graduation with honors. Bye-bye."

"Did anyone investigate the sex ring she frequented?" Mary asked. "What you describe sounds like something people like that would be involved in."

Jesus, I didn't need her getting in the middle of a sex club and wanting to put that on our to-do list.

"I have no idea. I have a theory. If Fiona wasn't doing it for the payoff, then maybe one of those perverts she hangs with had it in for her. Adam, my boyfriend, explained she was something called a top, the one in charge. But the way they found her, he thought she'd pissed off someone, and it was payback. He said probably another top gave her an embarrassing ass whoppin'. Just saying."

"Well, that is another avenue isn't it?" I said, giving that a moment to sink in. "Claire, do you know anything about her family, like where they come from or what her story is?"

"Connecticut, no, wait, the Boston area. I can't remember. We weren't that close. Her mother is a bitch with a capital B, and her father a pussy with a capital P. That whole family could do with years of therapy and drugs and still not be right in the head. That's about all I can tell you. You should talk to the private investigator Mahir's mother hired to dig up dirt on Fiona," she said.

"Do you know his name?" Mary asked.

"Nope, sorry. All I know is Mahir was pretty traumatized and went back to New York and is working somewhere in Manhattan. It's a shame what happened. His family had been through a rough time in Armenia and emigrated here and established new roots. We weren't friends, and I didn't know much about him other than what I told you, but when I saw him, he always had his head in a book and kept to himself. Kinda quiet and fragile. You never know what someone is capable of, but damn. I didn't think that skinny little guy would have it in him to overpower Fiona and then beat and rape her ass."

She had a point, if he were as she'd described him.

"Anything else you can tell us?" I asked.

"The woman was an attention whore. She loved pitting one guy against another for attention. Then add in jealousy, hormones, and possibly anabolic steroids, and what happens? An explosion!" she said as she remained still. It appeared like she was deciding if she were going to share anything else.

"You people aren't cops, so you can't arrest me. I may have used her computer once, and I may have found sick shit on it.

Extreme BDSM sites and that sugar daddy site that was on Dr. Phil. That's all I'm saying. I have a class in an hour, and beauty takes time, so I need to wrap this up."

She smiled as I handed her my card and asked her to keep us updated with anything that might come to mind.

As we walked out of the complex for grad students, I asked Mary, "Where do we start, boss?"

"I'd like to visit that high-end sex club while we're here—"

"Yeah, that's not happening. That crowd will take one look at you, think you escaped from a nursing home, and shut the door in your face. If we need to visit it, I'll be the one to do it.

"Now let's get serious. I think we should touch base with this Mahir guy and see what he can tell us. But first, let's get a copy of the police report. It will take too long if we go to the police for them to approve and process the report, so let's go to the county courthouse where it should be part of the criminal file. Unless they sealed it, it should be part of the public record."

"Hold up, slick," Mary said as she rummaged through her suitcase of a purse. She pulled out her phone and after a few false starts found what she was looking for. "The county uses online records. Here's the whole file. Come on, let's head to the car and print out the report."

"You mean head all the way back to the hotel to print it out?" I asked.

"Lee, don't be daft." She rummaged in her bag and produced a portable printer with a car adaptor.

Sweet Jesus, who is this woman?

"Mary, forget the printer. Hand me the phone, and let me skim the report."

Fiona stated she'd never seen the man. She'd identified him by voice only. He'd had a distinct accent she recognized, and she said it was Mahir Abajian. A fellow neurophysiology student in the PhD program. His alibi was loose, and based on her identification, he'd been arrested. The police had processed the crime scene and investigated, but nothing had tied him to the crime. Some clerk had been sloppy to allow a rape report to be put in the county file.

"I still think we should check out the sex club," Mary said.

"Drop it. No one from the sex club will talk to us. Technically, what they're promoting is sexual battery, which they'll argue all parties consent to, but the law still frowns down on it. If we go in, it'll have to be undercover, and I have other options to explore before we go down that road."

"I disagree. The guy in Seattle we interviewed at Benjamin's said she was heavy into sadomasochism," she said.

I glanced over and saw her searching for BDSM clubs and groups.

"I'm not saying we should discount it, Mary. But remember, Fiona was trolling websites and sex chatrooms. If she was doing it here, her search history might still be on her work computer in Seattle. Let's map this out, one step at a time. First, let's see if we can set up a meeting with this Mahir guy."

An hour later we reached out to Mahir who refused to speak to us by phone but agreed to meet with us the next day at a place in Manhattan.

CHAPTER
FOUR

Lee

W E TOOK A RED-EYE FLIGHT INTO NEW YORK. MANHATTAN HAS a life force, almost like its own ecosystem. You either go with the flow, or it spits you out. It reminded me of the Chicago buzz, and I fell right back into a routine of being hypervigilant, waiting for something bad to happen. Our appointment with Mahir wasn't until one o'clock, which left us time for lunch and to plan a way to get the information we needed.

"Lee, I should take this interview. My touch is softer than yours, and the boy might be unsettled by us bringing this back up. The word 'cop' is written all over you, and based on his experience, he may be reluctant to talk to us," Mary said as she forked her chicken salad.

She was right. After twenty-two years on the force, I still carried myself in a way that screamed law enforcement. The only thing missing was my sidearm. Law enforcement was in my DNA, coming from a family of officers and agents that traced back to my grandfather, the first of the family to walk the beat in Boston. We were a hardened, closed-off group who lived the life expected of us. If you dared to say you wanted to share your feelings you would be mocked by the rest of the family, so all of us learned to bottle up our fears. The one emotion acceptable to the Stone clan was anger, so much so we were encouraged to express it through the use of our fists. My brothers and I spent many an hour in the principal's office for disorderly conduct, only to be praised by my dad for being men.

"First off, Mary, he's a man, not a boy. I'll hand it to you; the interviews you've conducted produced some excellent results. However, since this one involves someone who might be a criminal, I'm going to do it. I've done hundreds of interviews, and this guy won't give us much time. We need to get to the crux of the matter. What would be Fiona's motivation in falsely accusing this guy? Did she wake up one morning and say, 'Today is the day I'll destroy Mahir'? That seems unlikely. Something happened to get her to that place," I said, pouring my third cup of coffee and feeling my nerves vibrate.

"There, right there. You already have it in your head he's guilty and just got away with it. Your whole demeanor screams he's guilty, and he'll become defensive—"

Before she completed her monologue, the phone rang, and Jackson's name appeared on my screen. I put the phone on the table, hit the speaker, and lowered the volume. "We're both here."

"Any progress?" he asked.

"Why?" Mary asked, filling her cup.

"Well, Mary, maybe because I'm the managing partner and want to make sure nothing you've done so far has opened me up to a lawsuit," he threw back. I heard papers spitting out of a printer and computer keys being pressed.

"Jacki boy, I provided you thorough documentation, even using bold print and yellow highlights. No one's escorted us from any premises, and there are no petitions for a restraining order pending. So, why are you really butting your nose into our business?"

I laughed silently. This woman was a real ball-buster.

Jackson cleared his throat and took a breath to calm himself before continuing. "Well, I see an interview is on tap with this Mahir guy today, and I wanted to review your strategy. I assume Lee will take the lead, and I wanted to brainstorm with you both."

"Jackson, we have this covered—" she started.

"Mary, we are now in a position where a misspoken word or accusation may cause a lawsuit, so I beg to differ that you've got this covered. I'd like to hear from Lee."

He could have been a little less confrontational, but I suppose his history with Mary warranted his concern.

"Morning, Jackson," I said. "I understand your concern, and I can assure you, we have this. I reviewed the case against Mahir last night and don't understand how the Cali police thought they'd make it stick. This guy's from a well-to-do family and never been in any trouble. I'd call him a nerd. The witness statements were thin, and there was no way to place him at the scene that night. The identification involved a voice ID from the victim because of his accent. But hell, half the program she was in is filled with people with foreign accents. So how she could identify this one under a moment of intense stress is questionable.

"He passed the polygraph, and during the interview showed no sign of fabricating his story. His mother, who's an attorney, sat in for the interrogation, and her abrasive manner seemed to set the lead detective off. I believe, from the encounter with her, he got a hard-on for this case. They didn't follow up on any other leads; although, there were several men Fiona had snubbed," I said.

"But maybe they didn't have accents," Jackson said.

Fair point.

"We'll never know, because they zeroed in on him, and that was it. Look, I'm no profiler, but this Fiona sounds like a narcissistic manipulator, a sociopath. I think she amused herself by toying with people's emotions. Somehow, this Mahir got on her radar, and she targeted him. My approach to him will be I assume he got twisted up in a game he didn't understand.

"Though, I might be wrong. For all I know, this guy might fly the same freak flag as Fiona. If I get that vibe, I'll change course with my questions. There had to be a reason the DA dropped it. The school wanted the whole thing swept under the rug, to get them both off campus as quickly as possible. This event wasn't national news. So, I don't think this guy is a serial rapist."

I checked the time; we needed to leave to make our appointment.

"I disagree with his strategy. I should come in with a soft touch, and Lee as a more jaded opponent. So far my gut has worked in getting information," Mary said, leaning toward the phone to make her point.

"This is where my experience comes into play," Mary continued. "This isn't an interrogation; it's a conversation. He's going to be defensive. His mother may be there. If she feels we're trying to get him to admit to something that wouldn't be in his best interest, she'll shut the whole thing down."

"Mary—" Jackson started.

"Am I the lead or not?" she asked, voiced raised; a few people turned to look.

Instead of answering her, all Jackson said was, "Lee has this. Call me when you have information."

Before she could continue her argument, he hung up.

It was clear she was deciding whether to call him back. Then she surprised me by saying, "I've got this check."

A few minutes later we were in a cab heading to the Upper West Side.

"That's odd; there are cars everywhere, and that's the address he gave us, isn't it? The one where all the people are going in and out?" Mary asked.

"It is." I instructed the cab driver to leave us a few doors down, so we could decide if we should approach. Mahir hadn't called to reschedule, so we walked toward the building for the meeting.

The steep stairs were difficult for Mary, but with a little help, we made it to the top, leaving her winded. I grabbed the door knocker and gave it three good taps. As I was about to ring the bell, I heard a woman's voice, and the door opened. In front of me stood a well-dressed woman, not much older than me. Her eyes were red-rimmed from crying, and her nose was swollen and red.

"Can I help you?" she asked, trying to regain her composure.

"Um yes, we're here to see Mahir. I'm Lee Stone, and this is Mary Collier. We had an appointment with him."

She seemed confused. "Mr. Stone, I'm his mother, and…"

A gentleman with dark exotic looks moved up behind her and placed his hands on her shoulders in a supportive way. I assumed he was Mahir's father.

"I see we arrived at an inopportune time. Would you tell

Mahir he can call to reschedule?"

The two looked shocked, and his father said, "Mahir died early this morning."

I saw Mary step back in shock, and I caught her before her heel caught the stone stair. "Oh my God, I am so sorry for your loss," she said, clutching her chest. "What happened?"

Mary, what the hell are you thinking? I wanted to say. You're a stranger; why would these people tell you that?

"The police are still investigating. What did you come to see Mahir about?" his mother asked.

Now I was sure we were unexpected. "It's not at all important—" I started before Mary blurted words I couldn't claw back.

"Fiona O'Dell. We're investigating her disappearance," Mary said.

Shock registered across Mahir's mother's face and was quickly replaced with anger.

"May that bitch rot in hell," Mahir's mother said with such hatred it felt like the temperature dropped twenty degrees.

Mahir's father encased her shoulders with his arms and said softly in her ear, "Lucine, do not bring that karma back to us." He gently kissed the top of her head.

Her face became grave, and she stood a little taller with stiffness to her. "Are you here on her family's behalf?"

"Oh, no, no," Mary said, touching her arm. "She may have taken a valuable product from our employer, and we were sent to find her and bring her to justice."

I was shocked and angry. Why would Mary cross that line? She was accusing Fiona of a crime when she had no evidence she had done anything wrong. I was about to make my apology for us both and leave before this got any worse when Lucine spoke.

"I see. Go back down these stairs. There is another flight of stairs to your right. When you get to the bottom, the door is unlocked. Go in and make yourself comfortable; we'll be right down."

With that, they turned around and went back into their house. We descended the stairs, but not without me asking Mary if she had lost her mind, and her telling me to hush.

We sat on a soft cloth couch, taking in the luxurious surroundings. These people were loaded and didn't mind showcasing their good taste. The first thing that popped into my mind as we waited was, *Did Fiona target Mahir because he was wealthy? Was she trying to extort an unfounded settlement from him to keep her quiet?* From all I'd gathered about Fiona, she wasn't above a hush-money scheme.

The Abajians entered the room, and before I could open my mouth Mary already had a sentence out.

"I'm so sorry for your loss and sorry to take you away from your loved ones." Mary sat forward on the edge of the cushion.

"Anything I can do to help extract justice against that woman…" Lucine said as her husband moved his hand over hers in comfort.

"If it isn't too painful, can you tell us anything about Mahir's contact with Fiona that may give us some insight into this girl?" Mary probed respectfully.

"I assume you're aware of the…incident," Lucine began, and we nodded. "My Mahir was a shy, gentle soul we raised to respect women. He was polite and thoughtful and never would have become involved with such a woman."

"Do you know how they met?" I asked.

"He said they were in classes together, and she started conversations with him. According to him, he politely shut her down. Mahir told me she was a flirt and had disrupted several relationships between classmates. My poor Mahir thought her attention toward him was a ploy to make him uncomfortable," she said, shaking her head.

"While the police investigated, it appeared no one put any effort into seeking other suspects, so I hired a private investigator. We found out Ms. O'Dell had quite the checkered past." Lucine's voice rose, and her head moved slightly back as her jaw jutted.

"I see," Mary said, in a conspiratorial tone. "What did you find out?"

"Lucine, what about the non-disclosure?" her husband interjected.

"Please, don't be crazy, Matthew. Mahir signed it, not me," she said with a cutting edge.

"But—"

"Enough! I want this out in the open." She turned to her husband in a silencing manner.

I wouldn't want to be her opponent in court. From our brief encounter so far, she was formidable. Since she appeared to relate to Mary, I remained shielded from her view, so she could tell her story to Mary.

"It was a terrible time in our lives. Mahir had always been a good boy, and his life was difficult as we emigrated from Armenia. But that isn't what you want to know.

"Mahir had attended Columbia undergraduate and wanted to spread his wings. We decided the California university system was a good match. So he enrolled in an accelerated masters and doctorate program.

"The night we received the call they'd arrested him was the worst night of my life. I had no idea he'd given a statement to the police. Once Ms. O'Dell had identified Mahir, and he was under arrest, we were on the next plane. We hired a criminal defense attorney and got him out on bail.

"Our attorney hired a private investigation firm, and the depraved life this girl lived was shocking—"

"Lucine, there is no need to go into graphic detail. I believe Mary and Lee can use their imaginations," Matthew said as he shifted.

"No, Matthew, it must be said. Ms. O'Dell frequented sex clubs and online sugar daddy services, which are nothing less than prostitution. Our investigator interviewed many students who had fallen for her particular brand of crazy and one who had stalked her."

"Again, Lucine, my love, this is just stirring up bad emotions," Matthew interjected.

She continued as if he hadn't said a thing.

"Digging into her background, we found she'd been part of a similar sex ring in Boston where she'd been at school last. We also found a student committed suicide because of his despair over finding out about a dalliance Fiona had with a professor.

"When the DA decided not to present the case to the grand jury, the charges were dropped. The school granted them both early graduation status, and Mahir returned home.

"He became more depressed as the weeks passed, and the doctors changed his medication. It is incomprehensible that one person could cause such destruction in life," Lucine said as she blotted under her eyes.

"Sometimes people that sick will continue to torment their victims. Do you have any reason to think Mahir has had any communication with her?" I asked.

"I don't believe so; however, the police have confiscated his phone. The phone is under my plan, and I can ask for a copy of his incoming calls and text messages. But I don't believe that girl would contact him and leave a digital footprint," she said.

"Would you be willing to share the report your private investigator put together with names and places?" I asked.

She reached for a small computer on the table and asked for my email address. Within a few seconds, the report sat in my inbox.

"I'm emailing you the card of the detective who's in charge of the investigation. I will email my investigator, Salvo, and tell him he has my permission to share any information he has with you. If you can prosecute this girl, let me know. My heart is saying she had something to do with Mahir's death."

"Again we're sorry for your loss and will pray for your son. We can see ourselves out," Mary said, giving Lucine a quick embrace.

We exited the home in silence as more people came and others left.

CHAPTER FIVE

Mary

I STUDIED THE PHOTOGRAPH OF FIONA FROM HER EMPLOYMENT package, as if the picture could come to life and explain her complexities. She was someone's daughter, possibly someone's sister, and, I perceived, no one's sweetheart. Unfortunately, all I could see was a beautiful girl with an ugly heart. Who was I to know her real story? Was she abused as a child? Did her neurotransmitters misfire and not send enough chemicals through her blood to reach her brain? Or had she sustained an injury to her frontal lobe? I needed to know what made Fiona tick.

"Fiona, who are you?" I asked the universe. "Where are you? Do you have what we want, or are we on a wild goose chase? Were you connected with Mahir's death?"

I opened my PowerPoint application and placed a circle in the middle, representative of Fiona. From there I linked everyone we believed had hurt her or had a reason to want to hurt her. The next grouping of lines was where she might go based on our information. Before I knew it, there were numerous lines, but none intersected at a common point.

The night passed before I realized it. I was so engrossed in my diagram that sleep eluded me. I dissected all there was to know about Fiona, and what I uncovered alarmed me.

I had twenty minutes before I needed to meet Lee in the breakfast area, so a quick shower and fresh clothes were in order. This would leave me enough time to devour a couple pastries and a carafe of coffee before we met.

Lee entered the room and interested female eyes swung his way. A handsome man at six feet four inches, a confident swagger, and a thick sexy mess of brown hair, added to his rugged looks. All he needed was a cowboy hat to round out many a woman's fantasy. His best feature was his eyes, the color of shards of thin blue glass. Lee had no idea women devoured him with their eyes, because he never looked around to see; his only focus was on his present task.

"Lee, you need a woman in your life," I told him as he flipped his coffee cup and put it on the saucer.

His lips twitched into a small smile as if something amused him. That mischievous smile kept me interested in what he was thinking.

"Mary, I was married for fifteen years, and it wasn't the most pleasant experience for my wife. I've been told I'm a hardass and difficult to please, and those are my good qualities. Many women have told me I set my standards too high, and I have no romance in my soul."

"A man has needs." I reminded him as I poured my second cup of coffee. "You're too young not to have a companion to enjoy life with, my dear."

"I don't want to get into this, Mary; it won't go well. You don't have to eat home-cooked meals when fast food is available," he replied, refilling my water. "When's your niece, Emma, due with the twins?"

"Ah, I see, a change of direction to throw the old lady off task of trying to organize a love life for you. To answer your question, Emma is due in three months. Now, let me continue. There is a lid—"

"I know, Mary; there's a lid for every pot. But, Mary, some pots don't need a lid. Now back to business—"

"Are you a Capricorn?" I asked. The man was stubborn and determined enough to be one.

"What's that?" He looked confused.

"When were you born? What month?"

"January 6. Is there a point to this question?"

"There you go, the mountain goat, the responsible one. Methodical, tough, unyielding. OK, we have to find you a water sign…" I was about to give him a list of qualities to search for when he snapped his fingers to get my attention and told me to focus.

I'd brought Emma and her husband together. I could do the same for Lee, if he gave me some room to work.

"First, I want to meet with the detective assigned to Mahir's case," Lee said. "His mother was holding something back. All she told us was he died, and we can't do much with that. Was he mugged? Did someone find him after he committed suicide? Was it accidental? If our case doesn't intersect with his death, then we need to move on.

"I spent a lot of time on Fiona's background to project where she may feel safe to go. I tried to narrow down a place she'd be comfortable enough to sell the information," Lee said.

He stopped while the server took our order, and I used that

time to fish out my murder board I'd printed out before I'd left the room.

He reached for it with a surprised expression as I handed it to him.

"What's this? It's like a picture of the London underground."

"This, my boy, is what you call a murder board. I've placed everyone we know about on this board, and together we can decide which leads to follow."

"Holy sh...hell, Mary, I'm impressed," he said as he reached into his messenger bag and took out a stack of paper stapled at the top left corner. "I took the FBI course on profiling when I joined homicide and worked a few cases with them. I read the report from the psychologist Mahir's family had hired for his case, and I did an abbreviated workup on Fiona. You know, to get into her head."

He handed me his notes, and I adjusted my glasses for proper reading. He'd circled the words "sociopathy," "manipulation," and "inability to form lasting friendships" several times. Lee had noted Fiona's childhood had been bleak and left her with abandonment and abuse issues to resolve.

"Well, we could have guessed that, but how does it help us find her?" I asked.

"Since she appears to fund her activities through, shall we say, certain men's generosity, I had Jackson tap into the sugar daddy site Claire gave us. Her profile had been inactive, but in the last three days, there's been some activity. Jackson took a chance and sent a query, and believe it or not, he set up a meetup scheduled Friday in Boston. That gives us two days to get what we need here and get up there," Lee said, sitting back, tapping the back of the spoon on the table.

I glanced at the report again. Fiona had attended college

and graduate school in Boston, but had left under a cloud of suspicion. There were no visible connections that would bring her back there. Boston wasn't exactly a hotbed of sexual activity. Something didn't fit, and it irked me that I couldn't find it.

I glanced up to see Lee studying me, as if he could see my deduction and induction process whipping at warp speed through my head.

"Lee, none of this makes sense."

"I can read your mind, Mary. You're worried Hightower is having us track her down as a personal agenda. Am I right?" he asked, blowing out a soft breath of air.

"It has crossed my mind more than once. Let's meet with the police detective, and if there's no connection here between Mahir and Fiona, we move on to Boston," I said. "Did you call and set up an appointment?"

"Yes, we'll meet at the station. She was reluctant, but, the fact we were following Fiona piqued her interest. And, Mary, I speak law enforcement, so please let me handle this meeting." He paid the bill and carefully placed it in his expense report compartment.

"Lee, that blonde over there has been trying to catch your eye. You want to amble on over there and strike up a conversation?" I asked, part tease, part question.

"Not my type, Mary."

OK, now we were getting somewhere. "What's your type?"

"Sensible, self-sustaining, and no drama," he replied without a thought.

"So, a woman who knows her way around a vibrator and binges on Netflix?"

"Pretty much." He chuckled.

I liked the way his dimples folded into his cheeks when he laughed. I was determined to find this boy his happily ever after.

The precinct appeared like any other in a large city, a hive of activity. Some people were seated filling out papers, and others were demanding attention of the officers at the front desk. This one needed a fresh coat of paint, and the gray tiles, once white, required a good wash.

I strolled over to the chest-high desk where an officer greeted visitors, and Lee took the lead. He was comfortable in this environment, a place officers called their house, and he relaxed, as if this was his home.

"I'm Detective Stone here to see Detective Hughes. God, sorry, Lee Stone," he said, shaking his head. "Old habits."

"Where were you stationed?" the younger man asked.

"Chicago, homicide."

The young man in the crisp blue shirt shot back, "The wild west."

"Yeah, you could say that." Lee smiled.

The officer turned to his landline and punched in some numbers. His conversation was brief, and he handed us each a laminated visitor's badge to sector five. He leaned over and pointed down the hall, telling us to take the first turn and follow the yellow line.

Lee pushed his way through a set of green doors with peeling paint showing decades of use. We entered a small room with old plastic chairs. Detective Annabelle Hughes, a petite, brown-haired woman with a gold shield on her waistband, stepped our way and offered an outstretched hand. We each introduced ourselves, and Lee's eyes focused on her in an assessing manner from the top of her head to her feet. His cop eyes searched and challenged hers, sizing her up as a police officer and as a woman. Interesting.

She directed us into a room with a metal table and five well-used chairs. She closed the door to the windowless room. Detective Hughes sat first, and Lee sat across from her. I sat at the end of the table to watch their interaction.

Lee gave a concise explanation why we'd planned a meet with Mahir and left out about 98 percent of the reason. The fact we knew a significant amount of information about Mahir took Detective Hughes by surprise. Her facial expression suggested she wasn't pleased we were ahead of the curve on what she knew in the ten hours since his death.

"How did you come by your information?" she asked, slouching back and tapping her pad. She didn't even try to hide her disapproval.

"Mahir's mother gave us access to the information gathered during the investigation of his arrest in LA," I answered. The situation was turning confrontational, and we would come out on the losing end. "Detective, may I call you Annabelle?"

She nodded but kept her eyes turned toward Lee.

"Annabelle, we have no intention of inserting ourselves into your investigation," I said. "Our interest is in finding the missing intellectual property."

Annabelle turned toward Lee and leaned forward. Was she trying to invade his personal space?

"I understand you were a homicide detective in Chicago?"

"Twenty-two years on the job."

She nodded her approval, and he leaned forward toward her, their faces about a foot apart.

"Why would you think Mahir had any information to help you find Ms. O'Dell?" she asked, licking her lips.

Was that a habit, a nervous tell, or sexual attraction?

"I didn't. We're gathering facts, and it led us to Mahir," Lee replied, maintaining an investigator's stare.

"And what have you found out about her?" Annabelle asked.

"If she's not a suspect in the case, why the interest?"

"I like to keep an open mind."

"We've just started our investigation. Well, in a nutshell, she has no friends, a loner. She enjoys being part of a crowd for the attention, and she's a fan of kink. We have a lead she's either in or heading to the Boston area, and that's where we're heading next."

They both took a moment to reflect on the information, and Annabelle spoke next.

"Do you have any reason to believe there's a connection between Mahir's death and Fiona?"

"That's impossible to say based on the limited information available. I don't know where you found Mahir's body, why he was there, what murder weapon was used, or what was going on in his life. Hell, I don't even know if Fiona was anywhere near Manhattan in the last few days," Lee said, avoiding overreach.

"I can tell you she was in New York as of two days ago, and she reached out to him by phone. The two had a short conversation, and we can place her in the vicinity of his death at the time of death. Since then, she may have shut her phone down." Although guarded in what information she shared, we knew Fiona was on her radar and a person of interest.

"Annabelle—" I started.

"Belle," she returned with a smile. "Please, Mary, call me Belle."

"That information is very helpful. Would I be overstepping if I asked if you've been able to pick up any activity on her phone? She has a meet set up in Boston with a person she thinks is interested in being her sugar daddy. If she's not pinging off your towers, it's a waste of time for us to stay."

"We're waiting for the judge to sign the search warrant to let us comb through her data. But that's all I can give you," she said.

Lee sat back, tipped his head to the side, and raised his eyebrows in my direction. A small smile played on Annabelle's lips, as she understood from his nonverbal cues I had said more than I should have.

Energy passed between them. Lee had more years and experience than she did, but her confident attitude said she had this under control and didn't need his input. Nor did she want it. Conflict was written all over this encounter.

"It seems we're doing all the giving, and you're doing all the taking in this conversation," Lee said, swiping his hand in a semicircle on the table.

"Were you expecting something different?" she asked with a raised eyebrow. "You're a civilian now."

"What Lee hoped," I interjected before he snapped back a harsh retort, "was to determine if we needed to stay here to follow up on leads. As you said, she was here at some point. If we can find her and determine if she has what we're looking for, that would end our case."

"I see. All right, Mary, call me about four this afternoon, and once we dump her phone, I'll tell you if she's here. That's the best I can do," she said with her eyes still boring into Lee's.

"You get breaks, don't you, Belle? The reason I ask is I saw Starbucks two doors down. How about I buy you a cup of coffee and pastry at four instead of calling you? I know you're busy, but I'd love to hear in person whatever information you can share," I said, hoping to defuse the tension and regain our footing.

She looked at me, and I suppose the mention of real coffee tipped her my way. She accepted the offer.

I patted her arm. I knew it. She, like me, was a caffeine fiend. We were compadres.

She offered her card, accepted mine, and then escorted us to the desk to turn in our visitor badges.

From the way he walked out of the building, I could tell Lee was about to unload on me for interfering. I shot him my stern look and advised him to zip it, and surprisingly he complied.

CHAPTER SIX

Lee

WE HAILED A CAB AND HEADED BACK TO THE HOTEL IN A SILENCE neither of us wanted to break. We were thinking about Mahir. Death could do that to you—take you into yourself. I remember those awful days after Debby died. Cancer had ravaged her body the same way it had destroyed my mind and heart. I should have spent more time with her when she was healthy, but I'd put my work ahead of everything. Why had I been so obsessed with making detective? It had never given me the satisfaction I needed; it wound up being different faces, same scenarios. I'd never effectuated any change in people; they'd effectuated a change in me as I'd sunk deeper into a black hole of hopelessness. Some of my colleagues had abused alcohol to medicate their pain and loneliness. I'd opted for too many nights at the gym, beating on the bag, as if it was a perp, or running on the treadmill as if I was running away from my life. At the end, when Debby had died, I'd felt relief and guilt, and the emotions, over the years, had led to numbness.

With everything Fiona had put the Abajians through, they hadn't deserved to lose their son. The death of someone is bad enough. But what about the people left behind who have to adjust their minds and hearts to the reality that there will never again be that laughter or hug at night? I'd had time to prepare for Debby's death, even down to making funeral arrangements together. Is it better not to invest yourself in love? Is it better not to care? This wound inflicted on Mahir's parents would never heal.

I glanced over and caught Mary studying me.

"I don't like New York," she said. "Everyone's in a rush. Where's everyone going? Look over there." She pointed at a park. "There's a little park there. Let's slip in for a few minutes. I need to settle my mind around what we just learned."

She got no argument from me. We exited the cab and ambled into the well-maintained area where mothers and nannies chased after children who had too much energy and made too much noise. But all the chaos reminded me these people had a future; unlike Mahir, who was dead because of a split second in time when one person crossed his timeline.

"I don't like this case," Mary said. "If it were just recovering a lost or stolen object, I'd feel satisfaction that, at the end, I'd recovered something of value, and there would be a happy ending. But this case, Lee, this case is dark, and I'm afraid the outcome will leave a mark on us."

I remained silent. I didn't need to affirm I understood what she meant. Because yes, this case was filled with ugly.

"Mary, it depends on how much of it you let into your mind and heart. Fiona is a damaged human being, and we can't fix her; that's not our job. You can sympathize with her because of the life she had as a child, but if she committed murder..." I stopped because what I wanted to say was she deserved an eye for an eye.

Instead I said, "If these are the kinds of cases Jackson's going to take, I'm not sure this is the job for me. I left the force for a reason, and I don't want to be sucked into getting into a psycho's mind. And, Mary, this girl is a psycho who might evade us for months."

"In a perfect world, what would you do as a job to make you happy or fulfilled?" she asked.

I took a few minutes to answer. I'd thought about it a lot, but options always seemed limited. "I'd own a carpentry business where I'd carve tables and sculpt wood."

She looked genuinely surprised. "That was the last thing I expected you to say."

"I like creating stuff, but as kids, none of us were ever encouraged to do things like that. We used our hands for fighting. I came from an aggressive family," I said, not happy to revisit my past.

Just then my phone buzzed, and the name Salvo Martucci, Lucine's PI, appeared on the screen. After a brief conversation, Mary and I were in a cab and on our way to meet him. We entered a building that had to be a hundred years old. The lighting and flooring were updated, but the ancient, slick plaster walls gave away the age.

On the third floor, we entered an office that had seen better days. The battered furniture and well-worn carpet suited the office's occupant. No secretary was in the waiting area to greet us, but Mr. Martucci, a stout, older man with worn shoes, was waiting for us and emerged from his small office. He introduced himself. When we thanked him for his time, he waved us off, as if we weren't disturbing him.

Once settled in a red leather captain's chair, I reached for my note pad to jot down notes. Mary, however, did something unusual; she sat with nothing to record our meeting. She just listened.

"Lucine called me and gave me the go-ahead to talk to you," Mr. Martucci said, tapping two files, each about three inches thick with papers and photos. "Tragic about Mahir. I liked that boy. I've known the family for about three years and watched him emerge from a shy teenager to a man. It infuriated me that someone would accuse him of such malicious behavior. Mahir is the kind of boy who made sure stray cats had food. The person who inflicted such violence on Ms. O'Dell had a sick, twisted mind, and that wasn't Mahir."

"I eyeballed the file Lucine gave us but will study it tonight. Looking at what you've got there, I'd say Lucine got an abridged copy. What's missing from hers?" I asked.

"I gave her the summary and highlights. There was no reason to give her every scrap of paper. My job was to gather the information, then filter through it. And to be honest, she didn't need to see some of the trash I uncovered. You can take these files when you leave, but at some point, I'll need them back. I scanned everything into my computer, but I'm a paper man. I like highlighting, and post-noting information by color codes, so don't mess that up." He looked at the file and then at Mary.

"What's your story?" he asked her.

"Not your concern, so don't go flirting with me and get your hopes up. We need to get cracking on the information; I'm not getting any younger," Mary snapped, and he chuckled as he leaned back in his chair.

"Fair enough. There's a lot of psychobabble from the shrink they hired. I always take that with a grain of salt. But considering the time my partner and I put into talking to people from her past and up to the time of the incident, I'd say the shrink was dead on.

"The girl had a rough start in life. Her mom was a drunk,

and Fiona went into foster care at seven. The family services department shrinks said she was highly intelligent, but she had what they called oppositional defiance disorder. She must have been a handful, and none of her foster parents were equipped to handle that big a problem long-term. By the time she was sixteen and had passed through several foster homes, her diagnosis expanded to the label malignant narcissist. The next to last foster family she was with, I think her eighth, asked for her immediate removal. They found her having sex with their son, and condoms weren't a priority for her. It's in the expanded report. They put her in a group home—"

"Wait," Mary interrupted, "we talked to her roommate, Claire, and she said Fiona's parents visited. How's that possible if she was in a group home?"

"If you'd hold your horses," he said with a quick raised hand, "Fiona was in the group home about a month when some do-gooders came along and took her in, as if she was some project. They homeschooled her and kept her on a tight leash. That mother was a control freak, and the father had a perv vibe, but surprisingly she didn't run off.

"When it came time for college, they must have known someone in the higher ranks. They were able to get her into a faith-based college, even though she just had a GED, and the college required a regular high school diploma. Her SATs were almost perfect, and her sad story about multiple foster care placements resonated with the school's mission.

"She appeared to keep out of trouble, nothing glaring stuck out on the undergrad level, and she graduated with honors. Fiona was a loner, but a loner who liked to party. She wasn't arrested for anything and maintained a low profile. Considering her background, I'd say she was smart and cunning enough to avoid the consequences of any mess she got involved in. The real trouble began when she hit graduate school, but by then she was an adult. She found a crowd heavy into that kinky shit, and she embraced it," he said with a judgmental tone.

"How'd she find her tribe?" Mary asked. "I'm sure it wasn't an activity offered by the school."

Mr. Martucci's lips parted a bit, and then he responded, "I don't know for sure; it wasn't relevant. In the early part of her graduate program, a similar incident as the one with Mahir, but not as brutal, occurred. She accused another student, Chuck Evans, who admitted to laying hands on her, but his spin was that she'd asked him to do it as part of a neurobehavioral experiment. That's when the gates of hell opened, and the school investigation team found she was a practicing member of a BDSM ring in Boston. The school didn't want state law enforcement brought in, so they asked them both to leave at the end of the semester, which was a month away. That was when she found her way to Los Angeles where the hedonism of its culture fed into her abnormal personality," he said, clasping his hands in front of him.

"So, no arrests made in Boston?" I asked.

"Oh, hell no. The school could never take that chance. Even a whiff of that could open a can of worms they couldn't contain. The school counselor played it off as Fiona was suffering from issues of rejection and abandonment, and that this made her feel unworthy and caused her to seek inappropriate attention. The boy said it was consensual and stuck to his story about it being part of an experiment. I couldn't get hold of the school records, but that's what the guy she accused said when I spoke to him. He wouldn't elaborate, and I let it go, but if we needed his testimony, I'd dig in a lot further," he said.

"So unresolved mental health issues?" Mary stated more than asked.

"I suppose, but don't we all suffer from that in one form or another? Anyway, bottom line, she was social with men but steered clear of women. The shrink Lucine hired went into a bunch of gibber-gabber about Myers-Briggs testing, which I snoozed through, and based on her reported behavior, made some assumptions. The words I grabbed onto were 'angry, self-centered, emotionally abusive behavior, greedy, and no empathy.' His report wouldn't hold water in court. If the case moved forward, he'd have to do actual testing, but he concluded that she was a sociopath, based on the available information. Although well on her way to behaviors that led to criminal actions, she hadn't hit there yet. Like I said, all psychobabble. She liked attention and knew how to get it; she also liked to play with people to see what it would take to break them. She's an evil person who needs to be locked away for life," he said, hitting his hand on the desk.

"I think that's a bit extreme," Mary said. "She's not a serial killer—"

"Yet. Give her time. That girl is unhinged. Is it nature or nurture? I don't give a crap. Why she targeted Mahir, I don't know. But he wasn't her first victim, and he won't be her last. Take the files, but get them back to me," he said, moving his eyes away from Mary to me. "You're a man. If you met this little cock tease, you'd understand the hold she could have over men desperate for her to choose them. She exploited men for sport, and any woman who got in her way? She tore their egos to shit. If she killed Mahir, there will be hell to pay. Lucine will not let this sit."

We thanked him for his time and took the files. As we left,

he yelled from his office, "You mark my words, that bitch had something to do with Mahir's death. She broke that boy in LA, and she came here to finish the job."

We spent the afternoon combing the file. It was a treasure trove of information about Fiona but didn't give us any real leads about where she was now. It didn't really help our case. So, we closed the files and headed back to meet Annabelle to see what she'd turned up. Her information would be more helpful than Mr. Martucci's.

Precisely at 4:00 p.m., I spied Annabelle as she pushed her way through the crowd. I hadn't realized until I saw her that my eyes had been glued to the door, awaiting her arrival. She smiled and signaled she was getting coffee.

"That's a nice-looking young lady, Lee," Mary offered and gave a short wave to Belle.

Mary was a busybody, and the best way to cut this obvious matchmaking off was remain silent. But that wasn't happening. Mary would not be silenced until her point was made.

"You two may have a lot in common. Hard-headed, you both know your way around weapons, and can tolerate the smell of decomp. I think you might want to explore this," she said, continuing with her unsolicited matchmaking.

I gave her the head signal that Belle was approaching to cut her off. She turned to check I was correct and flashed Belle a broad smile.

"So what've you got for me?" I asked before Mary could do something to make me uncomfortable.

"Lee, your mama would be disappointed in you," Mary said. "We're cultured people here. Belle, thank you for joining us. That's how you start a conversation. Then you give her a few moments to settle, and after a bit of small talk, you ease into business. Now, Belle, dear, how are you?"

Belle let out a short laugh, but her smile was bright and aimed at me. "Thank you for asking me, Mary." Then she turned to me and said, "I'm sorry to say I don't have much to offer. The judge wouldn't sign our warrant; he felt we didn't have probable cause to suspect Fiona had played a part in the murder. He didn't think we'd placed enough information in our affidavit to convince him Mahir was a personal target. From the scene, he felt it appeared more a crime of opportunity."

"I disagree," I said, leaning back and shaking my head.

"How can you disagree? You haven't even seen the crime scene or the body," Belle said, leaning forward and making it a point to meet my eyes. "Do you think I missed something in presenting my observations to the judge?"

"In a word, yes."

She looked startled, and she studied me as I studied her. I noticed her makeup was subtle and her jewelry was minimal. She didn't wear a wedding band. She tapped her fingers on the table and then leaned forward, engaging my eyes. What I saw in those eyes was spunk and fire. I could tell behind those eyes there was an intelligent woman processing information and drawing conclusions.

"You have a lot of nerve!" she said.

"Settle down, no need to get yourself in a twist. If you'd like to hear my thoughts, I'd be happy to share them," I said.

I could feel the tension building between us, but it wasn't unpleasant. I liked the spark in her and her ability to speak her mind unfiltered.

She lobbed a response right back that cut me off at the

knees. "You're not much of a detective if you can't *detect* I don't need an outsider who has no information about the case insinuating I haven't done a thorough job." She emphasized the word detect, as if it were disdainful to her, but I pressed forward.

"A stranger murder in that area of the city is unlikely. It has the lowest crime rate in the five boroughs, and the last murder was eight years ago. There hasn't even been a property crime, except for the occasional auto break-in. In a city this size, that's peanuts.

"An online article that popped up a half hour ago said the attacker had used a knife. A homicide where a knife is used usually indicates a personal attack." I could tell she was ready to argue, so I raised my hand to stop her. "The wound placement on the side indicates the killer was someone sitting next to Mahir, engaged in conversation with him. It wasn't someone who was walking past him and decided, 'hey, I think I'll stab this joker for the hell of it.' And coincidentally, the murder in Seattle was by a knife as well. And, something you may not know, Fiona's special type of kink was knife play. She knew her way around a blade," I said, looking over at Mary whose expression was a mix between alarmed and proud.

Belle thought a moment. I thought by the way she crossed her arms she might close herself off and leave. I gave her an incentive to stay.

"If you find any of the perp's blood, and it's AB negative, you might want to take a closer look at our Ms. Fiona." I let that hang, because they might not have run DNA yet, but blood type only took seconds to run.

Belle studied my face. It was clear she wanted to ask how I had that information but didn't want to give me the satisfaction. So I volunteered it.

"During some knife play at the sex club she belonged to in LA, someone went a little too far, and she had to be rushed to the ER. It was bad enough the doctor asked for a pint of AB negative to be on hand."

She opened her mouth, poised to ask a question, but I continued before she had a chance. "Yeah, I know HIPPA prevents that kind of information from being available. Well, she happened to dispute the charge on her bill because they didn't use the pint. Somehow, that accounting bill found its way into Ms. Abajian's investigator's file."

I could see a thought pass through her mind as she made connections.

"I see. That is useful information," Belle said. "I'd like to see that file."

"We can make that happen," Mary said. "Come by our hotel tomorrow morning, and we'll share it with you."

"Or you could just give it to me right now," she said as she smiled. The way her eyes lit up, I could tell she was anxious to see the file. And I was anxious to see her again, so I'd hold onto the file.

"Not a chance. It's not mine to give," I said. "It's someone else's work. And before you say warrant, forget it. There's less probable cause for a judge to sign a warrant to seize the file than there was to pull her phone LUDs. Play nice, and we will too."

"I could make a case for obstruction," she said, squinting to target me.

Was she playing with me?

"Look, Detective, I've been at this a lot longer than you. We can play this game all day. But I get bored easily, so do you want to meet tomorrow or not, because we're leaving the next day for Boston."

Although Annabelle seemed to be a stubborn woman, she realized she had no room to argue and trying to bully me would be useless.

"I'll be there at eight," she said, as she stood to leave.

"Don't you want to know where?" I asked, a little leery we were being set up.

"I wouldn't be much of a detective if I didn't already know that," she said, positioning her bag on her shoulder and sashayed away.

CHAPTER SEVEN

Lee

WHAT A NIGHT. FIONA'S FACE FLOATED THROUGH MY DREAMS. I was chasing her down blind alleys, and every time she was within reach, I couldn't get to her. She evaporated into a matrix of digital codes, reassembled herself, and ran again. How had I gotten to this place of being a glorified bounty hunter? Belle was right; solving the case wasn't my concern, and I should let it go.

I rolled over on my side, shook the ethereal face of Fiona from my mind, and replaced it with Belle's. Such a pretty woman and what a spitfire. Every time I was near her, my heart beat quicker, and my breathing was more difficult to control. *Whoa, that's crazy,* I thought. *I can't go there.* But she was the first woman who had held my interest for longer than a potential sweaty roll in the sheets. I had to shake that shit off! I wasn't up for a relationship. I wasn't relationship material anymore; that had died with Debby.

At 7:00 a.m. the phone buzzed, and Jackson's name came up on my screen.

"Hey, Jax, you're up early; what's up?"

"Mary said you got ahold of the PI's file, and it had great

background information. She also said the next Mrs. Stone will be there in two hours. Talk to me." He chuckled.

"Okay, first, take anything Mary says about my love life with an enormous grain of salt. Second, yes, the file was a well-documented biography of Fiona O'Dell from birth to present. While a page turner, it gave us no information that will bring us any closer to finding her. She has no patterns," I said, getting up to start the coffee machine.

"Well, not necessarily," he said.

"How's that?"

"The girl is hooked on kink; it's her fix. Every state she's been, there's a place she gravitates to and attaches herself. For whatever reason, her safe place is anything involving sex she can control. If she's in Boston, then she might possibly be back with her old ring. What's your plan when you get up there?" he asked.

"I don't know, man. She's a social ghost with no social media digital footprint like other people her age. Mary probably filled you in that she bounced from foster home to foster home. She has no connections, no relationships. Even her roommate, who lived with her almost two years, had limited reliable information. If I had access to her financials, I could track her cards. The best and the only lead is that Belle said Fiona spoke to Mahir two days ago, and it's my hope she's still here.

"But she might be on her way to Boston by now. I thought it might help if we talk to the guy, Chuck Evans, she accused of assaulting her in Boston before we have the sugar daddy meet-up. I'd like to get a read on him, but I'm not convinced he'll speak with us. If it were me, I'd want that chick so far in my rearview I might even go for hypnosis to wipe her from my mind." I poured the steaming coffee into the plain white mug, waiting to take that first hit of caffeine.

"How are you going to find this guy in Boston? He might have moved away," he said.

"The guy's in the PI's file. There's a last known address in Newton, and unless he moved in the last eight months, it's a valid address. The phone number he had isn't working. But this guy's all over social media, so I should be able to get a fix on him after Belle leaves. One thing I've learned is these schools are skilled at keeping unpleasant information tight. It's terrible the way they handle things by relying on the school to investigate the incident and leave law enforcement out of the loop. If Fiona hadn't gone to the hospital in such bad shape in LA, there's no way there would've been a record. The school would have investigated and dispensed their punishment.

"I'd like to know what it was about these two guys that drew Fiona to them as her fall guys. Mahir's family has money for a shakedown written all over them, but I don't get the feeling this other guy comes from money. I'll touch base with you before we leave for Boston," I said, stretching. "Jax, my gut says she doesn't have the missing drive. If she did, why not sell it, and then disappear? Why drive all the way to New York to extract some crazy-ass revenge when you can collect your millions and go?"

"Lee, we don't understand how this girl's mind works. We're just assuming she killed Mahir, but from what Mary says, the police disagree. Benjamin said the Seattle police aren't being aggressive with pursuing Fiona as a missing person. They're treating it more like she rolled out of town. From what they gathered, she lived in a month-to-month furnished apartment, and when they searched it, her clothes and personal items were gone. They didn't have enough probable cause to dig into her financials or put a BOLO out on her. So the only way we can find Fiona is with old-fashioned investigating.

"You've only been on this a few days, and she had just a small window before we were on it. If she's there and heading to Boston, that's great for us. Will she show in Boston, or is she playing a game; I don't know. The PI's file gave you all the background information it might have taken you weeks to get. Count that as a win.

"Talk to your police contact, and we'll chat again soon. And, Lee, I'm not kidding, Mary said Belle is the next Mrs. Stone. Word to the wise, don't let Mary get too far into your business."

I about choked on my coffee. "Jax, Mary doesn't know what she's talking about; leave it at that."

After an unusually long shower, I studied my appearance before I left the bathroom, and noted I needed a haircut. *Should I shave before I go?* I checked my watch. *Whoa, eight o'clock!* There was no time, and yet I cared. *What the hell?*

Two minutes later, I knocked on Mary's door. My stomach flipped and not in a good way when Belle opened the door, pastry in hand. It was clear she'd been there a while, judging from the little amount of breakfast left on the large tray.

"Ladies, what did I miss?" I stuttered. Mary chuckled, and Belle outright laughed.

"Mary was sharing some of her adventures with me. She has lived a rich life."

This wasn't good. They'd bonded.

"So, has this been a social breakfast or a working breakfast? And how long have you been here?" I asked Belle.

"Mary texted me this morning at about three, but I was up working the case, so I came over about six to get a jump on things," she said. I followed the gooey pastry she was eating to her lips and found it impossible to tear my eyes away from the way they parted.

Regaining my composure, I sat next to Belle. I refreshed her and Mary's cups of coffee, then poured my own.

"I see. Anything you ladies need to share with me?"

"Belle received a call from Lucine last evening. Lucine told her she'd gotten a call from an anonymous source telling her Fiona is leaving for Boston tomorrow," Mary said.

"Aren't you concerned about this tip coming from an anonymous source?" I asked Belle.

"Be real. Her PI is the source; she just didn't want to rat him out. I put Fiona on the board as a person of interest, and that will allow us to bring her in for an interview, if she's still here. Lucine is a high-profile lawyer, and my captain doesn't want her calling him night and day. So we've been tasked to track Fiona down," she said.

"Why is she just now a POI? You already knew she was in the vicinity before you had this information," I said.

"Patience, Lee, patience," Mary said, patting my hand.

"Lucine also received a call last evening about eight from an unidentified woman. But the content clearly was something Fiona would say. Lucine paraphrased it as, 'I haven't forgotten what happened. I was denied justice; now everyone will pay,'" Belle said, pouring a dollop of cream in her cup. "And before you ask, we traced the call to a burner phone."

"Busy phone last night. How do you know it wasn't Lucine or someone associated with her making the call to get the NYPD jazzed up?" I had a hard time thinking Fiona would be so obvious and announce her plans. "The call to Mahir was from a phone registered to her, why switch to a burner now? If she killed him, I'd think she'd be long gone—"

"Unless she has unfinished business," Belle interrupted.

"Yes, there's that, but this feels wrong. Anyway, that's your case to clear. Our task is to find the drive, and if Fiona has it, our job is done. If not, we regroup. Solving a homicide isn't on our agenda," I said.

Something that looked like disappointment flashed across Belle's face.

"Lee, don't be crazy. If we can help, then we should," Mary said.

I saw a glimmer in Mary's eye that was trouble, and I wanted no part.

"Look, Mary, we already have a plan. Fiona, or someone posing as her, is meeting Mr. Sugar Daddy in Boston. That's our best lead. If Lucine is playing a game to get the NYPD on Fiona's tail, then we'll lose valuable time waiting to see what unfolds." I sat back, crossed my arms over my chest, and stared Mary down.

"But what if we can work with Belle and catch Fiona here before she heads to Boston?" Mary tapped her index finger on the table and leaned forward, as if that would persuade me. "She's a psychopath, and if she killed Mahir and is going after his mother next, shouldn't we stop it?"

"First, we have no idea whether or not she murdered Mahir; although, my money is on yes. Second, I'm not buying that phone call. It sounds too convenient. It got Fiona on the board for Belle to work, but as for us, we need to stay single-focused. And that means following the money. We know Fiona probably needs money, and in the past, this was her way to earn it. Boston was a good revenue source for her in the past, so that's where we're going."

Unless Jackson changed the plan, that was the one I was sticking to.

"Did you get what you wanted from our file, or do we need to go through it with you?" I asked Belle.

"Lucine arranged for me to receive the entire file on a flash drive from the PI. That's what kept me up all night," she said with a bit of arrogance, as if she was one step ahead of me.

What game is this woman playing?

"Then why the hell were you here at the butt crack of dawn," I asked, angry at her for wasting our time.

"No need to be rude, Lee," she said with a scolding voice. "I wanted to discuss things with Mary. Collaborate with her, so our efforts didn't overlap. She's the lead on your case, right?"

There it was; she was trying to outplay me. I could feel my scalp buzzing, and my breathing picked up. I could not let this woman get to me.

A mischievous smile tickled the corners of her lips.

"I'll have my team stay on Lucine in New York and make sure she's safe while they track down Fiona, if she is here. Me? I'm packing a bag and heading to Boston with you."

Mary clapped in sheer joy. After I tried to stare her down, she mouthed the two words she knew would throw me off my game: "Mrs. Stone."

CHAPTER EIGHT

Lee

THE HOUR FLIGHT FROM LaGuardia to Logan was smooth, unlike this case we were working. The airplane touching down brought me back to where I'd started my life. The section of Boston where I'd spent my childhood wasn't an easy place to stake your claim in the world. Southie had vastly changed over the years. In my time, it was more a working-class population, filled with noise and lots of action. It was definitely a place that had its own set of rules, and if you weren't aware of them, there would be trouble. It was common knowledge that after a snowstorm, if you shoveled a parking space, by God, that area belonged to you for the duration. Try to park where someone else had shoveled, and see what happened. You might have a shell of a car when you returned, but nothing more. If you didn't know the Southie rules, things went bad fast. Now professionals and young families populated Southie, and street fights, once encouraged, now resulted in arrests. One thing never changed, if you came back home from wherever you'd moved, the family got together. I'd quickly put some plans into motion so it would be my eight family members and my two guests for dinner tonight. But before that, though, I had work to do.

A stop at the car rental proved a bit of a fiasco. Mary wanted to rent a Lexus, Belle a Dodge Challenger, and me anything small. These women didn't understand that navigating the streets of Boston could be much like an obstacle course and parking a fight to the death. However, the gods of driving were not on my side. Belle gave me the slip as I made a restroom stop and got to the desk first. We left the airport in a cherry-red Mustang. Not only did we leave with a sports car I didn't want, but we left with her driving.

We dropped our luggage at the hotel and verified via Facebook that Chuck Evans, the man Fiona had implicated in a college scandal, worked at Syntex Corporation. Another ordinary guy minding his own business who had the bad luck to cross paths with Ms. Fiona O'Dell. Had their paths crossed when she lived in her last foster home? Had he done something that caused her to carry a grudge? I suppose he could have, but nothing indicated this had occurred. We had to work with the premise Fiona had targeted him when they were both students. After verifying online court documents all we found were two traffic violations incurred in the last two years. Nothing indicated he was a man who looked for trouble or had trouble find him. To be thorough, we planned a stop at the precinct where the college was located to make sure we didn't miss any other police reports.

After stopping for a quick lunch at an old-fashioned diner I swiped the keys from the table before Belle could claim the car again.

"I think I should take the lead on questioning Evans," Annabelle said, putting on her seatbelt. Her authoritarian tone told me she'd made up her mind, and she thought I should fall into place. I should have known there'd be a catch to her forfeiting driving.

I'd known from the start it was a bad idea to bring Annabelle. What the hell was I thinking, letting her come along? Oh, right, Mary had convinced Jackson to give the okay.

"Not gonna happen, Annabelle. This guy has nothing to do with your homicide and everything to do with our case. You have no jurisdiction in Boston. The only reason you're riding shotgun is to help us access any police reports that might be on file," I said. To me, it was the end of the discussion.

Who was I kidding? Annabelle would only take the word "no" as a challenge, and then we'd work at cross-purposes.

"Hold on. Chuck Evans has nothing to do with your case. He's just noise in the background that faded years ago. You have no reason to believe Fiona has contacted him recently. All you're doing is spinning your wheels, getting background information about her previous victims. It's unlikely he'll tell you anything you don't already know. But, if I interview him and find out something I can use in my case, I can add him as a witness." Her voice took on a scolding tone.

I felt an argument brewing, so I found a place to park so we could discuss the issue. By discuss, I meant I was going to lay down the law.

"That's ridiculous. A witness to what? The fact they had the bad fortune to come across Fiona? Detective, you are an invitee in my car and sitting here because I'm letting you. You don't like the rules? You can leave right now." I was tired of her bossy attitude.

Thank God Mary had stayed behind at the hotel to pore through some records Jax had sent over or I'd probably be dealing with her too.

"But here's how this will go down. *I'm* the one who will contact him and get the information *I* need. If there's anything I leave out you think will help you, then have at him."

"You're a real sweet talker, aren't you? Bet you that attitude gets you laid every day of the week." Annabelle twisted forward and readjusted her belt. "Just drive."

Although we rode in silence, her body language showed she was gearing up for another argument. She certainly could dish it out.

Annabelle was the first to break the silence. "You realize you have no authority here, right?" she said, twirling her pony-tail between her fingers. *Was this a nervous habit?*

"As far as I can tell, neither do you. I don't recall you telling me that BPD has invited you in to talk about the Evans case. If you're doing more than just liaising, it's news to me." I felt my lips tip into a smirk I should probably have controlled but didn't want to.

We reverted to silence, giving her an opportunity to plan another run at me from a different angle.

"How did you go from a premier law enforcement agency to a private investigator?"

She had a tone of derision I was sick of hearing, so I let it lie.

"Was it booze? Or too many women?" she taunted.

OK, she wanted to poke the bear? Well, once he wakes up, she might not like it. I didn't like this side of her.

"I gave up caring. If the gangs want to kill each other, why not let them? It will save us money for a trial, and after trial giving the little fuckers food and shelter. If the populace wants to promote making Chicago a sanctuary city, don't expect law enforcement to explain why your loved one is dead because someone in the correction system had released a criminal five times. If women called time and time again about getting beaten but didn't leave and wind up dead, what did they expect? When you try to find a way to justify beating a confession out of a suspect, that becomes problematic on so many levels. Or if you have no remorse about drawing your weapon even before you have all the facts, knowing you might kill someone, that should raise a concern. It didn't make me concerned, not for a long time. Do you want me to go on?" I gripped the steering wheel; I knew she was studying me, and I didn't care. She'd stirred up emotions I'd bottled away for years. How'd that happen?

My eyes lowered, in what I hoped reflected my disapproval as she laid her hand on my arm. The swirl that started in my stomach might be either the beginning of a sexual sensation or anger welling. It was a total crap-shoot. When I raised my eyes to her, she removed her hand.

Neither of us wanted to wade into that pile of emotional shit. So, we moved to a safer subject.

"I'll keep this short. I want to find out why she chose him to target. In and out," I said, moving my eyes from her to the road.

"So why do you care? What's this got to do with locating your missing external drive? It's not likely Fiona will reach out to him. He's in her review mirror."

"Why would Fiona return to Boston? What's here for her? Why set up a meet from the sugar daddy site? None of it makes sense," I said more to myself than her. "Why not get another job and not list these last six months on her resume?"

She had no answer, and neither did I.

"Are you going to meet with her foster parents? I mean I

don't get why you're interviewing all these people that have a history with her and not those who are part of her present?" She stopped talking as she read a text and looked out the window.

"What?" I nodded toward her phone.

"Trace found long blonde hairs on Mahir's jacket. It looks like someone ripped them from the scalp. It appears he put up a struggle—"

"Aren't you jumping the gun again? People shed hair all the time; you don't know when they landed on that jacket. You have no timeline."

"Actually, we do. Mahir's mother had picked up three jackets from dry cleaning the evening before, and that jacket was one of them," she said as she texted back.

"Yeah, I'm not sure how reliable that evidence is; someone at the cleaners may have shed the hairs when putting the plastic over the jacket. It could have happened when Mahir went to work that morning. What if he took off his jacket to put on his lab coat and someone brushed against it? It's your case to process, I'm just sayin'. I'd like to have more information about the stab wound or know if they recovered the knife," I said. I could go on and on and make mental lists of alternative theories, which didn't solve my case.

After a pause, she said, "Thanks for inviting me to dinner tonight with your family." Her lips pressed together, like she had a secret.

I turned and studied her, deciding whether to throw her to the wolves that were my family and watch her squirm as their inappropriate behavior unfolded, or to give her a heads-up so she could prepare herself for the chaos known as Stone. Just because I had issues with her professionally didn't mean she should be traumatized for life after an encounter with my family. I'd throw a few crumbs her way, and if she were as bright as I thought, she'd put the pieces together and act accordingly. It wasn't fair to throw anyone into the lion's den. She had a right to prepare herself for what she was stepping into tonight. Although letting her go in unprepared might prove entertaining.

"So, just so you know, my family's a motley crew. All of us wound up involved with law enforcement one way or the other. My sister and two brothers on the right side and my youngest brother on the wrong side."

"What do you mean you have a brother 'on the wrong side'?" she asked.

"Jake is doing a five-year stretch for involuntary manslaughter. Before you ask, it was a bar fight. No one could foresee the guy he beat up had a weak artery in his brain, but you take your chances in a fight. Anyway, he's out in three months, so people might be talking about it at dinner."

"Is it a sore subject with your family?"

What a ridiculous question.

"Well, as you can imagine, no one wants to accept that a family member took someone's father and husband from their family. We're supposed to be the protectors, not the destroyers."

I saw her lips part to respond, but then close. Good. There was nothing to defend my brother's actions. Everyone was drunk and tuned up for a fight, but his punch had killed the guy, and mutual combat and self-defense were not defenses a jury accepted.

The building where Chuck Evans worked came into view, and as we parked, we maintained a comfortable silence. I had to admit I liked working with someone I could bounce ideas off without having to file all types of police bureaucratic paperwork, and she was easy on the eyes. Too bad she ever had to open her mouth.

As Annabelle released her belt, she said, "Families are funny; they can make or break you. I'm an only child and grew up in New York. I spent twelve years in Catholic school and hated every minute. When I went to college, I did a bit of hell-raising, did some under-age drinking, but the minute I graduated I knew what I wanted, law enforcement."

I nodded in understanding.

The doors whooshed open, and we passed through the large atrium. We approached the desk marked "information" and gave the attendant Chuck Evans's name and ours. He started to say something but then directed us to the waiting area to wait for someone to speak with us.

A tall, older man dressed in casual attire approached us and asked us what our business was with Chuck. We gave him a carefully crafted version. He thought about it and asked to see Annabelle's badge and my credentials. Once he was satisfied, he said something that shocked us.

"You'll probably hear it on the news this morning. Last night someone stabbed Chuck and left him for dead. He's in critical condition in the ICU at Mass General. That's all we know right now."

Our faces both must have registered shock.

"Chuck's a well-liked guy and I can only hope this was a random occurrence. Because to think otherwise would be just too much for me to accept that someone targeted him."

We tracked down the precinct that had jurisdiction of Evans's case. Belle called the detective who'd been assigned the case and waited for a call back. After he verified her identity, he gave her limited information. What happened to Chuck was alarmingly similar to what had happened to Mahir. He also had been stabbed while in a seated position. Belle provided her partner's contact information to the detective assigned to the case, so they could liaise and determine if the cases were linked.

I didn't want to jump to conclusions, but this was just too much to ignore. The modus operandi was similar; it involved a common thread, but what was the motive? Why now? People rarely start a killing spree without some trigger.

Also, I was worried this wrinkle could get complicated with Belle. I was sure she'd want access to Fiona. I couldn't let that happen until I determined if she had the external drive, and if so, retrieved it. As much as I hated having a secretive plan, I had to maintain control, or our case could go sideways.

CHAPTER NINE

Annabelle

"LET'S MEET IN THE HOTEL DINING ROOM IN ABOUT FORTY minutes. I texted David, my partner, and he'll call and get more information," I told Lee.

"OK. It's important we keep Mary focused," Lee said. "We're here to find out if Fiona has our client's drive. We're not here to investigate a homicide. So play this low-key, or she'll weasel her way into your case."

"How are you going to handle the meeting with Fiona? Do you have a place picked out? And do you have clothes that scream you're wealthy and ready to spend some serious money on her?" I asked. "You could use a haircut. You know, so you fit the bill."

"I'll need to talk to Jackson about the details later today. He's the one chatting with Fiona and setting up my identity and backstory. I also have to manage Mary's expectations. My gut says Fiona has nothing to do with the murders or my client's property," I said, walking toward the hotel entrance.

"How do you explain that the two men she accused of assaulting her were stabbed in a forty-eight-hour window?" I asked. To me, it was more than a coincidence.

"I don't have to; it's not my problem." He half shrugged. "But the question is, why now? What's her motive? She's a genius, and, I'd say, not a woman who'd do well in a women's prison."

It had become easier to talk to him. I'd begun to understand his triggers and my boundaries. I had to remember this was an NYPD case, and although I felt like I was working with another detective on this case, he was a civilian. I'd have to be careful not to let him step over that boundary.

After speaking to my partner, it was clear there was no news to share with Lee. The Evans case was still in its early stages. During the night, Chuck Evans had taken a turn for the worse, and had to have an emergency operation to repair a nicked liver. Everything that had happened to Chuck was another piece of the giant puzzle that was this case. As the newsfeeds reported, it appeared whoever had attacked him was sitting next to him, just like the person who had stabbed Mahir. This was too much of a coincidence to ignore. But, why would either of the victims have agreed to meet Fiona for any reason? Nothing on Evans's social media indicated he was afraid of anyone or that anything was abnormal. A walk might clear my mind, so after I unpacked, I headed out to chase down a light lunch and a bottle of wine for dinner.

At 4:30 p.m. I heard a light rap at my door. Lee and Mary stood on the other side, and Lee had cleaned up good, real good.

The black Henley gave him a sexy bad boy look, and the well-worn jeans encased his muscular thighs. His hair, although a little on the wild side, set off the scruff on his face. I was seeing him in an altogether different light and liked what I saw.

The man clearly knew his way around a gym, and as quickly as an inappropriate thought popped into my mind, I squashed it.

"So, you ready to meet the family Stone? It's not too late to bail," he said.

"Lee, behave. I'm looking forward to meeting your parents, and I'm sure Belle is too," Mary said to him, then turned toward me. "Belle, you look lovely. That green dress brings out the green in your eyes. I thought your eyes had more of cerulean blue, but in that emerald-green dress, well, Belle, those eyes are definitely viridian green. Wouldn't you agree, Lee?"

He shook his head and raised an eyebrow. "Mary, green is green unless you're looking at a box of crayons. But yes, Belle, you look absolutely amazing. Now, I wouldn't want our dog Raven to get at that dress when he greets us at the door. Dad tries to contain him, but it's a losing battle. Between myself and my brother, we should keep him from knocking you over, but stay behind me as a human shield. Raven's a black field lab. If he gets too excited, you may find his paws on your shoulders. If you don't brace for it, the next thing you will feel is your ass hitting the floor. So, if you're ready, let's hit the road."

Boston had such a different tempo than New York, and I liked it. As many years as I've lived in New York, I've never set foot in Boston.

"Sorry, Mary, I was lost in thought; what did you say?" I asked.

"I said my niece, Emma, and I used to come to Boston for the museums here when she lived in Maine. One time, Russians were hot on our trail—"

"Nope, not going down that trail, Mary," Lee said. "Jackson already told me not to let you talk about anything other than the case." Lee gave her the "zip it" sign.

"Well, I never. Jackson's not the boss of me. Technically he is, but that's open for debate—"

"Seriously it will be hard enough getting through a meal with my lunatic family. I don't need you jumping in there and adding more to their special brand of crazy. So can we please agree that we'll keep this on the level of just having a meal with people we need to tolerate and not stir anyone up? Because, I guarantee, you tell your stories, and my father will have to top you. Add in booze, and there's a chance the cake might land on the floor. It's happened."

Since his eyebrows were about to his scalp, I had every reason to believe what he said.

The Stones' home was at least seventy-five years old but well maintained. As we turned into the driveway, you could see people milling about in the house, and it appeared every light was on. Windows were open, and Lee's father was the first to see us and yell a hello from the living room. Then several people rushed out onto the porch.

Lee ran around to open our doors and instructed us to stay behind him until he was certain the coast was clear and the dog was contained. Just as we thought we had a clear shot to the house, this bolt of black lightning came bounding toward Lee, and we all braced. He was right; the dog was so wild it took three men to corral him.

His mother was the first to introduce herself. She was a short woman, who might give the appearance of being gentle but I knew it took a formidable woman to raise the men I saw in that house. Next, his father appeared, and instead of shaking my hand, he hugged me and stood back, assessing me. Then he shouted to the others in the living room, "She's good, boys! It's impossible she's a Yankees fan. You're not, are you?" he asked with a bit of concern in his voice.

"Benintendi and Betts, all the way." I smiled. I'd always been a Socks fan, but when the Yankees had signed Jeter I almost wavered.

A mischievous, proud smile spread across Mr. Stone's face.

"You know Lee played ball and could've been in the minors," he said, giving his son a side hug.

His mom broke in and asked if anyone wanted refreshments, and Mary offered to go help her with dinner.

It was so noisy in there. There were at least three separate conversations all happening at once.

By the time we sat for dinner, I felt like I'd been a part of the family for years.

"Belle, are you a lifer with the force, or are you taking your pension at twenty?" his father asked.

"I'm out as soon as possible," I said, and that surprised everyone.

"Have you got a plan, dear?" his mom asked.

Should I share my secret with them, or would they all laugh at me? Lee's eyes met mine and dared me to answer. Challenge accepted.

"I write books," I said with a bit of hesitancy.

"The hell you say," his father said with a laugh.

"You mean novels?" his sister asked, putting down her fork.

"I've written a few." I smiled and caught Mary's eye as she gave me a questioning look.

"Are they published?" Mary asked.

"They are," I responded.

Suddenly people were reaching for their phones, and I

could only guess they were going to Google me or go straight to Amazon. I waited as they tried to find me.

Lee was the first to say, "You had me there."

"OK, all you detectives, try searching for Cloche Hughes." And I waited.

Slowly each person looked up at me.

"How'd you become an author?" Lee asked.

"It started with a case when I first made detective and exploded from there," I said.

"Eight books. Not quite Lee Child but getting there," his sister said with a wide smile on her face. "And one was a *New York Times* Best Seller. How do you keep it under wraps?"

"The pen name," I said. "Cloche is the French for bell. Neat, huh?"

"Very," Lee said, with admiration in his eyes.

I became the focus of conversation, explaining how I crafted my books while everyone continued eating. I saw Mary wink at Lee and him shake his head and smile.

By the end of the night, I appreciated Lee, who was a beloved member of a close, albeit a dysfunctional family, who embraced us as their own. I learned a lot about Lee that night, just by listening and looking around. Without having to say a word, I realized Lee had been an honorable cop who may have lost his way. But, being honorable, he knew to get out while he still had a soul. I hoped this firm wouldn't be a long-term commitment, and after seeing his wood sculptures, I hoped he'd explore that passion.

His ribbons for athletics spoke to his ability to commit to a team. Pictures of happy days before his wife died opened my eyes to the man who loved and loved deeply. I hoped to find that kind of love someday.

As we left his family home, I got a text from my partner. Chuck Evans had never regained consciousness and had died an hour ago. Boston said they took into evidence blonde hairs on his jacket.

I passed the phone to Lee whose only comment was "Fuck."

Fuck indeed.

CHAPTER TEN

Lee

A S I APPROACHED THE BREAKFAST TABLE, I HAD THE uncomfortable feeling Mary and Belle were about to set upon me like hyenas. Their foreheads almost touched as they whispered and laughed, but they quieted down as I walked up. Mary's eyes danced when hers met mine, as if she had a secret. Belle's eyes swept up through her lashes creating a soft crinkle at the corners.

"Good morning. Coffee's right here on the table," Belle said. She motioned to the seat across from her, turned my cup over, and placed it on the saucer.

As I sat I asked, "Hear anything more about Evans?"

Belle adjusted the napkin on her lap, then handed me the milk for my coffee. I noticed the blood-red nail polish that accentuated her delicate, porcelain-like hands. This was new.

"What? No small talk? Thanks for inviting me to dinner. I enjoyed your family—"

Oh no, I would not relive the teasing I'd gotten from my family last night. Belle had learned way too much information about my past for my comfort. They'd embraced her as if she had been a family member for years.

"Belle, not to be rude, but there's a shitload of stuff to do today to get ready for my meeting tonight. Let's cut the chit-chat," I said. I didn't need to be caught up in going down the memory lane my mother had shared with her and Mary last night.

A brief look of disappointment flashed across Belle's face, but she quickly schooled her emotions. I thought Mary would say something, but she remained still with her lips to her cup, almost smiling. I could read her expression; she was formulating a plan I was sure I wasn't going to like.

"Fine by me," Belle said, and a stiff shrug followed.

When a woman said "fine," that was your cue to be on guard.

"First, to get you ready for tonight, you're going to need a professional haircut. Then, you're going to need some new clothes. I talked to the concierge this morning. He recommended an exclusive salon, and he booked you for nine o'clock. That's for a haircut, facial, and manicure—"

I put my hand up to stop her. "There will be no manicure or facial," I replied. That was my hard line in the sand.

"Of course there will be a facial and manicure, Lee," Mary said. "Your skin needs a good exfoliation, and with all the pollutants in the air, your pores are choking. You're supposed to be a wealthy man who's influential in the business world and takes care of himself. If you don't pamper yourself, then how can you take care of little Miss Fiona? You've got one shot at a first impression. If you don't look the part, she'll sense something is off, make an excuse to use the ladies' room, and bolt. Trust me; she seems the type who would dine and dash. Even if she doesn't have the drive, if she smells a setup, she's out of there. So, suck it up, buttercup. It's a part you have to play."

"That should take Lee about an hour and a half, Mary, and while he does that you and I will check out the clothing store the concierge recommended," Belle said. "Lee, by the time you're finished with the facial, we'll have two outfits ready for you to look at. You can meet us there, and we can choose which looks better on you. Is there a price range we need to stay in?"

Mary jumped in with an answer. "I checked with Jackson, and we can spend up to three thousand dollars for the whole shebang."

"Mary, that's insane!" I objected. "My whole wardrobe didn't cost three thousand dollars. That's a total waste of money."

"Lee, when was the last time you went suit shopping? Wait, don't answer that because it's rhetorical," Mary said.

"I understand you're stressed because of the tight time-line," Mary said.

I felt like they were acting like a tag team. One of them picked up where the other left off before I could even say anything.

"It probably seems overwhelming trying to get this all done because we have so little time. Like we've said, though, you've got to look the part. I'm going with gray, linen, three-button, and no cuffs.. And, Lee, you won't like this, but they're putting highlights in your hair."

I couldn't comprehend what Belle had just said. She want-ed me to add highlights like those metrosexual men? Like Hightower? She wanted me to fit into the artsy-fartsy, cham-pagne-sipping crowd? No way.

She read my body language as I braced for an argument and stopped me before I could even rev my engine. Her eyes met mine; she leaned forward, and her hands gripped the table edge. Then came the dreaded words, "I'm doing this for your own good."

I realized arguing was futile, so I did what most men do when it comes to arguing about clothes and grooming. I surrendered.

"After lunch, we can discuss your strategy for getting Fiona to trust you," Belle said, as if she was in charge of my operation. She was a bossy little thing.

"Thanks, Belle, but I've got that covered," I said. One thing I knew for sure, I knew how to handle a perp.

"Well, pray tell, how are you going to handle it? I think we should prepare by doing role-playing. Lee, this woman is a master manipulator, and you have no idea what path she'll take you down. She won't have enough time to do the total mind fuck, but she can do a brief version to reel you in for more," Belle said, moving her chair closer.

I glanced at Mary who appeared to be hanging on her every word. "Mind fuck?" I asked, turning back to look at Belle.

"Mind fuck," she replied.

"Let's hear it."

"OK, there are three rules to trapping a man. First, you create a comfort zone through establishing a pattern. Every morning you call at eight o'clock, without fail and say you love him. It becomes a comfortable pattern. Next step to keep his interest, so you aren't taken for granted, you create pain by breaking the pattern. Suddenly your calls stop. That makes a man wonder, *Why did she stop? Is she bored? Doesn't she care anymore? Is there another guy?* Thus, you've now inflicted pain. The guy becomes obsessed with finding out why you broke his comfortable routine. It also puts him in a sexually competitive state. Now, the door is open. He'll look for any bit of validation available, so you offer him a reward. That reward he's working for will hit him hard. This game is methodical, but the keyword is 'unpredictable.' And that's how Fiona works. Normally she has months to work her game. Her time with you is limited, so she'll have to amp it up and be ready. You need to prepare for everything she may throw at you."

I stared at Belle thinking, *Who is this woman?*

"Belle, like I said, I've got this," I replied as I watched the waiter come to take our order.

Once we'd placed our order, she continued. "Lee, the woman is a sociopath and, as you said, a genius. No offense, but do you honestly think if you go in without practice you can match wits with her? This date can't be an interrogation; it has to be a conversation where you subtly extract information. You'll have to flirt with her and make her feel protected and wanted. Frankly, Lee, that behavior doesn't seem to be in your normal bag of tricks. We only have a little time to make sure you're ready to feel comfortable engaging her and yet still manage to stay ahead of her—"

"Belle, I said I've got this," I repeated more firmly, but this time I wasn't sure I really did.

Mary, who had been quiet too long, finally said, "Lee, Fiona is half your age and smart as a whip. She's looking for money for a short period, so she's got her game in place. If she isn't convinced you can offer what she needs with minimal effort short term, she's onto the next mark. She may already have another date set up after you to go clubbing to hedge her bets. You have one shot; mess it up she's on the move. Do you want to be the one to tell the client we had her right in our hands and you let her go because you were too stubborn to accept our help?"

"Mary, I've been interviewing people for years," I said with an air of confidence. "Plus, I took the FBI profiling course. Trust me, I can control this woman."

Belle reached out and took my hand in hers. *What the hell?* She slowly stroked the pad of my hand, moving her thumb in circles, and turned my palm upward. Her green eyes met mine, and her face softened as she smiled. *Well, this is nice. Should I let her know I reciprocate her feeling and appreciate it?* Her thumb caressed my palm as she leaned into my personal space and looked into my eyes, almost in a hypnotic manner. *Whoa.* My skin tingled, and my heart rate sped up. The bottom part of my body engaged, and my cock came to life. Her eyes had a certain softness, but it was her lips that got to me. Those lips were moving, but I couldn't hear anything; it was like I was suddenly deaf. I watched her teeth lightly sink into her lower lip. All I wanted to do was reach across the table, no, jump across the table, and own that mouth. I had no other thought except I had to have her. Right now.

Without warning, she released my hand and sat back. My hearing returned with the broken connection, but other body parts refused to comply.

"And that's how it's done, Lee. You were putty in my hands. If you act like that, she's a goner. You'll have her where you want her," Belle declared.

"Lee, that was quite entertaining," Mary said with a mischievous smile. "I could read every thought going through your mind. Belle was in total control, and she could have extracted anything she wanted from you. If you're supposed to be a man who commands others and who's monetarily rewarded for your business shrewdness, then you better get your shit together and up your game."

I cleared the fog from my head and weakly and gravely

said, "I see your point."

"Here's the plan," Belle said. "We meet at the clothes place at eleven; that should give you plenty of time. An hour to finalize which outfit you're going to wear tonight. We'll grab lunch after that and prepare you for battling Fiona. What time is your dinner date?"

"We're meeting at seven thirty," I responded.

"OK, let's finish breakfast and move out. I've got this," Belle said, and Mary chuckled.

This whole preparation for my role as a sugar daddy left me exhausted and needing a nap. But Belle had other plans. Her plans involved lists and cue cards. For the second time that day, I found myself wondering, *Who is this woman?*

"All right, do we need to run through the psychopathy of a sociopath? Did I mention my degree was in psychology? Do I need to give you a crash course in knowing the positive triggers for a narcissistic sociopath?" she asked.

I rolled my eyes, probably rude, but I was in no mood for psychobabble. "I'm good."

"Are you? Are you really? Because I don't think you know what you're doing, and if you don't, you'll botch this whole thing up. She's our killer. Both of us know it. You're just too arrogant to admit you're out of your depth. You should step aside so the professionals can take charge." Her face filled with anger, and her voice escalated with each sentence.

"That's it," I said, returning her anger with my own. I stood, stalked to the door, opened it, and motioned her to leave.

Mary shook her head and grabbed the arms of her chair, as if ready to lift herself out and leave. I motioned her to stay.

I pointed at Belle and gave her the out signal with my thumb. Imagine my surprise when she leaned back into the overstuffed chair, threw her head back, and laughed. I had once again been played by Belle. First the hand rubbing, now the mind games.

"I got it, ladies. I can't be overconfident, and I have to stay on my toes and measure every word," I said.

When 7:00 p.m. rolled around, I looked like a man who owned the world. I looked at my bare wrist and worried if I had made a mistake not buying the Rolex Belle suggested. No, I could never justify that expense. I was ready to take on Fiona O'Dell. Only, I felt worried. Was I out of my league?

CHAPTER ELEVEN

Fiona

THERE WERE ONLY A FEW LOOSE ENDS TO TIE UP BEFORE I LEFT for Europe and my new job. I'd hit the motherlode of employment opportunities. I still couldn't fathom that a premier research lab in Berlin that had advanced beyond the point of manipulating DNA strands had reached out to me. My more than adequate salary would be commensurate with my abilities. I loved that they were going to cover my housing expense in a premiere part of Berlin. No doubt, by this time next year, I would hold a senior position and be working on a bigger and better product. Finally, someone appreciated my talents. But first, I needed traveling money. The money I had tucked away in an offshore account, out of the reach of the IRS, needed to stay there.

Now, what do I do with this guy I'm meeting? How should I approach him? On paper, he looked good, but he hadn't passed my background screen. Although PamperedSugarBabies. com assured me they'd verified him, something didn't fit. Many people avoided social media, but this guy was a ghost. It wasn't like I had a few weeks to work the money from this guy. I had two weeks, maximum, to secure some decent traveling money, and that meant I had to up my game. But if I upped it too quickly, he might sense a scam and bolt. I had to outthink him and do it with finesse. I didn't like going into a meeting without a plan.

My end game simple, relieve this sugar daddy of $10,000. But my plan needed work. The bait I would offer was my body. I was an expert at playing the femme fatale part. My dress cost a fortune, but you have to invest money to make money. The dress skimmed my skin and left nothing hidden of what I would offer him. Cutouts strategically placed in areas that should remain private were boldly displayed. The sleek, black dress had clearly been designed to have a man concentrate on every piece of available skin that could be his. I wanted him studying my body rather than thinking about how he would answer my next question. I wanted him thinking of how he would unwrap me as we negotiated terms.

I had already Googled the restaurant and determined the best seating position in each of the areas if things didn't go well and I had to leave undetected. How easily would he give up control? Men like him were usually control freaks. He wasn't on social media, and that was concerning because it squelched my ability to find something I could fake that I liked so I could bond with him over a "mutual" interest.

The mirror reflected what I wanted to portray, a desirable woman, every man's sexual fantasy. This dress transformed me into a living fantasy, possibly even a taboo one. Satisfied I'd hit the mark, I picked up my purse and headed for the lobby. Ah yes, as I swept across the lobby, heads turned and eyes followed me. I was ready.

The high-end restaurant in downtown Boston he'd chosen was acceptable. The elegant Japanese restaurant offered small portions of food for high prices and was highly sought after for nearly unattainable reservations. The glass and low light bathed its wealthy patrons in a golden glow. Yes, the ambience was perfect, and the tone thoughtfully set.

He saw me before I saw him and stood to the side of the table. I was going to have to rectify the seating arrangement. His chair faced the front doors, which limited my ability to leave undetected. Where he'd positioned himself gave him an unobstructed view of the entire room. If I were to leave, he would see it.

This seating arrangement wouldn't allow me to monitor who came and went from the place. What if someone from my past arrived, and I didn't know he was there until I felt a tap on my shoulder? I was well aware certain people make a point not to have their backs exposed, like law enforcement or controlling men who don't want other men looking at their dates. I watched him as he watched my every move. Did the position he was trying to place me in mean he wanted control of the situation? He didn't scan the room, envious of his prize, to see if any other men were watching me. Instead, he was tracking me like prey walking toward his trap. The look in his eyes concerned me.

My date had a roguish air about him, yet he could have easily graced the cover of *GQ*. His brown highlighted hair was perfectly styled and accompanied by the requisite expensive suit. So far, nothing should have triggered an alarm, but something, difficult to identify, had shifted me off-balance. His body was stiff and guarded, as if he didn't feel comfortable in his own skin. For some reason, it made my skin prickle. Unlike most men, who undressed me with their eyes, this man seemed like he was trying to find the seat of my soul.

His stilted greeting offered no warmth. Didn't he realize a cheek-to-cheek greeting, not a handshake, was the norm? As I shook his extended hand, I noticed he wasn't wearing a watch or any other jewelry, another tick that something was off.

"Ms. O'Dell, a pleasure to meet you. May I call you Fiona?" he asked with a bit of a rasp to his voice.

I nodded and smiled with a warmth that put most men at ease and had them begging for more. It didn't work on him. I did, however, continue capturing the attention of the men three tables over who watched my every move, so I wasn't off my game.

"Please, call me Mykus. Here, let me help you," he said and moved toward the chair behind me.

"If you don't mind, I'd like to change places with you." He tilted his head questioningly, and I didn't explain. Why should I? I should be able to sit where I wanted. I needed to set the tone for the night, me controlling the situation.

"Whatever makes you more comfortable," he said. He offered an insincere smile that soon flattened out to lips pressed together. As I walked past him, his body stiffened, as if he was on guard.

He didn't come around to push my chair in but waited for the wait staff to do it. Could he be married and have lost all sense of manners? Or was he placing himself in a dominant position? What the hell was going on? As I sat, I spied the bottle of wine already chilling. Had he already chosen the wine without giving me an opportunity to peruse the selection? Just as I collected myself from his faux pas, he asked the server to bring the menu and stated we were ready to place an order. The least he could do was compliment my dress or admire my appearance. No chitchat? He was cutting off my ability to find my bearings and set the tone.

This was ridiculous.

"If you'd give me a moment, I'd like to review the selection," I said to the server who bowed his head and departed. I needed some time to regain control and set the pace.

OK, so he wanted to play mind games? Then we'd have a go at it. I decided to see how far he'd permit me to push him.

"Mykus, I'd like to get business out of the way so we can enjoy our meal and time together."

He stopped and held the napkin he was about to place on his lap. His eyes engaged mine and remained focused.

"To be honest, I've never done this before," he confessed. "So why don't you lead me through this transaction."

Transaction. Oh, that stung. My gut screamed that this meeting was off, but no, I decided, I was just on edge to close the deal and was being paranoid. The man obviously felt awkward in this situation, and this was my chance to gain control.

"I prefer to think of it as an adventure," I said, licking my lips to put him off-balance and draw his mind to them. But my plan didn't work. He remained focused on my eyes.

"I'm game," he said, reaching for the prechosen wine to fill our glasses.

"Perfect," I said, leaning forward to give him an eyeful of my cleavage. "Pull out your telephone and open your browser." As I waited, I savored the wine. Merlot would have been preferable, but this Cabernet would do.

He looked perplexed but complied.

"Now, open your banking app, and once that's opened, go to the tab that allows you to access your FICO score."

His staged smile disappeared.

"I don't know what game you're playing, Fiona, but I have no intention of giving you access to my financial information. I'm here for a nice meal, and I feel we're already off to a bad start." His tone reflected annoyance as he put his phone back in his jacket. "Maybe this was a mistake."

He let the silence hang, and I accepted the challenge. I offered a sigh of defeat and smiled.

"Surely you understand that taking precautions is necessary."

His eyes met mine with such intensity I felt the need to reposition myself.

"Fiona, we both know that's not true. The service thoroughly vetted me, and we wouldn't be sitting here if I hadn't passed every checklist. This is a meet and greet to decide if we want to take this further. I'm not a desperate man seeking companionship, and I do not appreciate the way you've conducted this so far. I'm looking to spend time with a bright, engaging woman, not some high-end hooker. If I've misunderstood what the service offers, then I apologize, and we can end this meeting."

A "high-end hooker"? He'll pay for that if we leave together tonight. I'm going to have to up my game.

"All right, my apologies, Mykus, but as I said, I'm a cautious person. I certainly didn't mean to come across as you're painting me. Please, tell me about yourself. I want to know everything about you." I willed my body to relax; although, every nerve in my body fired as if electrocuted. He wanted the upper hand? So be it, but only because I was allowing him to have it under my conditions.

Mykus signaled the waiter to return to take our order.

Once we had ordered, he turned his attention back to me.

"Ladies first. Please, Fiona, tell me about you. You're a beautiful and intriguing woman. Is Boston your hometown?" he asked, lifting his wine glass to his lips.

"Yes and no. I'm a graduate student at Harvard and live in Cambridge." If I'd had the funds, I could have attended an Ivy League school. So a lie but still some truth.

His eyebrows almost hit his scalp, reflecting genuine surprise. Maybe I had played this wrong and should have chosen Boston University. Had I overplayed my hand? He'd said he wanted a bright companion. Harvard fit the bill.

"I see," he said as the server placed our appetizers before us.

"What are you studying?" he asked, not at all interested in the food.

"Oh, Mykus, academia is a boring subject. I'd rather hear about you." I wasn't about to reveal anything that had the potential to trip me up.

"What can I tell you that wasn't already provided in the vetting process? What secrets can I reveal?" he asked, leaning back, not reaching for a fork.

This was all wrong. Red flags flew up all around me. What happened to banter and flirting as foreplay? He was way too defensive and tight. On paper, the man had looked like an absolute winner. Was he really just socially inept with women? I'd give him a bit more rope before I left and move on to the next mark.

I softly giggled and tilted my head. "Whatever you tell other women you go on dates with." I wanted him concentrating on the way my lips moved and my mouth savored my food to bring his thoughts around to what my mouth could do to him later. If he thought he could unnerve me, he was wrong, so wrong.

"Harvard, that is quite a coup for your resume," he said, avoiding what I'd said and bringing the conversation back to me. "You look like you'd be more a west coast girl. I'd guess LA or Seattle."

I nearly choked. "No, I've never been to either place. I like the traditions of Boston."

He picked up his fork to spear a shrimp but stopped midair before it reached his mouth. "Fiona, you appear to be anything but a traditional woman. In fact, I'm fairly certain you like to live on the edge and dip your toe into the wild pond."

This was getting out of hand, and I fought to maintain my cool. I needed to bring it back to neutral territory, retake control, and set the narrative.

"Wild? Oh absolutely not. I'm a real bookworm; I worked hard to get accepted into my PhD program. All my energy is focused on paving the way for my future." I leaned toward him to whisper a secret. "My passion always was and still is forensic psychology."

His facial expression remained the same, but by the way his eyes dilated, I knew he was more than a little interested.

"I'm impressed. A super brain and beautiful woman. Quite the deadly combination. What does a forensic psychologist do?" he asked.

After wiping my lips, I took a moment to gather my thoughts before I responded.

"I can give you the American Psychological Association's definition, but it's short and boring. The APA's line is that it's the application of clinical psychologies to the legal arena. However, I like to make it more of a personal interpretation. My training as a forensic criminalist allows me to study crime and criminals. I want to know what makes people tick and get into their minds. Own their minds." A response crafted for a purpose.

He nodded, so I continued. "I identify and predict psychological, sociological, and economic characteristics that may lead people to commit crimes. And from there, I can control them. I find the human brain fascinating." I shrugged and waited.

"Do you have much experience with criminals?" he asked.

"Enough," I answered.

"Care to share?" he asked with a raised eyebrow.

"We keep talking about me, and it's you I want to focus on. What type of position do you hold in your company?"

God this had hit the territory that involved too much work. Without his eyes leaving mine, he failed to set his fork back on the table and dropped it. I think he purposefully dropped it to avoid my question. Or could he be as clumsy as he was dull?

"I own the company," he said, not giving much away.

Most entrepreneurial men liked to boast about their accomplishments. Not him. He patiently waited for the staff to remove the plates and brought the conversation back to me.

"I suppose your education brings you into contact with new medical discoveries associated with treating criminals."

"Such as?" I asked, not understanding where this was leading.

"Such as a gene-editing tool to manipulate behavior and illnesses. Isn't that all the rage?" he asked.

OK, that was it. Was he trying to commit some corporate espionage? Had my false profile somehow led him to discover I had worked for a company that was heavily invested in genome re-engineering? Whatever his reason, this was my cue to leave. Nothing good could come from this.

"How about we continue this when I get back from the ladies' room?" I asked. "We can discuss it over dinner."

He stood as I stood, and I made my way to the restroom, but a quick left took me outside the restaurant and on the curb hailing a cab. And that, ladies and gentlemen, was why I always have my mark's back to the door.

CHAPTER TWELVE

Annabelle

WHY THE HELL IS FIONA LEAVING THE RESTAURANT? OH MY GOD, *she's ditching him and hailing a cab.* Before I thought it through, I started my car and began following the cab. Once I had her clearly in my sights and could safely follow her, I called Lee.

"So, how's it going with Fiona?" I asked.

"What the hell is wrong with you? She went to the bathroom and will be back any minute," he said. "I have to go."

"I doubt that," I replied with a smug tone.

The silence was deafening.

"OK, I'll bite," he said.

"I'm right behind her in the cab she left in about five minutes ago. You might as well pay the tab, and when the cab drops her off, I'll head back," I said.

"Shit. Call me when you get back."

After Lee hung up, I called Mary who laughed and said she'd order coffee and cakes, and we'd meet in her room.

When I returned, Mary and Lee didn't seem upset, and I didn't sense any elevation of tension.

"Well?" Lee asked, turning off the TV.

I flopped into a soft chair, waiting for the onslaught of questions.

"What the hell?" Lee started.

"Pretty open-ended question," I said, and he glared.

"Look, my gut said things would go south. You didn't want to listen to me, and I felt you weren't ready to take Fiona on. I followed my gut and parked outside."

"Brilliant," Mary said. "If Belle had told you what she planned you would've been on edge."

He mulled it over, and I saw him struggle not to argue.

"Well, where is she?" he asked as he threw himself into the chair across from me. His posture was cocky.

"I have no idea," I replied, tucking my feet under me.

"What do you mean? You followed her somewhere."

"That's correct. However, by the time I'd parked and went into the hotel, she'd already left by another door."

"There you go; if that doesn't say guilty I don't know what does," Lee replied.

"No, it means the girl is street smart. Something you should have expected from her years in foster care. You probably set off her radar, so she bailed and used diversion tactics," Mary said with a shrug.

Lee took out his phone and opened an app. The app had a map with a grid, and on the grid was a blinking red dot. "There she is," he said.

I was stunned stupid. "What? How?" I babbled.

"I attached a tracking device to her purse when I dropped my fork while we were eating," he said way too nonchalantly.

"So why did you let me follow her to the hotel?" Anger

KJ. MCGILLICK

built in my voice.

"Hey, I didn't tell you to follow her; I said I'd meet you back here after you had accomplished what you'd decided to go do."

"So you let me follow her and waste my time so you could have a laugh?" I was pissed.

"Do you see me laughing? Your little adventure helped," he said.

"How?"

"You said she used diversion tactics," he said with a shrug. "We wouldn't have known that about her if you hadn't followed her. Now we need to figure out her next move."

"OK, I guess all we can do is sleep on it. Maybe tomorrow we can catch her off guard. Anyway, nothing more to do to-night," Belle said.

"Can you send me the app and login information? That way I can follow her too in case we aren't together or if I'm up before you," I said to Lee.

With a few thumb strokes, I had the login information, in-stalled the app, and left.

It was impossible to sleep. I had no reason to believe Fiona had killed anyone or committed a crime. And oh, by the way, Belle, are you doing something illegal by using this app? Are you stalking this woman? God. I'll think about that later. She'll never find the device, so no harm no foul. Right? Keep telling yourself that.

With nothing else to do, I opened the app, and low and behold the dot was moving. Moving at 4:00 a.m. *Where the hell was she going at 4:00 a.m.? Should I wake Lee?*

I threw on my sweatshirt and pants, and as I was walking

to his door, I called his cell.

He answered immediately. "What?"

"Fiona's on the move."

"I know," he responded.

"I'm standing outside your door. Open up," I said.

"Can't."

"Why?"

"I'm following Fiona. Gotta go, I'm parking," he said.

"Where are you?" I asked before he hung up.

"The airport, and I'm about to—shit, I just lost the signal. She must have checked her purse in her luggage. Let me see if I can catch her in the airport departure area before she passes through the security gate. I'll call you back."

We were once again in the dark.

CHAPTER THIRTEEN

Lee

SCOURED THE AREA OF THE AIRPORT THAT WAS OPEN TO THE PUBLIC, but it proved fruitless. Fiona was gone, out of my reach until her plane landed and the tracking device re-engaged.

The sudden shrill of my phone ringing broke my concentration, and I answered.

"Good morning, Lee," Jackson said. "I spoke to Mary already, and I'm up to speed. She told me about the fiasco last night, but we've hit a bit of luck. Fiona called her old roommate, Claire, out of the blue and asked if she could stay with her for two nights. After that, she told Claire, she's leaving the country. All Fiona would tell Claire was she was in Boston, and when she'd returned from a date, her room had been searched. She was frantic. She'd sensed someone had been stalking her, and this break-in validated her fear. Apparently, Fiona has arranged a meeting with someone in LA who's going to help her with some business. Claire called me looking for you and told Fiona she'd try to help her. Fiona's supposed to call Claire when she lands. I'm texting you Claire's number. Touch base with her, and let me know your plan," he said.

"Copy that," I replied. "My gut told me Fiona doesn't have

the drive, but if she doesn't, why all the cloak and dagger? And why is she leaving the country?"

"Well, you've got to make contact and get the information. Once Fiona leaves the country, she's sure as hell out of our jurisdiction. My head's ready to explode. I don't like the shady way Benjamin originally got the information under the government's radar. I'm beginning to think we've been had. Who tossed her room and why? I don't care if you have to confront her; get this done. We have no way of making her give us the drive. This is so goddamn frustrating," Jackson said.

"I hear you. We can't arrest Fiona; well, Belle could. I'm thinking of letting Belle take the lead on this when we confront her. She can flash a badge and see where it goes. I know Fiona damn well won't talk to me," I said. Letting Belle take the lead with Fiona didn't sit well with me, but I had to put my ego aside.

I had to admit, something about Belle drew me in. She was confident, feisty, and didn't work for my attention. And why did I like that she fell right into a rhythm with my family like she'd been a part of them for years? I needed to manage my expectations. Once this job was done, I'd probably never see her again.

I called Belle, looking forward to her picking up the phone. Jesus, was I turning into a sap?

"Are you and Mary together?" I asked, merging onto the highway headed back to the hotel.

"Of course. And you're on speaker," Belle said.

"I'm on my way back. You two need to pack your stuff. Mine's already packed; just grab it from my room. Check out, and be waiting in the lobby for me to pick you up. Mary, call the airlines and get three seats for LA for the next plane out; that will give me enough time to pick you up and get us back to the airport."

"Whoa, what? Why LA?" Belle asked.

"Because that's where Fiona is heading. For some reason, Fiona called Claire and asked to stay with her for a few days. Apparently, someone tossed her room while we were at dinner. Get the tickets, and we can discuss this later."

There was an uncomfortable silence.

"What's wrong?" I asked.

"It's unlikely I'll get an approval to follow Fiona to LA, so I may need to go home. Boston is one thing, but we aren't any closer to getting an arrest warrant much less an extradition order," she said.

She was right; she wasn't on an unlimited expense account.

"It's Saturday. When's your next day off?" I asked.

"I don't have to be back until Wednesday," she replied. "Why?"

"Do you want to follow this through?"

"Of course, I do! I'm emotionally invested in this at this point, and I want to play it out to the end," she said.

"We can front your ticket, hotel room, and meals if we make you an official consultant for our case. You in?" I asked with more hope than I cared to admit.

The smile in her voice translated over the phone. "I'm in. What's the plan?"

"Honestly, I have no idea. I'm going to call Claire and see what Fiona said to her. By the time I get back, I hope I'll have more information. It's weird that Fiona called Claire. They didn't seem close or like they even got along. Maybe she didn't have any friends to call, and Claire was her last resort. But she sure was stringing a lot of guys along; why not call one of them?" I said, more thinking out loud than needing an answer.

"Let me get things rolling, and we'll talk about this when

you pick us up. I've got this," Belle said.

"Thanks. Fiona leaving makes things a lot more complicated. I hate to admit it, but I'm not sure what our next move should be after we get to LA," I said.

"That's because we don't have enough information. Just get back here, and we can brainstorm," Belle said.

I liked brainstorming with Belle, it felt comfortable.

After I hung up, I called Claire. I asked her to let Fiona stay, and told her we'd be in touch as soon as we landed. Her reaction surprised me a bit. I'd expected her to be apprehensive, or that I'd need to talk her into it. However, she seemed excited by the prospect and was all in.

As I pulled up to the curb, Mary and Belle put the bags in the trunk, and we were off.

"There's a new development; I don't know what to make of it," I said as Belle fastened her seatbelt.

"I have news too, but you go first," she said.

"Fiona told Claire she thinks someone is stalking her. Claire said she saw some guy hanging around the complex, possibly someone Fiona knew when she attended school. He definitely wasn't a student. Claire said he looked like someone from the sex club that had picked Fiona up a few times. Claire reported the guy to security, but since he hadn't done anything illegal, they just made a report. I suppose I see why Fiona would want to avoid hotels after a break-in," I said.

"Gaining access to hotel rooms is easier than most people imagine," Mary said with an authoritative tone.

"Do tell," Belle said, as she turned and smiled at Mary.

I looked back at Mary in the rearview mirror and could see she was revving up for a long-winded speech. When she had that look, nothing could stop her.

"First, the perpetrators obtain an ordinary electronic key, even one that's long expired, discarded, or used to access spaces like a garage. Many keycards use electromagnetic fields known as radio-frequency identification. By holding an RFID reader near a keycard, a hacker can capture the card's response and then use it later to create a new card with the same properties. Within minutes, the device can generate a master key to the facility. Several companies are working on software to override this defect. But there's no industry standard," Mary said. She tried to balance her cup of coffee while putting her head between the two of us.

Again, I asked myself, *Who is this woman?* I wasn't going to ask her how she knew all of this because another long speech would ensue and open up more questions I didn't need answers to.

"Well, it begs the question of who would do this, and why?" I said to divert her from a further explanation.

"The list of suspects is endless," Mary replied, sitting back. "This woman has been screwing people over for years. She's a master manipulator who's probably left a trail of unhappy bodies in her wake. I'd start with someone in Boston who knew her from her past and found out she was back in town. Maybe a former sugar daddy. One of them would have the funds to hire a person to hack the lock and search the room."

"But why? What could she possibly have that a previous sugar daddy would want? Jewelry he gave her?" I asked.

"I don't know; I'm just spitballing here. For all we know, it was a staff member looking for something to steal. Right now, I'd focus on who was watching Claire and why she felt she had to report it to security," Mary said. "And like I've said from the beginning, the sex club is involved."

"God, this case is getting way out of control. I'm not in this to solve not only a murder but a stalking case as well! All I want to know is if she has the goddamn drive. And I'll say it again, this case should have been turned over to law enforcement. You said you have news?" I said, turning to Belle trying to change the subject. I was getting frustrated.

"Oh, right. This might dovetail with what you're saying and might have something to do with the break-in. This information comes from our investigation. Since it's an ongoing investigation, I can only tell you so much, though. Mahir's mother had been keeping tabs on Fiona almost to the point of stalking her. We think Fiona caught on and came to New York to confront Mahir and make sure his mother backed off. But remember at this point it's speculation. So, Mahir's mother possibly had a hand in the break-in," Belle said, which prompted Mary to lean forward again.

"Why would she? What did she imagine she'd find, the murder weapon?" Mary asked.

Yeah, that didn't make sense. No one would carry a murder weapon around. And unless Fiona packed the knife in her check-in luggage, she'd have a hard time getting it on a plane.

"What if someone was planting something instead of searching for something?" I asked.

"How would they even know she was there?" Belle asked.

"That's an easy one. Lucine's private investigator has been keeping tabs. Remember he tracked Fiona by phone. Why not follow her in person? Lucine feels like Fiona ruined their lives; her son is dead. Sometimes months pass before an arrest is made," I said. "Maybe things were progressing too slowly in the investigation, and Lucine wanted to speed it up."

"OK, I can buy that, but what's he going to plant? A knife?

That would be crazy. Like you said, why would Fiona carry something like that around? We never recovered the murder weapon, but my guess is she tossed it in the river. And a new one wouldn't produce valid evidence if it wasn't the actual weapon. Somewhere in the hilt of the murder weapon we'd find a trace of blood. And the shape of the blade would need to match. I suppose he could plant blood-splattered clothing, but again not likely. He'd need access to Mahir's blood. The only way to do that would be to get it from Mahir's clothes or scrape the blood off the sidewalk or bench. But by then it would be dry and useless," Belle said.

God, it felt good to interact with someone who thought just like me.

"How about a souvenir?" Mary asked.

"What?" Belle replied.

"I see where she's going. If the PI found out about Chuck Evans's death, it's possible he devised a plan to set Fiona up as a serial killer who takes trophies. I mean what are the odds two people from her past die within days of each other, and she's in the vicinity? What would it take for his mother to get a lock of Mahir's hair? She could place the hair in a bag and plant it. Then call in an anonymous tip, and if someone came with a search warrant, they'd find it." It was a good theory. "But what about Evans, how would Lucine get something of his?"

"What if someone broke into his place and took something with his DNA? Possibly a watch or ring? I'd need to consider all aspects to determine if this could even be a workable theory," Mary said.

Now we were off on a wild goose chase, and I was too tired to participate. I needed to keep my mind focused on more realistic theories.

"Well, even if that was a viable plan it didn't work well. Fiona's gone because she got spooked. Even if someone alerted the Boston PD through an anonymous tip, and if they had probable cause to search, by the time they did, too many people would have had access to her room," Belle said.

"OK, what if someone planned to kill Fiona and make it look like a suicide? Or maybe they wanted to make it look like she came in during a robbery and got killed? Strangulation would be quiet," Mary offered.

"Fine, but if the guy was lying in wait, why isn't she dead right now?" I asked.

"I don't know, Lee. It's too much speculation. For all I know she never went into the room once she found out her room had been searched. Maybe she left with the clothes on her back," Mary replied, sitting back.

"What if someone was after the drive? Like someone who knew she had it, and she planned to sell it?" Belle asked.

"Now, that's a more plausible theory. But would Fiona be carrying the drive around with her and risk losing it? It's more likely she put it somewhere like a safe deposit box," I mused out loud.

"What if she'd taken a flight from Seattle to LA and put the drive in a safe deposit box in there and is going back for it? Maybe she's working with someone. She could have given it to a partner. And what if she fed Claire the stalking story so she could stay under the radar and not have to use her credit cards while she cleaned up loose ends?" Mary said.

"These are all good working theories, but for now, how about we leave them all on the table and see what Claire has to say when we land? By then, Fiona should have made contact with her. I'm not pussyfooting around anymore. We'll confront her and get an answer if she has the drive," I said.

"So, are you going to beat a confession out of her? Or do you have the unrealistic expectation she'll say, 'Yes, I did it'? Not a good plan either way," Mary said.

My face heated with embarrassment.

"I'm still ruminating, Mary."

Belle laughed and added, "She's right, not a good plan, Lee."

"You've got a better one?" I asked, with an edge to my voice.

"I'd like to wait and talk to Claire," she said. "Get a sense of her how she comes across, facial expressions, posture, if she's nervous, and see if Fiona confided anything in her. And I think we need to look at the sex club members as well."

"I'd say that's the better plan, especially the sex club part. And, Lee, I'd put Belle on point on this. Fiona's already seen you, and she might bolt if she sees you before you see her."

"Mary, Belle and I are at two cross purposes. She's looking at Fiona for murder. If Belle interviews her and has a reasonable suspicion Fiona committed the murder, she'll arrest her and take her back to New York. That doesn't get us any closer to the drive unless she has it on her when she's arrested. If Belle arrests Fiona, we're screwed anyway, because they'll take whatever's on her as part of her personal effects," I said. I knew this was the reasonable route; I just wasn't ready to surrender.

Belle stiffened, but as I pulled into the rental car bay to deposit the car, we had to put the conversation on hold.

As we walked toward the departures entrance, I received a text from Jackson. "The drive is in play. It's up on the web for an auction, and bidding begins three days from now."

CHAPTER FOURTEEN

Lee

S ERIOUSLY, WAS I REALLY BACK IN THIS HELL HOLE AGAIN? I HAD avoided the entire state of California my whole life, and here I was, back again, within a week.

As we approached the building complex, I called to let Claire know we were downstairs. She answered on the first ring and said she'd be down and we should wait outside the building. Odd.

When she arrived, her bloodshot eyes made her look sleep deprived. Her hands trembled slightly—from fear, too much booze, or too much caffeine? I expected her to ask who Belle was and what she was doing there, but she just glanced at her and tilted her head, gesturing toward a semi-secluded area in the back of the building.

Once seated around a stone table, Claire clasped her hands together, took a deep breath, and looked carefully around the area. What was going on? Something had this girl spooked.

"I'm glad you're here," she said, looking at each of us. "That man I told you about came back this morning, and I snapped a picture of him. Do you want to see it?"

"Yes, that would be very helpful. Would you email it to

me?" I asked.

Within moments, the image was on my phone, and the three of us huddled to view it.

"At this point, he's dangerously close to stalking. Did you call campus security or the police?" I asked.

"No. The police acted like I was wasting their time before, and I sure as hell am not going through that again," Claire stated. Her face looked tense, and anger flickered in her eyes.

"I can run his picture through facial recognition," Mary said, as if she had that kind of pull. It was highly unlikely.

"Mary—" I started as I sat back and rubbed my face with my hands.

"Don't start with me, Lee. I don't like to pull this out of my bag of tricks often. But a few years ago, I sued the government in an age discrimination suit and won an obscene amount of money. Anyway, that's a whole other story," she said as Belle smiled and leaned in closer. "I have access to the best facial recognition databases available. If you give me permission to send this picture off, I will."

"Mary, I don't know if I can do that," I said.

"Not you." Mary shook her head in disgust. "Claire. She holds the copyright for the photo. She took it in a public place where this clown has no expectation of privacy."

Belle laughed out loud.

"Sure, be my guest," Claire said, and within seconds Mary had sent it off.

"Tell me what you know about this guy," Belle said. "Or sensed about him."

"He had a few disturbing tattoos on his forearms, and he had a knife strapped to his belt. The knife was in a leather sheath, and it was long, like you would use for hunting. He was wearing torn jeans, battered motorcycle boots, and different shirts that were the same style each time he came around. His eyes had sort of a sinister appearance, almost snake-like. He seemed so focused. Like the surrounding crowd meant nothing to him; he was waiting for something—"

Mary's email dinged, and we waited a moment for her to open the message.

"Winner, winner, chicken dinner. Ladies and gentlemen, meet Jeremy Stamos. Mr. Stamos is well acquainted with the law and not in a good way. He's been a resident in three states and arrested in all three for some variation of aggravated assault and battery. Once he was even charged with rape but not convicted," Mary said. She continued reading silently for a moment; then she looked up at me. "Mr. Stamos apparently had some trouble right here in LA. I'll give you one guess where."

I shrugged, as if I didn't care.

"Fire and Ice. A secretive and private sex club. Which if I remember correctly, is the same club that the PI reported our little Miss Fiona belonged to when she was here. Do I need to connect the dots?" she asked.

"I'll admit it is a bit of a coincidence," I said. "OK, put that to the side for one minute. Claire, have you heard anything more from Fiona since she called you last?"

She shook her head no.

"Hold on," I said, opening the tracking app to see if she'd popped back up. Nothing.

"Did she leave any contact information?" I asked, and again Claire shook her head. "God, this is so frustrating. I hope this hasn't been a wasted trip."

"We had no idea where she was heading when she left Boston, and this is still a possibility. Maybe she's taking care of business. Or what if she got spooked by Stamos? Let's not give up yet. Claire, the minute you hear anything, please let us know," I said.

We said our goodbyes and headed to the car.

"Now what, Sherlock?" I asked Mary.

"You're not going to like it; I want to look at the sex club," she said.

"Don't be ridiculous. It has nothing to do with our case. There's no reason to believe Fiona will be there, and it's just a waste of time," I said, hoping she'd drop it.

"You got something else better to do?" she asked, knowing we didn't.

"OK, you pest," I said, hoping she'd catch my tone. "We'll do a drive-by, just so you can see it and move on. It's probably some dingy old warehouse in some run-down section of town."

Belle typed in the address from the police report and flashed me a wicked smile. She turned the phone for Mary and the two of them laughed.

"What?" I asked not liking being kept out of the joke.

"Just head toward Mulholland," Belle said. I was sure we were making a mistake going there.

After sitting in traffic for nearly an hour, we approached a mansion behind black, wrought iron gates.

"There, pull over there, and let's talk about this," Belle said, pointing at a spot to park.

"There's nothing to talk about," I said. "Mary wanted her curiosity satisfied, and now it is. Now, we're going."

"No, wait, just pull over," she said, touching my arm. I must have lost control for a moment at the touch that sent an electric jolt through me, and I complied.

"All right, now what?" I asked.

"Turn off the car, and let's reconsider a minute," Belle said.

"I already have a plan," Mary said.

"Not interested," I replied.

As we sat silently, I heard a consistent beeping from somewhere in Belle's handbag.

"You want to turn that off? It's giving me a headache," I said, as she rummaged through her bag.

"Yeah, give me a minute to shut it off," she said. She pulled her phone out and frowned as she looked at it.

"What?" I asked.

"You know that app that's tracking Fiona? It's beeping," she said, opening the app. She stared at her phone in disbelief and then looked at me.

"She's inside," she said.

"Get the hell out of here. If you're having a laugh at my expense, it isn't funny, trust me. There's no way my phone didn't pick that up, and yours did," I said, sure it was a joke.

I pulled my phone out, and realized I'd closed out of the app when we'd visited Claire and hadn't relaunched it.

"Well if that's true, why didn't it notify me before this?" I asked.

"The possibilities are endless. Dead battery, low signal, or interference from all the waves in the area are a few," Mary said. "Who cares, as long as we've found her? What are you going to do, grab her up when she comes out?"

"That would be a great idea, if it didn't involve prison time for kidnapping," I said. "We could just stop Fiona and tell her who we really are and give her an opportunity to explain."

"Lee, that's a wonderful idea. 'Hello, Fiona, we've been

stalking you from one end of the country to the other; would you care to chat?'" Mary interjected.

I turned to Belle and asked, "Thoughts?"

"You still have the wealthy sugar daddy cover, right?" she asked.

I nodded.

"I say when she leaves, we go inside, and say we're new to the area, and we're interested in membership," she said.

I looked at her like she'd lost her mind.

"There's no way I am stepping foot inside some pervy palace. What possible information could we get?"

"Lee, I don't know. But what I do know is that we don't have a lot right now, and sometimes luck drops right in your lap." she said.

"What if they ask us for a reference?" I said, hoping to stop this before it got too far.

"And what if they don't? You can't go throwing negative vibes out there; let's just do this," Belle said.

"Yeah, Lee, let's," Mary threw in.

"There's no 'Mary' in 'us,'" I said, and suddenly spotted Fiona walking out of the door, and a black car pulling forward to meet her.

I'm sure Belle kept speaking, but I couldn't tear my eyes away from the car. As the gates opened to let the car out, it was impossible to tell if anyone else was in the back seat. I quickly pulled into the drive before the gates closed.

"Mary, you stay in the car and stay low. Belle, you're with me," I said, sliding out of the car.

"What's my cover?" she asked hesitantly.

"My wife."

That brought a mischievous smile to her lips.

We held hands as we walked up the stairs together. At the top, we took a moment to collect ourselves, and I noticed a camera. What happened next startled me as much as Belle, I kissed her. Not a sweet "hello" kiss, but one filled with passion. I longed to stay like this all day, but an intercom voice interrupted us asking what we wanted. I quickly explained we wanted to talk about membership and determine if it was a good fit. I don't remember the specifics of what I said because my mind was flooding with happy neurotransmitters.

As the door unlocked, Belle whispered in my ear, "Let me take this; I worked vice and speak their language."

A well-dressed man waited in the hall to greet us.

I made the introductions and was shocked when he said, "I see your mother is in the car. Please invite her in; it's far too hot to sit in a car. I insist."

Oh my God, what now? Everything was going to go to hell in a handbasket. Before I could say anything, Belle interceded.

"Thank you. She'd love that. Darling, wait here a moment, and I'll go get her," she said. Before I could argue, she was gone.

The man and I chatted about the fact I was considering moving here, and that my wife and I wanted to seek out the options for our unique brand of entertainment. As the host was about to suggest real estate agents, probably club members, Mary and Belle walked in, and introductions were made.

"Since no members are using the facility, why don't you join us?" he said to Mary.

Her back straightened and a broad smile broke across her face. "Lead on," she said.

After an hour tour, which was more like a palace than a club, we were offered refreshments in our host's office.

Seated in a soft leather chair, I broached a question I hoped wouldn't get us kicked out.

"I have a concern," I said.

He tilted his head. "Oh?"

"When we were coming in, we noticed a very young lady leaving. She looked like she was barely out of her teens," I said.

He laughed. "Don't let her concern you one bit; she's a member in good standing, and there has never been a problem. She's well past the age of consent, and she's a well-practiced dominatrix. In fact, if you'd care to attend our party tonight, subject to a background verification of course, she'll be there," he said with a smarmy smile.

"However, madam," he said, looking at Mary, "I'm sorry, but we cannot invite you."

She nodded, accepting the disappointing news. "I understand I might dampen the festivities. But these two will have a good time for me."

"Such an open-minded woman," our host replied. "This is how we proceed. I'll verify your credentials. I'll email the information about the party tonight. It will include where it is to be held, dress for the evening, and your admittance code. If you decide we're a good fit, I'll arrange for your membership to be placed on the board's agenda, which often takes up to a month. Tonight's activities will be subdued, so no worries," he said.

I placed my arm around Belle's waist, as he accompanied us to the door. "Masks are optional and provided at the door. For new members, I encourage them. Old members may be a tad inhibited around new members. Or the opposite can occur, and they become a tad too over enthusiastic."

We thanked him and left.

I waited for the rapid-fire conversation to come from Mary in the back, but none came. I had to turn to make sure she hadn't died of shock in the back seat.

"Did you have a stroke back there, or are you stunned stupid?" I asked, looking in my rearview.

"You're being set up," she said.

I stiffened and looked at Belle.

"She's right," Belle said. "I worked vice two years in some form or another. During that time, I liaised with the FBI in large human trafficking cases. I've seen my share of BDSM gone wrong and people needing medical attention."

Why did my mind flash to Belle in leather and boots? That's not to say it had to be leather, it actually could be—

She snapped her fingers to bring me back, and Mary smiled as she turned her head.

"First, we didn't tour the whole building. I have a feeling there are some rooms in there that allow illegal activity to occur, including rooms where more serious violence might be acceptable. Those high-security locks are there for a reason. Second, no club would ever give you entrance through the door before you were vetted. I wouldn't put it past them to have run the car plate and determined it was registered to you and not your alter ego. These places have people who belong to law enforcement and the judicial system. Third, the fact the party is being held off-site should cause a series of alarm bells to ring wildly in your head. They set up a front to give the appearance a party is going on; you drop your guard and go, and zap, your life is never the same. I'm trafficked overseas, and maybe your body parts are removed and sold. Either way, we're going nowhere near that place," Belle said, gently placing her head on the headrest and closing her eyes.

"What about tipping the police off about the party tonight?" Mary asked.

"What's the probable cause? Rumor and innuendo? An email from an untraceable IP? No, our best move is to switch out this rental car in case they put a tracker on it and lie low," Belle said.

A tracker? Jesus, that hadn't even crossed my mind. She was way ahead of me and made me wonder if my investigation skills were waning. Or maybe my mind was still back on that kiss and what I'd wanted to follow that kept vividly playing in my mind.

"I'm heading to the airport to get a different rental car," I said. "That way, if they track this one to LAX, it might appear we left. And it will be easy to pick up a new one."

"Good choice," Belle said.

"Are you going to do a drive-by tonight to check out the party?" Mary asked.

"Not on your life," Belle said.

"OK, if you think they made you, and there's a possibility of trafficking, then leave it to me. When you get the email with the party location and entrance code, I'll forward it to a contact and leave it with him to deal with," Mary said.

I laughed, but Mary didn't appreciate the humor.

"Are you serious?" I asked her. I found this incredulous.

"Obviously you haven't been privy to the exciting life Mary has lived these last few years," Belle said.

"Obviously I haven't. Are you buying into her story?" I asked Belle.

"People, I'm right here," Mary said. "I've got contacts with the mob. I'm on a first-name basis with Israeli intelligence and a phone call away from several FBI agents."

Our eyes met in the rearview mirror, and I realized she was telling me the truth.

"Alrighty then, you take point on this portion," I said to Mary.

Just then a text came in from Claire. Still no Fiona, but that guy was back.

"Belle, look at the app and figure out where Fiona is right now."

She opened the app and hit refresh. "Right now, she's...at Claire's complex. I don't know if she's inside, but the tracker says she's there," she said.

I hit reply and typed: "Thanks, I guess she decided to move on."

"Is Claire playing us, or is Fiona playing her? Let's head over to the complex," Mary said.

"And do what?" I asked.

"Knock on the door. If Fiona's there, we can ask her our questions and be done," Mary said. "I'm done playing with this case. Now let's get a move on; I'm getting older every minute."

I didn't like this one bit, but what other option did we have.

Mary's plan was flawed, but it was the best we had. Time was winding down, and if we didn't confront Fiona now, we might lose her.

"I'm the one to knock on the door; you two stand to the side," Mary said.

After three short raps, the door opened, and Mary stepped back.

"Can I help you?" the voice asked.

Fiona.

CHAPTER FIFTEEN

Fiona

"CAN I HELP YOU?" I ASKED, SURPRISED TO SEE A NICELY DRESSED older woman at my door.

A man and a woman suddenly appeared on either side of the older woman. It took me a moment to recognize the man, but then it slammed into my brain—Mykus and some chick I'd never seen before.

"You! Didn't you get the message when I ditched you in Boston? What are you, some freakish stalker?" I demanded. Over the years, I'd had trouble with men who didn't know when to let go. Or men who thought they meant more to me than they had. But this guy was a stranger who'd had one date with me that had ended badly for him.

Well, that remark seemed to catch him off guard. But it didn't cause him to step back. Odd.

"May we come in?" the older woman asked. She started forward. These people were way too pushy, and they had crossed a line showing up here.

"You may not. Who are you people, and what do you want?" I asked.

The older woman said, "I'm Mary."

"My name is Lee Stone, and I'm a private investigator. Your former employer, Benjamin Hightower, wants me to have a word with you," he said.

What. The. Hell. No. This was not happening. "Hold on. Are you telling me that prick sent you across the country and back again just to make sure I'd keep my mouth shut? You can tell that asshole his secret is safe with me. He can call off his dogs," I said, starting to close the door.

Lee's hand went up to block the door, and it sprang back toward me.

The younger woman stepped forward and flashed a badge.

"I am Detective Annabelle Hughes with the New York City Police Department, and I have questions for you," the petite, attractive woman said. "Now, I suggest you let us in. We may be able to clear this up and be on our way."

NYPD? What the fuck was going on? I could refuse to talk to her; she had no jurisdiction in California. But something in her stance told me she'd be persistent if I didn't cooperate. We couldn't meet in here. I hadn't been here long enough to see if Claire had her stash of coke somewhere in plain sight. What a can of worms that would open up. I didn't need them nosing around, and I didn't want to get an intent to distribute charge hung on me.

I grabbed my keys from the table, closed the door, and tilted my head, indicating they should follow me. We walked to the end of the hall where there was an unoccupied room. I opened the door and invited everyone to take a seat.

As they sat, I studied their body language and then their seating arrangement. I assessed who was in charge. It was apparent Lee was the alpha, but it was almost too close a tie with the detective to call it. But I quickly determined Lee, with all the alpha signs going on, would be my adversary.

I leaned back, crossed my legs, and placed my hands on the arm rests. I was prepared. Looking at Lee, I said, "You first," letting him know I was the one setting the agenda and pace.

He removed a pen and a small pad from his jacket pocket and flipped it open. The way he performed this small task suggested he was a former detective with law enforcement.

"So, why did you leave your employment without notice?" he asked, as he clicked his cheap pen.

"Why's that any of your business?" I asked, looking him straight in the eye.

He didn't answer for a moment, and I could see by the way his eyes focused on the wall he was deciding what information he wanted to share with me.

"It's my business because a project you were a part of is now missing and up for auction. Also, a man you were in a hotel room with the night you left was brutally murdered. Another man in the same room was left in a coma," he said.

How should I answer without saying something that would lead to more questions? He seemed to be accusing me of the murder. What do you do when you're on the defensive and have nowhere to go? You play for time and then go on the offensive.

I looked at Detective Hughes. "And you, why are you here? Are you here to question me about a crime that happened in Seattle?"

She looked a little put off and returned my stare. Good.

"I have questions about a crime that occurred in New York," she said.

"Don't you have to Mirandize me? Or, at the very least, have me sign a waiver," I asked. I knew she didn't, but I thought it would make her take a step back. I wanted to show them all that this wasn't going to be easy.

"I'm investigating the murder of Mahir Abajian," she said with an inflection in her voice that issued a challenge.

"Well then, you're wasting your time. I didn't even know he was dead. This is the first I'm hearing of it."

"That's odd, because you contacted him not more than a few days ago," she said with a smug smile.

"So?" I returned. She wasn't going to box me into making any statement that would require follow-up questions and answers.

"Next you're going to say you had nothing to do with Chuck Evans's death either," the older woman said with disdain.

My eyes met hers for a second and then swept back to the detective.

"Detective Hughes, right?"

She nodded.

"I have no information or knowledge about either of these deaths. Tragic as they are, it's absurd that you think I knew about them or had anything to do with either of them."

I wasn't going to allow this to continue. I knew it wasn't irrational at all for them to think I'd had something to do with Mahir and Chuck's deaths. After all, I had accused both of them of battery and rape, so I could see how someone might think I could be linked to both deaths.

I'd let my pace slip and needed to bring it back and close this down. My next attack would be the old lady. She appeared to be their weak link.

"And you," I said to her. "How do you fit in here?"

"I'm a private investigator and his partner," she said, with a bored shrug, hitching a thumb toward Lee.

I had to stifle a laugh. "Are you now?"

"Enough," Lee bellowed. "We're not here for your entertainment. I want answers."

Well, I wasn't about to give him any. He had to realize this was wasting all our time.

"What makes you think I owe you any answers?" I asked him, while maintaining my composure.

"Because you want to clear yourself, so we can all move on. The valuable information you had access to while working for Benjamin Hightower is missing, leaving you a primary suspect in its disappearance. You were the last one seen with those two men, again leaving you a suspect in their murders," he said. As the muscle in his jaw clenched.

"Seriously. That's what you have on me? That's what makes you think I'm a thief and murderer? I didn't hear one shred of evidence in that accusation," I responded, standing to leave.

"Sit down," Detective Hughes ordered.

"Excuse me?" I asked, annoyed. "You have no authority here, and I don't see why I should stay here any longer. If you think I stole something, get a warrant. If you think I killed someone, arrest me. But since you have no grounds to arrest me, your time is up, and I'm leaving because you can't hold me here."

"What were you doing at Fire and Ice today?" Lee asked without taking his eyes from his notepad.

I studied him before I formulated my answer. If he weren't such a dick, he would be appealing in a rough sort of way.

"You do realize there are laws against stalking?" I asked.

His face fell slack. He knew where I was going; I had him right where I wanted him.

"How did you know I was in California much less at Fire?"

"It's called investigation," the old lady answered with authority.

I saw an uncomfortable look pass over the detective's face as well as Lee's.

"I see. What state issued your private investigator's license?"

"Colorado," she said, with a touch of pride.

"I assume Lee's license was issued there as well."

He nodded, but I could tell he knew where I was going with this.

"And what state are we in right now?" I prompted. This wasn't my normal way of dealing with unpleasantness. Honey usually worked best, but this situation called for vinegar.

"Don't take me for a fool, young lady," she snapped.

It wasn't nice to gloat when you were about to kill your prey. They already knew their interview with me was about to die.

"I'm merely pointing out that your license isn't valid here in California. So that makes one man's surveillance another man's stalking. How would it look, you following me from Boston to LA?"

Lee looked livid, and I could almost hear Mary's dentures snap together.

"Now," I said to Detective Hughes, "I will tell you I didn't have anything to do with those murders. But that's all I'm telling any of you unless you're bringing me in...but wait, you can't do that, can you?" I gave a snide smile. "So, I suggest we end this nonsense right now."

"You." I pointed at Lee. "You tell Benjamin he can have you stop following me. His secret is safe with me. If I find out you're continuing to follow me, I will file a police report."

"Why'd you try to disappear?" Lee continued, as if I hadn't

just threatened to have him arrested.

"I'm done here, and make no mistake; you are on legal notice to stay away from me."

He reclined deeper into his chair, as if he were settling in for the long haul. I didn't like that. This wasn't going to happen.

"It's a free country," Mary said with a false smile and shrug. "We can go wherever we please. We can't help it if you happen to be there too."

That did it; I snapped. I couldn't have these people following me around.

"Ma'am, you do not want to cross me. Trust me, I don't play well with others," I warned.

"That sounds like a threat to me," Lee said to the detective.

He was sorely mistaken if he thought he could scare me. "I'll refer you to California Penal Code 422 PC to make that assessment," I said.

I couldn't tell who was more agitated, Lee or the detective. But it was Lee's hand that started to twitch.

"I've got things to do. You can find your way out, I assume?" I said.

"Why did you leave without telling anyone?" Lee asked.

Was he really going to do this? What was he hoping to accomplish?

"Would it satisfy you to know that I got a better job offer? I just accepted a job at a premier lab," I said, monitoring my tone.

"But you already had a job at a premier lab," he said.

I studied their faces, and it was evident that none of them knew Benjamin's secret. They truly believed I had stolen some intellectual property, and that's why they were here.

"What was your relationship with Dennis and Ryan?" Lee asked.

This man was relentless! "You mean the men from the lab?" I asked with innocence only a practiced actress could muster.

"Don't play with me, little girl," he said, spitting out the words through clenched teeth.

He had come here for a confession and to retrieve some stolen property and would leave with neither. Too bad. I clearly had the advantage, and he knew it.

"Two co-workers I partied with; what's next?" He stood, walked to the window for a few moments, and once he'd regained his composure, moved back behind the detective's chair.

I looked into his eyes and then to the detective's. Brilliant. I still had him where I wanted him. I knew I should leave, but I wanted to see how this was going to play out.

"Were you with them the night Dennis was murdered?" Lee continued.

I licked my lips and watched his eyes follow the tip of my tongue. The detective stiffened. She realized what I was doing.

"Since I don't know when he died, I can't tell you where I was at that time," I said. taking a breath to lift my chest.

I watched his breathing increase, and the vein in his neck pulsated. Lee was moving ever closer to the edge.

Suddenly, the old lady stepped in. "See here, you little sociopath. I've about had it with you. I didn't have an opinion one way or the other if you stole the drive. But now I'm fairly sure you had a hand in the theft. I'm just wondering if you were in cahoots with those other men."

"You people should take this show on the road; it's quite entertaining. First, you accuse me of theft, then murder, and now you're labeling me with a mental disorder? Your employer better have deep pockets for the lawsuit coming his way if any of what you're saying about me becomes public. I'd caution you to watch what you say. Let's recap. Wasn't it you who admitted to stalking me? Now, stop me if I'm wrong, Detective, but didn't Mary make an admission against her interest with that statement, right in front of an officer of the law?" I let that hang before I said, "People, I'm done here. As 'fun' as this has been, this conversation is over. If you want any further interviews with me, you can feel free to reach out to my lawyer."

These people had taken up enough time, and they had balls to accuse me of murder and theft. I had business to attend to, and time was money. Claire didn't know it yet, but she was about to be paying me a hefty fee for me not telling them about her little coke problem and her side gig of selling whatever product she didn't use herself. I had the upper hand for now, but I was going to need money to stay one step ahead of these people, and Claire was going to pay.

As I stood to leave, Mary said, "Don't leave the jurisdiction. We might want to talk to you further."

That produced an unfiltered laugh.

"You watch too much TV, Mary. Tell her, Detective Hughes. Tell her there's nothing keeping me here."

When I reached the door, I turned and said, "Good luck with your case. And tell Benjamin I still have it. But his secret is safe. He'll know what I mean."

Lee straightened; for a moment, it looked like he was going to walk toward me, but he stopped. No one said anything.

Back in Claire's room, I watched from the window as Mary, Lee, and Detective Hughes exited the building. They appeared to be in a heated argument. As I was about to turn away, I saw Claire approaching the building. She stopped and started talking to them. They started arguing with Claire, leaving her in a defensive position. Within seconds, they were all looking up at the window, staring at me looking down at them. As if in slow motion, my brain rewound everything I'd witnessed, and the pieces clicked into place. Claire was working with them. Son of a bitch! Yep, there was the body language. Her hugging her bag, afraid I'd found out and closing herself off from them. Leaving the group still talking, she walked toward the building, looking up and watching me, and I began to formulate a plan.

I heard the elevator doors slide open and then close. The key slid into the lock, and I waited for the turn of the handle. Claire walked in and stopped to take the temperature of the room. I'm certain she could tell things were about to get frigid.

"Did we have visitors?" she asked, placing her keys on the tray.

"You know *I* did," I said, staring her down. I was not in the mood for games. "So, when did you start conspiring with those three?"

"I didn't. I don't know what you're talking about."

Her body language said she was lying.

"Don't even try to lie to me. I see I'm going to have to leave, since you've exposed me. But before I do, here's what's going to happen. We're going to the bank, and you're going to give me twenty thousand dollars in cash from your safe deposit box," I said. As she started protesting, I raised my hand, cutting her off. "I arranged for you to supply the drugs at Fire tonight, so think of it as my cut. Or you could think of it as paying me to keep your secret from the police. Either way, I'm getting paid."

"I don't have that kind of money, Fi. I had to invest it in the new supply," she whined.

"Oh my God. Seriously? I'm starting to think you've been

working with those people with the hope they'd arrest me for something. God knows what crap you fed them about me! You know, if it hadn't been for me, you wouldn't have the connection with Fire, so cut the crap," I said. "You owe me! You think it was easy creating a relationship with a mob-backed sex club? Now, get your bag and your keys, and let's go. I have some product to deliver on my way out of town."

With cameras strategically placed in the bank, it was challenging to maintain any disguise. My hair pulled up into a baseball cap along with large sunglasses was my best hope. As Claire signed the registry, I checked a text I'd received from Steven verifying he'd be picking up the drugs in an hour from the safe deposit box.

We brought her box to a viewing room, and Claire opened it cautiously.

"Don't have twenty thousand dollars? Really, Claire, there has to be a hundred thousand there, so throw another five thousand on the pile," I said, opening my bag. "You'll more than make it up tonight. Those rich fucks know how to party."

Once the money was in my bag, we moved back to the vault. I removed another empty security box. I placed the drugs Claire had given me for tonight's party in the new security box, closed the box, and slid it back into its cubby. Within the hour, Steven would be retrieving it from here.

"Well, Claire, we've had some good times together, but the run is over. Goodbye and good luck," I said. "Oh, and did you hear Mahir is dead? Such a tragedy."

"Yes, Fi, I'm aware," she said. She got the message.

I couldn't fly with this much cash; I'd needed to keep about three thousand dollars and deposit the rest. But not in an offshore. Maybe a bank that did business in the US and Germany and that didn't like US rules about reporting cash deposits. Three doors down, there was the perfect bank for what I needed, so I headed there. I'd get a new account and access to my funds in the States and in Berlin immediately. Perfect.

A week from now, I'll be on a plane out of here.

CHAPTER SIXTEEN

Lee

As we walked to the car, I glanced up at the window one last time. Fiona was watching us; a moment later, she turned away.

After our public outburst at each other and Claire, we remained quiet, but we were gearing up for the next round. I held the door for Mary to enter the car, and she shook her head at me in disapproval. Belle didn't wait for me to open her door, she was in, buckled, and ready to go before I'd even gotten to her door. I looked between Mary and Belle and realized the minute I started driving all hell would break loose.

"Before I get in this car, let me just say, we're not continuing this conversation until we're back at the hotel. LA traffic is an accident waiting to happen, and I won't be a willing participant because you two were screaming at me and distracting me."

Mary opened her mouth to say something, but I held my finger up, stopping her. I started the car and headed back to the hotel. Everyone was quiet, but my thoughts were anything but calm.

I'd had no control over the situation in there with Fiona.

How had that happened? This had been the second time she'd boxed me in; I started replaying the whole interview in my mind and dissecting every sentence and innuendo.

I was lost in thought until Mary broke the silence.

"We've been played."

"Mary, so help me. I don't want to raise my voice, but right now if I hear the name 'Fiona' said out loud, I will lose my mind," I said impatiently.

"What? No! Not by Fiona," she said. "By Hightower."

Belle turned to look at Mary.

"Mary, remember, he's our client, and we signed a confidentiality agreement," I cautioned. "I can guess where this is headed, and we should talk to Jackson about this before it goes any further."

"Do you think he's having you track down something that doesn't even exist just so he can find Fiona?" Belle asked. "I mean, what are the chances a whole server was wiped with no backup anywhere? And why put the entire focus on her and not the other two? I'm having a hard time swallowing the whole scenario."

I sighed. My mind had been spinning with these same questions over the last week, and the answers remained the same. I didn't trust Hightower. The minute he'd admitted to an inappropriate relationship with Fiona an enormous red flag went up for me. Should we have challenged the story he gave us? Possibly, but to what avail? I'm not privy to Jackson's finances, but I guessed a cash infusion was a welcome addition. Maybe, I was willing to believe him because it benefited us.

"OK, how about this plan? When we get back to the hotel, Mary and I can brief Jackson on what happened with Fiona. Once we get his input, we can meet back in my room and work on a plan. How's that?" I asked.

Before anyone answered, the tracking app beeped, alerting us that Fiona was on the move.

Belle launched the app and said, "She's at a bank. Do you want to go?"

"Where's it at?" I asked.

"Three streets down," she said. "Keep going straight."

As we approached, Fiona exited through the revolving door. As luck would have it, we were stuck in bumper-to-bumper traffic. This gave us a free, legal parking space to watch her enter another bank three doors down.

"I don't like this," Mary said, leaning forward. "That bank is on a watch list because they're suspected of cooperating with terrorists. Last year, they paid several million in fines for their non-compliance with US banking regulations."

As we were ready to turn, Claire exited the same bank Fiona had just left.

"What the hell is going on! Were we bamboozled by them both?" I asked. "All right, this is what we're going to do. We talk to Jackson and get his input. Belle, you reach out to your precinct and find out what's going on with the Mahir case. We meet back in my room in one hour."

Both nodded.

"Do we continue tracking Fiona with the app?" Belle asked.

"The batteries for the tracker are probably almost dead," I said.

"My head hurts. I have so many questions I thought I had answers to, but after today everything is utter chaos," Belle said, turning to look out the window.

I don't know what possessed me, but I reached for Belle's hand and squeezed it. At first, I was worried she would snatch her hand from me. But instead, she squeezed mine back. She looked over at me, and the look she gave me was one I hadn't seen in years. It said, "I care." Something was growing, changing between us, and we both felt it.

"Tell me about your wood sculpting," she said.

Well that had come out of nowhere. Was my agitation showing so clearly that she was trying to calm me down? Funny, how she picked to talk to me about sculpting.

"God, I've been whittling with wood for as long as I can remember. It started out when my brothers and I were small, and my great-grandfather would sit with us on the front porch and teach us how to scrape the wood with a knife. From there, we graduated to a larger thing like a Welsh love spoon. People would custom order them from me, and I got so good at them I made a tidy little profit. With those profits, I bought more supplies and tools. From there, I progressed into making furniture."

"Do you still carve wood?"

"All the time. I recently finished making an oak dining room table for a friend. It took me six months to make, but it's a beauty," I said, remembering the feeling of pride I'd had when I'd finished.

"Why not do it for a living now? If the pictures at your parents' house were anything like what you can create now, you'd make a fortune," she said.

"It's a pretty niche market. I still do it because it relaxes me, and I love it. It's my passion, but I wouldn't even know how to go about starting a business," I said. As I thought about starting a new business, this feeling of exhilaration and fear washed over me.

"You realize you could sell your products on the internet, don't you? And with word of mouth, you'd have more orders lined up than you'd be able to handle," she said. "All you need is a website, social media, and boom, you're ready to go."

I'm sure my face looked like a bomb had exploded in front of me. The reality that I could make a go of it had never entered my mind.

"People do it all the time. You register your business with the state, get a web designer to design your website, and do a few publicity stints, and that gets the word out about you. Before you can catch your breath, you'll be hiring an assistant and expanding into a warehouse," she said, getting excited.

"We'll see," I said. "Mary, you're quiet back there."

"I'm sitting here taking this all in," she said.

Was that good or bad?

"I have a great handle on QuickBooks. I'll just throw that out there."

"There you go! A business is born," Belle said, gracing me with a beautiful smile.

"Gives me something to ponder," I said. "Back to business."

"You give any more thought to what you want to do about tonight's party? Have you changed your mind?" Belle asked.

"No. I still think it's a bad idea," I replied. I relied on my gut, and it rarely let me down.

"Why, because we've already talked to Fiona? Or you don't want to get naked in front of strangers?" Mary asked.

"Both. The plus side would be we could watch Fiona interact with people in an environment where she felt comfortable. But the downside is she's already told us she thinks we're stalking her. These people are her tribe, and if she unmasked us, so to speak, we don't have a clue what might happen. We could get arrested, or get our asses kicked, or worse. So considering she already knows we were at the club, it follows she's already alerted them," I responded, letting go of Belle to turn the wheel.

We arrived at the hotel, parked, and agreed to meet in my room in an hour. Mary and I went to my room and Belle to hers.

"That's the girl for you, Lee. Don't let her go," Mary said, as if issuing an order.

I smiled. But agreeing with Mary would be dangerous territory I didn't want to tread yet. "Let's table the matchmaking. Let's do a video conference with Jax, so we can bring him up to speed," I said.

Jackson answered on the first ring.

"Jax, we've run into a situation, and we need some direction from you," I said. "We just had a face-to-face meeting with Fiona."

"Go on," he said.

"Well, it wasn't what we expected. To be honest, she controlled the meeting, and I take full responsibility for letting that happen. As expected, she denied everything, but that's not why we called in," I said.

There was silence, and as I was about to continue Mary spoke. "She said to tell Hightower to call off his dogs; his secret is safe with her. Now that could mean anything, but I took it to be a personal issue. Her exact words were she still had 'it,' and his secret was safe."

There was more silence.

"Hold on; I'm calling him," Jax said.

We waited as he placed the call. However, we didn't wait in silence.

"You're very good at woodworking, and I think you should only stay on with us for the occasional skip trace and follow your passion instead. We rent our office furniture, and I'm not a fan of renting anything. I'd be willing to spend up to a hundred grand for you to design and build what we need to make that office what it should be," Mary said, looking at me intently.

"Mary, that's crazy!"

"In case you hadn't heard, I won a multimillion-dollar age discrimination lawsuit. They paid excellent money to compensate me. I earned every penny. I brought people to tears. I was a star witness. But regardless of that, I now have more money than I'll ever need. How do you think I became a managing partner? By my wit and charm? So there's your offer. You can still work your job with us as a freelancer, but I'd like to give you a start in your business. If you could only see how your face lights up when you talk about the sculpting. Don't let the chance go by to stay in what you consider a safety zone," Mary said.

I was about to respond when Jax jumped back on and patched in Benjamin Hightower.

"Sorry, guys. I brought Benjamin up to speed. Let me turn this over to him," Jax said.

Benjamin appeared on my screen, and he didn't look happy. He looked like he had aged at least ten years overnight. The purplish discoloration under his eyes gave him a sinister appearance. His lips appeared a pale, waxy color, which was alarming.

"I want to thank you for your hard work. It sounds like we've reached the point where you'll need to bring Fiona back to Seattle so I can speak to her," Benjamin said.

"I'm sorry; I must have misunderstood you. Are you saying you want us to invite Fiona back for a chat?" I asked.

"That would be a place to start," he said.

"And—" I started.

"And if she declines? Well, you are a bounty hunter, aren't you?" His voice held a tinge of annoyance.

"No, I am not. A bounty hunter captures fugitives and criminals for a monetary fee," I said.

"Yes, well isn't that what I hired you to do? In my opinion, Fiona stole my drive and that makes her a criminal," he replied.

"This is something you and Jackson need to discuss. However, Fiona isn't a fugitive, and right now there's no evidence she's a criminal. The woman might have a personality disorder, but she hasn't been arrested. In this instance, I could justify she falls under my job description of skip trace. She skipped; I traced," I answered, a bit annoyed.

"Semantics. She has something I want, and I'd like you to bring her to me," Hightower insisted.

Was he for real? Was he suggesting we kidnap Fiona?

"Let's start with what she has that's yours. I assume it isn't only the drive we're talking about any longer," I pressed.

"No, it's something more personal," he replied with hesitation. "But I still believe she has the drive. The fact she mentioned the other issue leads me to believe she's cooking up an extortion plan."

Could the man be any more cryptic?

Jackson appeared back on the screen.

"Benjamin, what you're asking Lee to do is tantamount to kidnapping."

Good. Even with all that money at play, Jackson was standing firm. What was with Hightower? What did Fiona have he didn't want to tell us about?

"Do you know where she is right now?" Hightower asked.

The app still displayed a location, so I confirmed we did.

"I'm leaving right now to board my company jet. I'll be

there in three hours. Then you'll take me to her," he said.

Hightower said he'd call when he was close and disconnected.

"OK, Jax, there are several problems here," I said as he came back on screen.

"Like I can't figure the liability facing us, right?" Jackson said.

"First, Fiona already warned us that she considered what we were doing as us stalking her and this will verify her claim. Second, how do we explain how we found her? The tracker is an invasion of her privacy, and it further proves to her that we've been stalking her. Third, what if this gets out of hand, and he becomes violent; are we then accessories?"

He rubbed his forehead, as if to draw answers and guidance from somewhere.

"All right, this is what we do. Don't tell Benjamin about the tracker; you tell him you had her under surveillance. You tell him she might be at the party tonight, and give him those coordinates. Nothing more. If he wants to crash the party, so be it," Jackson said in an exasperated tone.

"How will he get in?" I asked.

"That guy at the club said he'd send you an invitation code; did you check your email?" Mary asked.

I checked, and the invitation was there with a code, address, and instructions. The dress code was explained along with the reminder that masks were optional.

"I suggest you give him that information, and if he wants to chase her down that'll be on him. It won't be considered stalking; well potentially it might be, but it's him and not you. God, what a legal mess this is becoming," Jax said, removing his tie and unbuttoning his collar.

"This is turning into quite the clusterfuck. We work for someone who may be lying to us about the proprietary information that was stolen from him. What's the real reason he's not being straight with you? And in following Fiona, we stepped into a murder investigation that might have nothing to do with her," I said.

"Right, and that's where we need to draw the line. We have no business at all in Dennis's murder in Seattle, Mahir's in New York, or Evans's murder in Massachusetts. I realize the detective is with you, but you need to make sure your fingerprints, so to speak, are not on any of her reports. Nothing we gather can be shared with her. We on the same page?" he asked.

"Yes. Some lines have been blurred, but she's smart enough to sharpen the line when doing her reports. And, Jax, straight up, I don't think Fiona had anything to do with the murders. She might be a sociopath, but all my years of experience say we would be going down the wrong path to look at Fiona for the murders," I said, looking at Mary who nodded.

"Well good thing that's not our call, because we weren't hired to solve a murder," he said. "Lee, as former law enforcement, we want to solve this crime, but we now have a new role and have to adapt to it. Get with Benjamin when he arrives. Give him what he needs, but stay away from Fiona."

"Will do," I said, and we disconnected.

CHAPTER SEVENTEEN

Annabelle

MY PHONE FLASHED; IT WAS MY PARTNER, DAVID, AN unwelcomed intrusion on my little piece of solitude.

"Hey, what's up?" I asked.

"We got the analysis back on the hair," David said. "Hey, where are you? I went to your place to surprise you and bring you some Chinese, and you didn't answer."

I considered taking him into my confidence. But David had feelings for me, and he might misinterpret me following Lee out here. Keeping David at a distance at work was challenging enough. Telling him where I was might cause a significant rift between us. If David said anything bad about me, the squad would undoubtedly take his side.

"I decided to take a mini vacation and flew out to California," I said. It wasn't a lie but wasn't the entire truth.

"Yeah, I'm aware," he said, with a slight edge to his voice.

"How?" I asked both surprised and angry. I could guess what he'd done to locate me; I just didn't understand why.

"I was concerned when you weren't at home, and your answers to my texts sounded off. So, I pinged you," he said.

"David, that is wrong on so many levels. We're going to

have a serious talk about boundaries when I get back, but this isn't the time. What did you want to tell me about the hair?"

"It's a wig, made from real hair but definitely treated, so we're back to square one. I'm waiting for Boston to give me the results of their test. If their sample is from a wig as well, and it matches our wig, then we might have something to go on," he said.

"Since it's blonde and long, you think someone's trying to set up Fiona?" I asked.

"It would appear that way, or possibly the perpetrator wanted to look like her so when she approached they wouldn't suspect anything. Or she might have worn a wig to make sure none of her real hair fell at the crime scene. But, that's not all. No DNA from her hair could be picked up in a struggle. Now, I saved the best for last," he said, with a hint of mischief in his voice.

"Go ahead," I said, falling into our usual dance.

"This is so good it requires an exotic dinner when you get back," he said, and that was our pattern, but something felt different. I couldn't think about that now, though.

"Done. What gives?"

"Curare, or I should say a curare-like substance, likely coated the blade, because they found traces of it in the wound," he said.

"You mean like the stuff Native Americans used to lace the tips of their arrows?" My stomach clenched.

"Yep," David said, and I heard his hand hit the desk for emphasis. "Believe it or not, you can buy it on the Internet."

"So, the perp had the advantage of surprise and then paralyzed the victims to maintain control of the situation," I said.

"It seems that way," he replied.

"Well, this puts a whole new twist on things. All of this points to Fiona who had a motive, but we still have no evidence at all. Either she did it, or someone who hates her went to a lot of trouble to make it look like she did it," I said. "It could also be a man in disguise. I can't see Mahir or Chuck not noticing if a man dressed like a woman approaching them. A man would put them more on guard."

"To sum everything up, we have more information than we did, but we still aren't even close to figuring out if the killer was a man or woman. The only thing that ties this together is Fiona."

"Alright, keep me posted. Any other updates on our other cases that can't wait?" I asked.

"Nope," he said. "Just don't forget about our dinner when you get back."

"Right," I said knowing I would need to find some way to get out of dinner. His feelings toward me made me uncomfortable. He was pushing me to the point where we needed to have a difficult talk. We needed to discuss some ground rules so we would be able to continue working together. The call had almost made me late. I needed to get a move on for our meeting in Lee's room.

I barely tapped on the door, and it swung open. Before Mary and Lee could say anything, I told them about my phone call.

"David called, and I've got an update to share."

Mary poured coffee and arranged pastries on a dish as I made myself comfortable as I sat across from Lee. They both seemed distracted and didn't seem to be paying attention to what I was saying.

"Hey, you look upset; what's up?" I asked. Lee's body

seemed tight and guarded, and his face was pinched with conflict. He looked haggard.

"Belle, sometimes it's difficult working in the private sector. I have a fiduciary duty to our client, and yet my years of law enforcement are screaming at me and messing with my head," he said, rubbing his face.

My God, what'd happened in the few minutes I'd been gone?

"Lee, let me," Mary said, placing creamer and sugar on the table. "I'm a partner, and I will make the executive decision what to share and what not to share. This case is a mess." Well, this sounded ominous.

"Benjamin Hightower is flying in; he wants to confront Fiona," she said, raising her coffee to her lips.

"Well, that doesn't sound so bad. Hightower does have a stake in this whole mess. It's his property that's missing," I said. But, by the way Mary avoided my eyes and Lee sat back and looked toward the window, I gathered that was only the tip of the iceberg of what was going on.

"So there's more, and you can't share it?" I asked. "You both realize that if he said he's going to hurt Fiona, you have to say something, or you could be accessories to a crime."

"Not helping," Lee said, still not moving.

We sat in silence while I leapt to the worst conclusions.

"I'll pick him up when he lands," Lee said. "I have no concrete reason to believe he'll harm Fiona. So I'll provide him with information about where Fiona might be tonight." He looked at me, as if I had some power to lessen his sense of doom.

"I see. Has Hightower indicated he's going to do anything other than speak to her?" I asked.

They both shook their heads no.

"He's paying you to gather information, and there's no

crime in that job, unless it reaches a stalking level. What you do with that information is the important part. If you're leading someone to a place where they can hurt someone, then that's where you've got to stop. I'm not telling you something you don't already know. But I get the sense you want me to intercede," I said.

"Right now, if we do anything, it feels like we're trying to be the thought police. It's not a crime to think about something. How do we know what's in Hightower's mind, and what he plans to do?" he asked.

"Lee, seriously? If you're working this hard to justify what you're doing, then it's wrong. You know that. Let's break this down so you can make a decision. You don't need to answer me, just listen.

"You have to meet him. He's your client, and if you don't go, it would be unprofessional and rude," I said, and he nodded. "Let me play devil's advocate for a minute."

"Oh, I like this," Mary said. She poured a second cup of coffee.

I had been around them enough to know that three cups of coffee was her limit, and I'd have to cut her off soon. After three cups, her thoughts were sporadic and not well thought out.

I settled back and planned the best way to present my thoughts.

"I gather he hasn't been completely honest with you, but everyone has secrets they're ashamed of or want to keep private. Both he and Fiona have indicated she knows a secret of his. If she feared for her life, I don't think she would have told you she knows Hightower's secret. She would have kept it to herself and then disappeared. We can wrack our brains as to what the secret is, but in the end, does it really matter? The only thing that matters is, if you're convinced he'll hurt her or kill her to keep his secret, then you can't aid and abet him."

I watched their reactions and decided to continue. "I'm not at all suggesting this is what you should do, but what's the harm in telling him where she'll be tonight. She might show up, or she might not. I'm pretty sure he's not stupid enough to try to bring a weapon into a sex club. I'm also sure they provide some type of subtle surveillance. If he approaches her and the argument gets heated, the club has to have personnel to handle that type of situation. What's the worst that could happen?" I asked.

While I had my own suspicions on what could happen, I wanted to know what Lee was thinking.

"He has two hands and the ability to choke her," Lee said.

"Cameras are everywhere—" I started.

"We don't know that," Lee said.

"True. But these are rich and powerful people. I honestly don't see the club owner leaving them unprotected," I said.

"Aren't you forgetting one thing?" His eyebrow raised as he leaned forward, balancing his forearms on his legs.

"What?"

"If this party was a setup to trap us, as we suspected, then I'm sending Hightower into a dangerous situation," Lee said.

Boom. There it was.

"And if Fiona is part of it and she gets her hands on him, we helped her turn the tables on him. Once he goes in, there's no guarantee he'll leave," he said, rubbing his face with his hands.

"Here's my two cents. Hightower's your client, so you have to protect him to the best of your ability. But he's also a highly intelligent man able to make his own decisions." I paused for a moment to see if anyone wanted to jump in. Then I continued.

"I say you lay out all your information along with the risks, and let him make up his mind." It seemed like an easy solution.

"I can't let him go in there alone," Lee said.

"Why not? If he wants to risk it, that's on him," I said, not understanding.

"That's not how I work, Belle. If he goes in, I go in," he said.

"What makes you think he'll get past the door?" Mary asked. "The invitation is addressed to you and Belle. If he goes alone, he could possibly pose as you, but could he get in without anyone questioning why he was coming alone? And if he goes as himself, they didn't vet him, so they won't let him in. And if you go with him, they aren't going to let two men walk in when the invitation clearly says man and woman."

She had an excellent point.

"When's he arriving?" I asked.

"In three hours," Lee said. "What were you going to tell us when you came in?"

"The hair on Mahir's jacket was real hair but from a wig," I said.

"How did someone determine it was from a wig?" Mary asked.

"No root, so it was processed hair; therefore, no DNA," Lee said.

"Do you have any idea how long the hair was?" Mary asked.

"No. Just that it was long. Why?" I asked.

"And you have no idea if someone planted those hairs after the crime or if they shed during the crime," Lee said. "It's too wide open to even speculate. However, the fact similar hairs were found at both crime scenes leads me to believe they were planted."

"God, that just makes it all the more confusing doesn't it?" I said.

"In a way," Mary said. "But at least you can deduce it's someone who knows Fiona. Who else would know to plant a similar hair?"

We all agreed.

"But is it someone trying to frame Fiona, or some whack job leaving a calling card that the killing was done on her behalf or at her behest?" Lee asked.

"What do you mean? Like she hired someone to do it and left a clue it was her but not her?" I asked.

"No. I mean someone who thinks Fiona hasn't been treated fairly and decided to set the scales of justice in balance," he said. "Maybe someone decided to plant evidence."

"That's a possibility I hadn't considered," I replied as I watched Mary go for her third cup of coffee.

"Any more news to share?" Lee asked.

"Something odd showed up in the tox report and in the surrounding skin of the wound. We won't know specifics until the results come back from the mass spectrometry, but something similar to curare was found in the wound—"

"Curare is a muscle relaxant used in anesthesia and, in the past, in arrow poisons by the indigenous people of South America," Mary interrupted.

"What are you, Wikipedia?" Lee asked. "How does this figure in, Belle?"

Mary jumped in again. "Curare competes with acetylcholine, a chemical that carries information between nerve and muscle cells, and blocks transmission of the information, paralyzing someone. They can still process information but can't move."

"OK, how in the ever-loving hell do you know this, and should I be afraid of why you know these things?" Lee asked.

I lowered my head into my palms. This was getting more and more complicated. We still hadn't narrowed down our suspect pool one iota. In fact, it just kept growing. All I'd really concluded was the murders hadn't been random.

"Not that this isn't a fascinating who done it, but again we're completely out of the boundaries of our original mission in the case," Lee said. "Are we still looking for a stolen drive? Do we even still think there actually is a stolen drive? Or now that we've located Fiona, is that the end of all of this?" he asked.

"I don't understand why you must be such a party pooper, Lee," Mary said. "I honestly don't give a flip about the drive. I told you from the start the drive was a red herring. Frankly, I'm more interested in who killed those men and why. So if we need to make up a reason to stay on the case, then I'll say there is a drive. Hightower is still sticking with his story about the drive, so I'm good. I'll pretend I believe him."

"Will you still 'be good' if someone gets hurt?" Lee asked.

"Everyone in the game is apparently playing by their own rules, Lee, except for us. So yeah, I'm good," she said.

I felt like a spectator watching a ball volley back and forth. An amusement, but I needed an answer.

"What about Hightower?" Mary asked. "What are we going to do if he goes off halfcocked to crash this party?"

"I could accompany him," I said. Why I offered even I didn't know. It certainly wasn't well-thought-out.

"No, absolutely not," Lee said. "If he wants to put himself in danger after we explain to him we think he may be in danger if he goes to the party, then that's on him. It appears Fiona had nothing to do with the murders, so why do you need to follow any more leads about her?"

"There's no conclusive evidence whether or not she was involved in the murders. That door is still open. It appears she didn't do it, but did she have a hand in the planning?" I asked.

"Let's wait to talk about this anymore until we see what's going on with Hightower," Mary said. "Now, I'm going to take a nap. You two take some time and get to know each other in case you decide to pursue this together tonight."

"Thanks, Mary," I said and touched her hand as she took a few pastries for a snack. She winked at me and left.

CHAPTER EIGHTEEN

Lee

"Thanks for staying, Belle. My head's not in a great place. Now that we have some down time, how about we make good use of it, and you tell me about yourself?" I asked.

She smiled and snuggled down into the couch, getting comfortable, and I hoped she would tell me more about herself. I thought there might be a tender heart hiding behind the wall she'd put up to the world. Had she closed her heart off for a reason? Or hadn't she found a worthwhile person to trust?

She pushed a strand of hair behind her ear and said, "How about this instead? I'll tell you something about me, and then you tell me something about you. It can't be something like, 'My favorite color is red.' And, if you show me the real you, I just might have pictures to go along with my story," she said. A bright smile emerged that made me want to push her down on the couch and gently kiss her lips. "I'll start. Because I've met your family, I already know a little about you.

"I grew up in the Bronx. When I say that, I'm always afraid people will cringe because the Bronx has a bad reputation because of crime and gangs. But there are actually one or two pockets left that have a nice, almost suburban feel. My parents and I lived with my grandparents, the warmest, most loving people, who spoiled me rotten," she said.

She retrieved her phone and showed me a picture of a small brick home in a well-kept neighborhood. In the photo, her grandparents were sitting on the front stoop playing with a beagle, clearly enjoying their time together.

"So, you had a happy childhood?" I asked. It appeared an easy question.

"Not quite," she said. "When I was growing up, no one talked about mental health issues, but my family seemed riddled with them. My mother had severe anxiety and depression, and in my family, no one acknowledged it or suggested she get help. We all had to walk around on eggshells, so we didn't make her angry. And on the occasions I crossed some invisible line, known only to her, I'd get the shit beat out of me for the smallest thing. Sometimes she used her hand, sometimes a brush," she said, staring at the picture.

"What about your dad? Didn't he do anything to intervene?" I was shocked by what she'd told me.

"He wasn't around much. But when he was, all I remember about it was the fights he and Mom had. They were verbally abusive toward each other, and their fights always ended with him beating on the walls. I had my grandparents as a buffer, and though not ideal, my childhood toughened me up," she said, with a twinge of discomfort. "Now you."

"The neighborhood I grew up in was tough, and you learned to claim your territory on your street about the time you entered kindergarten. Your friends from the neighborhood remained your friends for life; no one seemed to move away from the community. I had a small group of friends I did things with, and some of the stuff we did...now I wonder how we didn't get killed. We explored old buildings and climbed trees that were a few hundred years old, and from those adventures there were lots of broken arms or legs. We all played on the same baseball team, and old man O'Hara always donated our baseball team uniforms. My dad drank too much, but my mom tempered his mean streak when it got too bad. When she saw he was getting too drunk, she would get him to get up and dance. Then either one of my brothers or I would take his bottle and hide it, so he couldn't drink anymore. We rotated the job of hiding the bottle, spreading the risk," I said.

"OK, now that we each got something negative about ourselves out of the way, I'll tell you a positive," Belle said. "I'm a classically trained pianist, but living in an apartment, I haven't practiced in years. But, you can bet your boots if I had some sheet music, I'd be able to pick it right back up. Another positive is I learned to ride the public transport system at an early age. Today, a child like I was, might be taken in by child services for being left unsupervised. But because of how I grew up, I can go anywhere in the world and figure out how to get somewhere by bus or train. It's quite a skill," she said with a laugh.

"That's impressive," I replied. "I know something else about you. If I remember correctly, you said you attended an all-girls Catholic school—"

"Um, yes, but not by choice. Oh, one good thing about going to that school, I didn't have to worry about fashion because we all wore uniforms," she said.

"Ah, the Catholic schoolgirl uniforms." I laughed.

"I can imagine what you're thinking in light of Fiona exploiting it, so don't say a word. Back to you," she said.

"I loved baseball when I was a kid. There was a time I

wanted to go pro. But one evening while I was doing a prank, I broke my arm, and it didn't heal right, so that blew that dream away. I then learned how to play soccer, which I ended up being so good at that I got a scholarship to play in college. My father never came to any of my games, because, according to Patrick Stone, soccer was a game played by European sissies."

I didn't tell Belle about the arguments Dad and I'd had every few weeks when he'd pressured me to quit the team.

Belle said, "I had a slew of Barbies that remain in their boxes to this day; I despise dolls. Maybe because I had no one to play dolls with. I preferred listening to classical music and looking at paintings than playing imaginary games. Nancy Drew was my favorite book series, and I'm sure that's where I got my love of investigation. Early on, I learned to ride horses, and when I can, I still ride.

"In school, basketball was my favorite sport, and I played rotating forward, even though I was shorter than most of the rest of my team. My mother forced me into cheerleading, and I hated it, so don't tease me about it. I always had good grades, and I was in the National Honor Society in high school. I didn't have a lot of friends; I guess I was an introvert, and being the youngest in the class was difficult. But being introverted didn't stop me from playing Lucy in our school's *A Charlie Brown Christmas* play."

We went back and forth, sharing stories until Belle laughed so hard she had trouble catching her breath.

As I reached across to wipe a tear of laughter from her face, I felt an intense need to kiss her. I reached up and held her face between my hands, searching her eyes for permission to kiss her. I leaned in, and lightly kissed her nose and then each cheek. Looking into her eyes, as I leaned in to kiss her, I thought, *this is crazy.*

She nipped at my bottom lip as my lips parted, and I slipped my tongue in and our tongues seemed to dance together.

The blare of my phone ringing tore us apart. I was tempted to let the call go to voicemail, but I saw the caller was Hightower.

I caught my breath and picked up my phone. "Stone."

"It's Hightower; I'm ten minutes from landing. I've got a driver on standby and will meet you at the hotel in an hour and a half. Meet me in the restaurant," he said. When I confirmed, he disconnected.

Well that killed the mood. "Do you want to continue this tonight, after things settle down?"

"Definitely," she said as she wrapped her arms around my neck and brought me in for a preview of the possibilities.

After a discussion with Jackson, we decided Belle shouldn't be at the meeting as it might be a conflict of interest. Although disappointed, she understood and settled in her room to watch some HBO.

At the restaurant, Hightower approached our table and immediately reached for my hand. A handshake a little too firm that ended with a double clasp. He nodded dismissively at Mary as he sat.

The server took our order and left us to attend to our business. The fact Hightower had ordered a double scotch on the rocks with the smell of liquor already on his breath didn't sit well with me.

"I want to get this cleared away before we start," he said. "I think you've done a great job tracking Fiona down. However, we are no closer to securing the drive than we were at the start. So, what are you going to do about that problem? I want solutions not excuses."

This wasn't going to be easy; he'd purposefully put us on the defensive. I took a sip of water to pace myself before I spoke.

"Benjamin, I understand your zeal for finding your drive, but there is little evidence that Fiona has it—"

"Of course she has it!" he interrupted. "Why would she run if she didn't have it?"

"Maybe Fiona didn't like the work environment and has another job lined up," Mary offered, testing the waters.

He ignored her and continued maintaining eye contact with me.

"I have one man dead and another recovering from a severe drug overdose, and neither are in a position to put the drive up for auction. So that leaves her. Tell me about these murders she's supposedly involved in," he said, accepting his salad from the server.

"We don't have any proof of her involvement," I said. "All we know is that two men from her past were murdered." I had no intention of sharing information Belle had given us in confidence.

"That's it? Two of the biggest police forces in America are investigating this, and you're telling me that's all they have? There's no evidence?" he asked in a terse tone.

"Benjamin, you don't understand how long it takes to gather evidence and sort through it, much less analyze it. The police are not in the business of supposition and speculation. It may be awhile before Fiona is implicated in a crime, if ever," I said.

"Benjamin," Mary said, "we're working closely with a NY detective. In fact, she is here in the hotel working on the murder case as we investigate Fiona's involvement in your missing drive. And there's nothing yet that has implicated Fiona in the murders. Just bad luck at knowing both victims.

"What Lee said is correct. The detective has shared with us that Fiona is still a suspect in a big pool of suspects. However, there is nothing of significance, yet, tying her to the murders. Now, should I call the detective to join us, or is the discussion you want to have with us confidential about what Fiona refers to as your 'secret'?"

I about lost my mind. Had Mary gone off the deep end? Why would she betray Belle's confidence?

He placed his fork down and looked from me to Mary.

"Fiona said she was pregnant, and it was mine. A night of too much drinking and not enough protection. I thought she'd terminated the pregnancy. But I suppose she found this was a way to extort money from me. I suppose her angle was for me to pay her hush money to avoid a scandal that could ruin my business or make me pay child support; neither works for me."

That wasn't what I'd expected at all. "What proof did she have that the baby's yours?" I asked.

"Seems after week seven all you need is a cheek swab from the father and blood from the mother. And voila, DNA confirmation of paternity," he said, shaking his head.

Oh God, this gave him even more motive to want to harm her.

"So that's my secret. Call the officer down, please," he said.

"She's a homicide detective, and it doesn't work like that, Benjamin. Belle's not on your payroll. She won't and can't share her information with you. She's here conducting her own investigation. Now, understanding all that, would you still like me to ask Detective Hughes if she would like to join us?" I asked.

The man looked taken aback; clearly he wasn't used to being spoken to like that. Yet when challenged, he changed his tone and politely requested I call Belle and invite her to join us.

As Belle crossed the room, I realized what a beautiful, confident woman she was, and I felt a stirring I hoped would be satisfied tonight. Our eyes met, and I sensed she felt the same. After a side jab from Mary, I noticed Hightower raking his eyes over her in a way that caused me to want to punch that fucker's lights out.

I made the introductions, and Belle sat across from Hightower so she could gauge his reactions. An old investigative technique. He wouldn't take his eyes off of her in obvious sexual appreciation.

"Detective Hughes, I realize this may put you in an uncomfortable position, however, I would like your opinion of Fiona," he said as he poured her a glass of water.

"Mr. Hightower—"

"Ben, please call me Ben," he said as Mary and I exchanged glances.

"Ben, I have not formulated a professional opinion about Fiona. I may have an impression based on my interaction with her, but I don't have an opinion on how that would impact your case," she said as she took a sip of water. He observed her every move, much like a predator watches its prey.

He suddenly began asking her questions in rapid fire. The only thing Belle would say, however, was "It's an ongoing investigation, and I can't share any information." Eventually, I told him Belle and I had been vetted by the sex club, and we'd been given a code for the party the club was hosting that night.

"So, you believe she'll be there?" he asked with a little too much enthusiasm.

"To be honest, I'm concerned it might be a setup to trap us—" I started.

"That's ridiculous, Lee," Hightower broke in. "Why would people you don't know go to all that trouble just to trap you in some place? I want you there tonight looking for her."

"I'm sorry, Benjamin, but we're not your employees, and we make decisions about what we're going to do based on information available to us. From the information we have available, this club has had some problems with violence. Neither Belle nor I have any experience with this type of activity, and the reward doesn't outweigh the risk," I said.

"You're both trained law enforcement, right?" he pressed.

We nodded.

"So, what's the problem? You can read a situation, and you're trained to defend yourselves."

"Walking into an unknown situation is reckless. Plus, Fiona is aware we know she visited there today, and she may have alerted them," I explained.

"And yet they sent you an invitation," Hightower retorted.

"Yes, they did." There was no use in arguing with him. "We won't put our lives in danger. What we will do is continue watching Fiona. With the auction three days away, if she's the one who does have the drive, she'll be preparing for the sale."

"Unacceptable," he said. "There's a good chance she'll be in there tonight, and I want to talk to her."

I was ready to snap off a snide answer when Belle interrupted.

"I'm certain Lee would be happy to give up his invitation, and you could use it in his place." She smiled.

Had she and Mary conspired to give me a heart attack?

"Would that include you accompanying me as my partner?" he asked.

Again before I could answer she replied, "No, it would not. Any further contact with Fiona may compromise my case."

"Then the decision is made. I'll go alone," Benjamin said.

"It's an unwise decision," I said.

"Noted," he replied. "Forward me the invitation, and I'll contact you sometime tomorrow. Detective Hughes, would you like to help me prepare for my role tonight and maybe give me some tips on how to blend?" he asked.

"Sorry, but again that would be frowned upon by the NYPD," she replied.

"Then if you all will excuse me, I need to do some research for tonight. I have to say, Lee, I'm disappointed in you. Maybe you're not the right fit for this job?" he said.

"Maybe, Benjamin, but that's something you should take up with Jackson," I replied. I was sure his little speech had been for Belle's benefit. This slimeball was getting on my last nerve.

He gave a short nod and left.

When he walked out of hearing distance, Mary said, "He's going in there to find that girl, and when he does, he'll hurt her."

"I disagree, Mary. I think she'll find him first," I said.

"Did I miss something?" Belle asked.

"Oh what the hell, she's pregnant or at some point was, and the baby is his," Mary blurted. "Who cares? What scandal? A sexual harassment suit? Join the line. People are getting numb to it at this point. I don't buy any of it."

I could see the shock on Belle's face. "I didn't see that coming, at all. With all the guys she's probably slept with, how would they confirm paternity before the baby is born?"

"Apparently there are tests you can do when a woman is seven weeks pregnant that can verify paternity," I said.

Belle sighed. "I don't know what to think at this point. This just keeps getting crazier."

"Well, since you kids won't need me any more tonight, I'm going upstairs to get a bit of rest. Are we going to bring Jackson up to speed?" Mary asked.

"I'm sure Hightower's on the phone right now giving him an earful. So I'm going to just wait for my phone to ring," I said.

Mary laughed and asked if we should follow Benjamin tonight to keep an eye on things. I told her I would consider it, and she left.

"You really considering following him?" Belle asked.

"The guy is in over his head—"

"Lee, it's his head, and he's a dick. Why would you care at this point?" she asked.

I hoped she was trying to talk me out of following him because she had her own plans for me later.

"He's our client, and he's no match for Fiona. Fiona's like a shark circling its next meal, and she's going to eat him alive."

CHAPTER NINETEEN

Lee

T HERE WAS NOTHING MORE I COULD LEARN FROM REVIEWING THE files we had, and frankly, I was stumped. Why were we still here? We should be going to talk to Ryan who was at home recovering. A knock on my door interrupted my thoughts. I looked through the peephole and saw Belle.

"Did you take a nap?" she asked, looking toward my bed.

"Yeah, just a power nap."

"I got some news from my partner about the knife wound," she said as she stretched her neck as if to loosen a kink.

"Your neck hurt?"

"I've been sitting hunched over my computer for so long my shoulders are locked up, and I have a wicked headache."

"Come over here and let me rub your neck and shoulders," I said, tilting my head toward the sitting area. She gave me a questioning look and followed me over. As I sat in the large chair with my butt toward the edge of the seat, she sat cross-legged between my legs and tilted her head down.

"If you loosen your shirt, I can get better access to your shoulders," I said. Belle turned her head to the side, caught my eyes, and smiled. She pulled her shirt off her shoulders.

"God, you're tight. It feels like you have rocks under your skin," I said as I pushed and prodded her shoulders. "This might hurt when I press on some trigger points."

I pressed into her muscle. "Tell me if I hurt you."

"Oh my God, that hurts so good. Right there, ah..." she said in such a way that I wondered if this were a good idea.

I leaned in closer to put leverage into my thumbs and asked, "So what did you find out about the knife wound?"

"Oh right." She smiled. "I almost forgot. The pathologist determined the knife was inserted with such force that the hilt left a bruise on the skin. But here's the kicker. The perp twisted the knife in a full circle at least twice, shredding Mahir's organs and muscles in the area. Which means, he or she had to reach around and hold the left shoulder for leverage. Doc said with that in mind the perp was probably at least as tall or taller than the victim."

"So, you're saying they're assuming it was a man who did this?" I asked. If so that threw a whole new light on this case.

"The doc said the brute force alone necessary to twist the knife like that was a major consideration. But he wouldn't commit on paper just yet because of the drug on the knife," she said, turning her neck to give me better access.

"What about Evans?" I asked, gently squeezing her shoulders.

"Apparently, he put up more of a struggle. The perp only got in a jab and a quick pull out. But again, like Mahir's, his wound was on the right side. The doc should have more by tomorrow."

"So am I hearing we can probably rule out Fiona as a suspect in the case?" I asked.

"Not necessarily. What if Fiona was working with

someone, and she was the bait, and someone else approached the victim while she had him distracted? Fiona is linked to this; we have to figure out how."

"Your upper back is a mess, and it's not just from the computer today. How about I get some lotion from the bathroom, and you take off your shirt and bra and lie on the bed. If you do that, I can get better access to the muscle attachments," I said, waiting for Belle's answer. She didn't say no.

She turned and smiled. "How do you know so much about all of this? You're a massage master. I'm putty in your hands."

I kept working at the small muscles in the neck and leaned in toward her. I'm sure she felt my breath on her skin. "In the advanced stages, my wife's cancer went into her bones. Massage was the only relief from the pain. I became great at reading trigger points and knowing how to release the tension. Your back is a roadmap of too many days and nights hunched over a computer. I've got the skill, and you've got the need, so you decide. Do you want to walk upright the rest of the day or hunched over?"

I sensed the mention of Debby hit a tender spot as she tensed and then released. I waited to see if she wanted to discuss it, but she let it pass.

"OK, I know they have the good stuff here in the bathroom; I've checked it out. It's the large bottle marked body lotion. You go get it, and wait until I say to come back in," she said, standing. I looked up at her, and she placed her hand on my cheek and said, "Thank you."

When the coast was clear she called out, and I returned with a bottle of lotion that had Kadota Fig written on the bottle. What I wasn't prepared for was the sensation that slammed into me seeing her lying in bed under the covers with her back bare. Her pants draped over one arm of the chair, and her shirt and lacy black bra were neatly arranged on the seat cushion. Sweet Jesus. I wondered if her panties matched the bra and if I would find out.

"Great, you found it," she said with a wink. My mind immediately went to visions of her naked and showering in my bathroom. My own private porno flick. *Stop it.*

"Would it be OK with you if I took my shirt off? This stuff can get messy," I said. *What the hell was I doing? Yeah, like I didn't know exactly what I was doing.*

"Hey, you're the one looking after me. Whatever makes you comfortable," she said, turning her head away from me and resting it on her folded arms.

I couldn't get my thoughts or the lower part of my body back under control. *What to do, what to do. Get my head in the case.*

"I don't want to startle you. I'm crawling up behind you, and I'm going to straddle you." My voice sounded low and raspy even to me. The last thing I expected was a laugh. And I about lost my balance when she pushed up a bit on her arms, giving me a glimpse of her breasts.

"God, Lee, you sound like a training session back at the academy," she said as she lay back down.

I managed an "um" as I squirted the lotion on my hands to warm it up.

I inched my way up to her hips, encased them with my knees, and leaned back. It seemed as if I had been here before, but that was impossible. The Sam Hunt song *Body Like A Backroad* came to mind as I explored her long smooth back. My hands started out slow with elongated upward strokes. But soon I was down around the hip area, probably not an area that needed much attention from computer work, but I was a guy who gave it my all.

"Wait, do I see a tattoo here?" I asked, looking at a partial inked picture peeping out from under the sheet covering her left hip. It kind of shocked me.

"Yes, you do. Go ahead and take a look," she said, turning a bit on her right hip to elevate the left hip.

Whoa, now that was playing with fire. But how could I resist? I pulled the sheet down about two inches, and I saw a burst of flowers. Well, that was unexpected. "Is there a story behind it?" I asked. I hoped it didn't entail a guy.

"In college, a drunk driver killed my best friend, and it's sort of my way of honoring her," she said.

"Oh, I'm sorry for your loss," I said, placing the sheet back over her hip. When she settled, I started the upward stroke along her spine and was rewarded with a groan that assured me my effort was appreciated.

I was getting lost in the texture of her skin and the moans of pleasure when her phone rang and flashed her partner's face on the screen. Damn, if that didn't break the spell.

"Let it go to voicemail," she said lazily without moving her head.

"What if it's important?" *Why should I care?*

"It's my day off. He's just trying to keep track of me. I'll get it later. This is too good to let go of," she said in almost a whisper.

Trying to keep track of her? That didn't sound good, but right now wasn't the time to ask about it. I made a mental note to talk to her about it later.

As I continued, she rolled from her stomach to her back, and I didn't stop her. Instead, I admired her full breasts and noticed the look of lust on her face. Her eyes were half opened, half closed, and her lips slightly parted. I lowered myself so skin was touching skin. My arms slid forward, and I slowly leaned down. When my face was so close our breath intermingled, I touched my nose to hers. Her eyes invited me to come closer, and I accepted the invitation. My lips gently dropped to hers, as if they were traveling home, and we'd done this for years. What started out as light feathery kisses turned into nibbling of lips and that traveled to earlobes. And then all my inhibitions left me as I kissed a trail from her ear down her neck to her breasts.

The scent of the lotion wafted to my nose; that scent would always be a reminder of this day. All my senses were overwhelmed. Overwhelmed with the sight, smell, and taste of Belle. I watched her eyes make love to me, just by their movement. The hum of the sexy noise from her throat sent what I was holding back into motion. Save for the moment it took to retrieve a condom, we didn't break our body contact. As our bodies found their rhythm, everything felt so right. So right I couldn't remember when a release had felt so emotionally charged. It was at that moment I realized I couldn't let Belle go; she had imprinted on my soul.

My emotions were all over the place as I explored every part of her body. No, not explored, worshiped. She'd had a full life, which I read through the scars left behind. She laughed as I regaled her about the history of each of my scars, which bordered on criminal. Laughter turned sensual, and we hit our mutually exhaustive release. I partially collapsed on her, and she tried to catch her breath as she continued to give me small butterfly kisses.

As we lay there enjoying the quiet, we heard a hard rap at

the door. I put my finger to my mouth to indicate we should remain silent, and she nodded. The knocking stopped, but it was replaced by my phone ringing. Hightower. I let it go to voicemail, hoping for a reprieve. No such luck. He must have remained outside my door, because the knocking started again only in a more rapid succession. I decided to wait him out. When I was confident the coast was clear, I got up and checked the peephole. He was gone.

I turned to Belle. I was still naked but surprisingly comfortable being so. I suggested she check her voicemail, and I check mine.

As she listened, her face turned from passive to angry. She tossed the phone on the bed, and the only thing I heard was, "Son of a bitch!"

After I listened to mine, I felt the same.

"You first," she said, with a nod toward my phone.

"Hightower. He's determined to go tonight, and he wants to talk strategy to see if you've changed your mind about accompanying him. What part of 'no' does that man not understand?" I asked, leaning on my arm, facing her. The man was a pain in my ass, and that wasn't a good feeling to have about a client.

"If you think it might help, I might consider it. I worked vice, and I'm not easily shocked," she said, waiting for me to respond.

"Yeah, that would be a hell no. That man seems to have a problem with boundaries. There are so many reasons that isn't going to happen, the least of which is I don't want you to get in trouble back in NY for your actions here," I said.

"Are you going to let him go in there unprotected?" Her tone suggested it wasn't a wise idea.

"Look, he didn't hire me to be his bodyguard. I wasn't comfortable giving him the invitation, but he paid for the information, so technically it belongs to him. He wants to play, not knowing what the rules are, and I can't stop him. I'll brief him on what information we have about the place, and if he decides to move forward, that's on him. What I will do is set up a stakeout close to him in case he gets into trouble and reaches out," I said.

"I hope your dislike for him isn't clouding your judgment," she said, turning toward me.

"Don't be ridiculous. I agree with what you and Mary said earlier. It might be a setup. And I don't intend to put myself in danger for a man whose intentions don't seem honorable. What did your partner want?"

"I have to call him back to put all the pieces together, but there may come a time, if this continues that a reassignment may be necessary. Like it or not, law enforcement is still a male-dominated field. Don't get me wrong; no one has ever stopped me from getting a promotion, but I don't fit in when it comes to 'man talk.' I draw the line at inappropriate jokes and refuse to step over the friendly line. David has feelings for me that aren't reciprocated, and he found out I'm in LA, and he's snooping around. If he found out I'm here with your firm, he might try to make something of it that may get ugly," she said. "I could be transferred to a less than desirable area."

"As much as I want to say I'm appalled by that statement, it's true that the force is a male-dominated occupation, and different rules apply. They shouldn't, but sometimes, they do. What will you do if that happens?" I asked.

Without hesitation, she said, "I'll quit. My apartment is rent controlled, and I have a tidy little sum in the bank. I'd move west some place where there's lots of land and write full time. I never considered owning a home, but the past year I've increasingly thought about it. But New York real estate and taxes are prohibitively expensive, even with all the overtime I work. So, I've always got a plan B in my back pocket." She smiled.

I kissed her nose and asked her if I could do anything to help the situation, and she said no. She was a woman who knew her mind and gently put boundaries in place.

"Are you concerned you'll be reprimanded for being here?" I wanted her to say no because I wanted nothing weighing on her mind to make her want to leave.

"It's a hazy line. I can do whatever I want on my time off. But let's face it, I sort of stepped over a line when I took a job consulting with you without clearing it with my lieutenant. Am I sorry I did it? Absolutely not. Again, if anything happens where I need to leave the force, I have a backup plan," she said.

"It sounds like you have a 'go bag' packed and ready to leave at a moment's notice."

"Well, I'm sort of a minimalist. I'm not married to my apartment, and my furniture is a lot of hand-me-downs. My mom loves to redecorate every three years, so she gives me all her furniture, which is new furniture since most is for display. I don't have a car to worry about, and my wardrobe fits in two suitcases. So when you say a 'go bag,' it would be two, and I'm gone. The furniture would be donated to Goodwill, the keys left under the mat, and it would be like I was never there," she said, putting her bra back on.

I shook my head and laughed. "You're in the wrong government agency. The CIA would kill for a woman like you."

A rapping on my door started again. I gave Belle the

signal to stay while I put my pants on. She continued to dress, and I peeped out the hole. Mary. I told her to hold on while I made sure Belle was dressed.

"What do you want?" I asked as I opened the door, and she walked in without an invitation.

She surveyed the room and smiled.

"Hightower is bitching to Jackson because he can't get ahold of you. Jax called me, and we're to meet in Hightower's suite in twenty minutes. Maybe a quick shower and a wet head will provide some cover," she said, giving me the once-over.

"Want me to come, Mary?" Belle asked.

"No. If he's going to do something stupid, no need for you to get in any deeper," I said.

"You need some plausible deniability," Mary added.

"Why don't you stay and straighten things out with David," I said.

"Do you still want to follow Hightower tonight?" she asked, as she retrieved her phone.

"Depends on how stupid he plans to get. We'll find out when Mary and I meet with him," I said.

"Any more on Fiona?" Mary asked.

Belle checked her app, but nothing showed up.

"Look, Lee, I don't like Benjamin any more than you, but my opinion is we should keep an eye on him. What if he gets in trouble?" Belle asked.

"And what if that means going to his rescue? How's that going to sit if we have to call in the local law enforcement?" I asked.

"I see your point. OK, let's chat again after you talk to him. How about I order dinner, and we meet in my room in about an hour and a half?" Belle asked.

"Sounds like a plan. I'm jumping in the shower. Mary, how about you tell Hightower I'll be there and walk Belle to her room?"

Mary smiled and tapped the side of her nose with her finger. Whatever.

CHAPTER TWENTY

Lee

WHILE I SHOWERED, ALL I WANTED TO DO WAS REPLAY THE afternoon's activities in my mind. How had this happened? Is such intense feeling even possible in such a short amount of time? Love takes time to grow, so surely this must be lust or infatuation. However, I can't say I've ever been infatuated with anyone. Ever.

I'd loved Debby, but I can't say I was infatuated with her. We'd grown up in the same neighborhood, and although I'd dated a lot of girls, Debby and I'd always seemed to gravitate toward one another. We'd been friends first and then became lovers. Her sense of humor had taken me out of dark places, and her bubbly personality had grabbed me by the collar and taken me along for her particular kind of adventure.

We'd left Boston so she could complete grad school in Chicago, and the culture shock of Chicago had jolted me. I'd thought I would do anything for her smile. But in the end, my job came before us and our marriage. I was determined to climb the ranks quickly and doing so sacrificed my time with Debby. I had just made detective when she got sick and the achievement felt hollow. My thoughts returned to Belle.

Belle, a complicated woman, led a complicated life. I found it amusing that she would be ready, willing, and able to pick up stakes in a day and morph into a new life. It had taken me six months to change my life once I'd decided to do it. Belle was spontaneous, a useful attribute in life and as a detective. Even as a younger man, I'd never possessed that ability. Everything in my life had to be planned and structured. My philosophy epitomized the phrase, "slow and steady wins the race."

Belle's partner, David, might prove to be a complication to what was happening between us. If he turned on her once she confronted him, a slew of problems could follow and put a wrinkle in her career. Unrequited love is never good. I needed to determine his intentions. Wait. Did that really just go through my mind? My God, I was already planning a future with her when we hadn't even established a present. And why should I claim someone's life and determine how they should handle their relationships? *Snap out of it.*

As I rinsed the remaining shampoo from my hair, I forced myself to focus on my meeting with Hightower. I realized chances of it going sideways were high, and it could happen quickly without warning. This was not a good position to be in. He seemed like an arrogant prick, and once faced with all that available flesh at the party he might divert from his self-imposed mission and immerse himself in the sex play. Which wouldn't be bad in the long run if it kept him off Fiona's radar, should she be there.

That Fire and Ice place was bad news, though. How could anyplace be safe when it encouraged people to beat the shit out of loved ones and strangers? Rumors painted the club as a significant drug use hub, but that was the extent of the illegal activities. We couldn't find any claims that the club or its patrons participated in distributing or human trafficking. And nothing from our research indicated Fiona did drugs.

I shut the water off, towel dried, and did a quick assessment of my appearance. A shave might be in order, but the scruff on my face needed to wait until later. A quick text to Mary had her waiting at the door when I left my room.

"Mary, what's your secret? How do you have all these contacts at your disposal?" I asked. It seemed preposterous, but every time we needed something done, she had the means to get it accomplished. And even better, the information she provided panned out. If it were me, I'd need to dig around, call in favors, and wait days if not weeks for a turnaround.

"It's a long story, but the bottom line is, money talks. I'm able to pay people to do things on an expedited timetable. And, don't forget, we're working with a generous budget in this case. Last year, I worked a case with the FBI that gave me the opportunity to cement valuable relationships. One was and is a criminal, and the other a foreign intelligence agent. But enough about that, I need to discuss something before we talk to Benjamin. There are so many moving parts here that we've spent no time parsing fact from fiction," she said.

"Such as?"

"Well, for one, Claire. She sure as hell is in cahoots somehow with Fiona. I can't figure out if she intended to help or hurt her. If hurting was her play, what's her endgame? And what about that man Claire said she sensed watching the place. Did she purposely give us a false lead?"

"No, Stamos is definitely in this mess somehow. Remember he traced back to the club. But there's not enough information to determine if Stamos wants to hurt or help Fiona. The fact he's showing up more is troubling. If we had more manpower,

I'd follow him myself. Times like these makes me miss working with the police force. My gut says he's the key to something, but I don't know what yet. We've been working this case less than a week and learned a lot. But to what avail? Why are we still here? Can we get to the drive before it's auctioned in cyberspace?"

"I've got someone monitoring the auction and tracking down the IP origin," Mary said nonchalantly.

"No way. You are so full of shit." I laughed as I shook my head. "I don't care how much money you have, that kind of trick would take serious hacking skills and organization."

She stopped in the hall and scoped out the cameras. In spy-like fashion, she moved us out of range and turned to the wall.

"Lee, you can trust me when I say the best of the best are intent on finding the location of the person running the auction. We know so little about what we're searching for and its potential uses. My sources say this gene-altering tool is even more advanced than CRISPR. There's no research published on this new tool, and yet it's rumored to be invaluable. Think about the term, gene-editing tool. Can you even begin to imagine its enormous potential?

"Gene editing is a technology that gives scientists the ability to change an organism's DNA. It allows the user to add, remove, or alter genetic material at particular locations in the genome. Hightower's project has the potential to revolutionize science. It's believed to be faster and cheaper than any method out there," she said. "I don't want to imagine the potential disaster if it fell into the wrong hands, like the Russian government."

"Yeah, but I'm sure they had the opportunity to buy it from the Germans, just like Hightower did," I suggested.

"Yes, but now Benjamin has streamlined it more and probably increased its efficiency by working out the bugs. My source says it has the potential to wipe out populations, if used for nefarious purposes. It also has the ability, once perfected, to be the market leader in a cure for diseases. Flip that on its head, and maybe Big Pharma doesn't want it out there curing disease. It's a big deal, Lee, trust me. So even if Fiona doesn't have it, we might be on the trail of whoever does."

"All right, now, more the point, what are we going to do about Hightower?" I asked.

"I've asked my friend, let's call him Tyler, to monitor the location you were sent via satellite to determine if there really is a party planned. From what he can tell, food and beverages are being taken to those coordinates, and there is activity at the place," she said.

What the hell? I wanted to laugh, but I began to trust what she was saying. Jax had hinted that her involvement with the FBI had left her with foreign contacts, so I let it be.

"So," she continued, "we need to get Hightower ready. He's got to be careful. And in the end, we can't control what happens if his emotions take over when he sees Fiona. So, he wants to talk? Let's talk."

We turned away from the wall and continued to his room.

I'd barely knocked on the door when he opened it. He quickly pulled me into the room.

"Come in, come in," he said, hurriedly closing the door.

"You seem a little jumpy," I said.

"Not at all. I'm anxious to talk this through so I can get ready for tonight," Hightower said. "I put together a plan, but I want your input."

Oh, this should be good.

"Here, sit." He motioned toward the large seating area. "Can I offer you anything?"

We declined. He poured himself two fingers of what appeared to be whiskey into a cut-crystal tumbler. I hoped it was his first, but something in the way he touched the furniture as he walked past it told me it wasn't.

"I hired, shall we say, a high-end escort familiar with this form of entertainment to accompany me tonight," he said.

"OK, stop right there," I said, inching forward in the chair. "What you're going to tonight isn't entertainment to these people. It's a lifestyle they take seriously. The members pay thousands of dollars in fees to make sure their confidentiality is maintained so they can practice their particular form of kink. Did you read the rules in the email? They specifically forbid escorts and only allow people they've vetted into the party. These people are not playing," I said.

He brushed my question off with a dismissive wave and said, "I took those as suggestions."

I saw Mary wanted to say something but stopped herself.

Hightower's lips turned up into an odd smile, and he asked where Belle was.

"Why?" I asked.

"I understand from reading the expense reports that I'm paying her a consultation fee, and I want to consult her," he said with a challenging stare.

This was not going well at all.

"Forget about Detective Hughes; focus on tonight and the auction for the drive. I want to be clear about our role. Now that Ryan is home recuperating, is he excluded as a suspect?" I asked.

"No one is in the clear, Mr. Stone. Not even Dennis," he said, draining his glass of the contents.

"So what? You think Dennis had a partner who still has the

drive in play, or is Dennis working solo in the paranormal realm orchestrating the sale?" Mary asked.

He ignored her, as if she was an inconsequential gnat buzzing past his ear.

"I think you should skip this party tonight, Benjamin, and I think we should all pack our stuff and head back to Seattle. We should spend more time investigating Ryan, someone we haven't even interviewed," I said.

He met my eyes and stood to get a refill.

"You might want to go easy on that stuff," I suggested. "These people aren't throwing a cocktail party, and they will possess implements that can hurt you. If you get yourself in a position where you need to roleplay, booze can dull the senses, including pain."

He stared at me, as if deciding whether I was giving him a lecture or offering him advice.

"Okay, if we can't talk you out of this, what can we do to help you get ready for tonight?" I asked.

"Who will be at the party?" he asked.

"How would I know? I met the head man this morning, and he didn't offer me a guest list. Mahir's mother's private eye reported the membership is comprised of a variety of professional people like politicians, lawyers, doctors—people who have money to pay the ridiculous fees to belong. No celebrities, but there are what he termed foreign diplomats—"

"So Fiona may be in contact with people who are representing governments that might want to purchase the drive," he interrupted.

As I mulled that over, my phone buzzed with a text message from Belle telling me to meet her outside Benjamin's room. She had news that couldn't wait.

"Can you excuse me a second? I need to step out for a moment to take a call. Mary, would you join me?" No way I was leaving that man unsupervised in there with Mary.

We stepped out into the hall, and Belle motioned us over to the window.

"David sent me some footage from Abajian's security camera from the day before he was stabbed."

She showed us the footage.

"Now, I realize it's fuzzy, but who does that look like?" Belle asked with a mischievous smile.

Mary grabbed the tablet, removed her glasses, then put them back on, and held it at arm's length.

"No idea," she said, handing it to me.

I moved the tablet forward and back trying to see it, but I was as stumped as Mary.

"Jeremy Stamos!" Belle said.

"You sure?" I asked, finding it incredulous.

"Go ahead; look again. Move it millisecond by millisecond, and when you get to point 16:03, stop it."

I followed her instructions, and by God at 16:03 a clear picture of his face came into view. He hadn't tried to disguise himself at all.

"Look, let's finish up with Hightower, and we'll meet you back in my room," I said.

"Whoa, slow down. Aren't you going to tell Hightower about this?" she asked.

"No, why?" I asked.

"Well, even though it's inconclusive, this footage suggests Fiona and Jeremy might be working together. And we know they're both in town, and both tied to Fire and Ice. I think Jeremy may sniff around the club tonight. Jeremy has no idea, for that matter neither does Fiona, that we aren't going to be there tonight. What if they're planning something? We might be able to handle what they throw at us but could Benjamin? You have to tell him about this," Belle said.

I thought about it and had to agree. We all walked back to his door and knocked. Hightower opened the door, and when he saw Belle, he smiled broadly.

"Detective! Please join us," he said, welcoming us in.

Mary and I went back to our seats, but Belle remained standing.

"Please, Detective, have a seat." Hightower offered a seat next to him.

This man was working my last nerve.

"Detective Hughes has uncovered information we need to share with you that may or may not have anything to do with the drive. It's about an associate of Fiona's, and he has some precarious ties to Fire and Ice. We have him on video surveillance around Mahir's home—"

"Mahir?" he interrupted.

"Yes, Mahir, the young man Fiona accused of assaulting her here in LA and who was recently murdered in New York," I said.

"Continue," he said, with a rolling-hand gesture.

What a pompous ass.

"The camera at Mahir's parents' home caught this man in town at the same time Fiona was in New York, shortly before Mahir's murder. So with her connection to him and the club, we need you to be alert if you recognize him," Belle said.

"I don't understand; what does this have to do with me?" he asked, confused.

"Probably nothing, but you're going in our place, and

Fiona has no idea we won't be there. So if she has something planned for us, you need to be on guard," I said.

"OK, let me see what he looks like."

As Belle passed him the tablet, he asked his name, and she replied, "Jeremy Stamos."

I don't know if his face or name caused the harsh reaction, but Benjamin dropped the tablet and visibly paled.

Belle rushed to him. "Are you OK? Here, lean back," she said.

As quickly as he had spaced out, he regained his composure. "Sorry, must be the whiskey. Forgive me. I'm going to go splash some water on my face. Please excuse me. I'll be right back."

As he left, we all exchanged glances but kept silent.

He was gone long enough that Belle was just about to go check on him when he returned and took a seat.

"Did you recognize him?" she asked.

"No," he said. But the way he fidgeted and averted his eyes said he was lying.

Belle and I exchanged looks, and she continued. "He has a criminal history of violent crimes, so I wanted you to be aware."

"What kind of violent crimes?" he asked.

"Aggravated battery and rape," she said.

He stood, walked over to the window, and looked out, lost in thought. He turned back and what he said got our full attention.

"Fiona got me involved with him in a threesome, and all I'll say was it did not turn out well."

"I don't want to embarrass you, but was it violent?" Belle asked.

He kept his eyes on hers and said, "Yes."

"OK, I've heard enough here," I interrupted. "Once again, I'm going to say I think it's not only a bad idea for you to go tonight, but now I also think it's reckless based on what we know and what you just told us about your history with Jeremy."

He walked toward us at a quick pace and said, "Thank you all for your advice; I've got it from here." And he left the room.

With no reason to stay, we quickly left as well.

"He's determined to go, and there will be trouble tonight," Mary said.

"Lee, if you don't want to stake the place out later, that's fine. But I'm going, and Mary's going with me," Belle said.

That brought an air punch from Mary.

Shaking my head, and knowing this could turn into a total clusterfuck, I knew I'd be going.

CHAPTER TWENTY-ONE

Annabelle

"**H**OLD UP, GUYS. I JUST GOT A VOICEMAIL FROM BOSTON PD asking me to call. Lee, your room is closer; let's go there," I said. *That's odd that Boston would call me instead of David,* I thought.

Lee stopped as he read a text. "Son of a bitch!" he exclaimed.

"What?" I asked.

"Hightower wants, no insists, we join him and his 'date' for dinner at seven thirty in the hotel restaurant to complete the plans. I'm going to go see him and put a stop to this," he said as he took a few steps away from us.

"No," Mary said, touching his arm. "Lee, he's the client, and he can ask us to do certain things. This dinner won't make him change his mind. And I, for one, want to see who he's chosen as his companion. Don't forget, this could just be a party. These people may not have identified you, and everyone might be getting excited about nothing. If this woman's expertise is BDSM, she's probably been to parties like this before. She should be able to give us a heads-up on what a 'normal' party is like so if she gets a sense something isn't right, she can make sure they leave."

"Just agree to dinner, Lee," I said.

I watched him struggle with the decision before he finally typed "OK."

"Mary, I know you're technically my boss—" he said, running his fingers through his hair.

"Nothing technical about it Lee, I am your boss," she said with a broad smile.

"Not helpful, Mary. I've got to be honest with you, I'm not sure I'm cut out for this line of work. It's taking everything in me not to go back to that room and have it out with him. He's arrogant, shady as hell, and has the morals of…well, I don't know," he said, looking at the ceiling and then back down again. "Plus, I'm worried that we're setting Fiona up. He could really hurt her."

"Lee, Fiona's perfectly capable of taking care of herself. We don't even know if she'll be at that party. I understand your frustration and your concern. When you do skip tracing you're in control of the situation, but in this situation you're being micromanaged. This was a bad job to be your first client-based job. The fact the man is definitely hiding something, and we don't know what his agenda is with this girl makes it all the more confusing. I don't know how this will end. But my gut? My gut says we need to buckle up because we're heading into some bumpy territory. Will we crash and burn? Maybe. Something is definitely wrong here; I agree. I know this has been difficult for you, but I'm glad to have someone with your experience working with me. If I had someone green working with me on this case, I can't bear to think what a mess I'd be in right now," Mary said.

He nodded and slipped the magnetic card in the slot of his hotel room door. It flashed red twice before it turned green.

Some would take that as a sign.

"This isn't just about Benjamin's personal agenda with Fiona. We need to keep on track. A biotechnology product was stolen, and it's now up for auction. Every time science makes an advance for potential good, along comes the shadow of bad. For every good scientist and doctor out there like Jonas Salk trying to better our civilization, there's also evil like Josef Mengele working another angle," I said trying to soften his frustration.

"I get your point, Belle. But, what if Hightower is a Josef Mengele, and we're helping him to recapture a tool that can do more harm than good?" he asked, closing the door behind him.

"Lee, you're being a bit dramatic and letting your dislike of the man cloud your judgment," Mary said. "I get why you're suspicious of him. He even admitted to acquiring the tool under questionable circumstances. But hell, as far as we know, what he did may be common industry practice. I don't have enough information about that, so I won't be the judge. We were hired to find the drive; Fiona was a lead. I don't think any of us believe she has the drive. Is there a chance we might be wrong? Yes. Should one of us be in Seattle checking on Ryan and close him out as a suspect? Without a doubt. But, we're here in LA complying with our client's directions. Let this play out tonight. Tomorrow, we tell Hightower we need to return to Seattle and talk to Ryan. Ryan's still an employee, and under an obligation to cooperate."

"You know," Lee said, "it bothers me that Hightower makes excuse after excuse why we shouldn't follow a trail that may lead us back to Ryan. Or explore the possibility of someone working with Dennis."

"You're right to question why his focus remains on Fiona, and he hasn't encouraged us to expand the field of suspects,"

Mary said. "What are you thinking?"

"What if Hightower had Ryan or Dennis steal the drive for him so he could sell it for an obscene amount of money on the dark web? What if Dennis was his partner, and after Hightower took possession of the drive, he had Dennis killed to keep him quiet? And to cover his tracks he sent us on a wild goose chase?" Lee said, pacing as his speech picked up.

"Stop, just stop," I said raising my voice to gain attention. "Everyone take a breath and refocus. The problem with this case is that there are three issues at play, and we don't know if they're interconnected. If the drive was stolen, and that's a big 'if' because there's no proof it was, that's one piece. Next piece, why were three men who had a connection to Fiona murdered? And third, why is Hightower so desperate to get his hands on Fiona? I'm not buying the whole pregnancy thing. Yes, she may be or may have been pregnant, but come on; that's not black-mail material. It seems like there's something more—"

"Maybe she has a tape of the threesome, and she's using it as blackmail?" Mary said, as she started a pot of coffee.

"I don't see that happening. With today's strict laws about revenge porn she wouldn't take that chance," I said, and Mary nodded.

Lee rubbed his hands across the top of his head, mussing his hair in frustration. "The theories keep piling up. Normally, we start with motive and work around that angle. But here the motives are tangling us up. Here's what I say. Go back to the beginning. Split this out. Are the murders of Mahir and Chuck relevant to the drive? More than likely not. If the murders are connected to Fiona, it's personal and not part of our case. Does the murder of Dennis and drugging of Ryan have anything to do with the drive? Possibly. But what proof is there that Fiona had anything to do with what happened to either of them in that motel? None. We've uncovered nothing to suggest such a theory. So we," he said, pointing between him and me, "need to divest ourselves from the murders and come back to the drive. We have two more days, and it's gone. The drive has to be our priority."

"That's a valid point. The murders will likely take weeks or even months to investigate. But retrieving the drive is time sensitive," I said.

"OK, so have we beat this dead horse to death?" Mary asked. "I'm pouring; who's drinking?"

"Pour me a cup while I call this guy in Boston back," I said, standing to move to a quiet area so I wouldn't interfere with their conversation.

I heard Mary and Lee continue talking in the background and gestured for them to lower their voices.

"Pinkerton," the deep voice with an obvious Boston accent responded on the other end.

"Hi, this is Detective Hughes from New York; you called?" I asked.

"Yeah, I've been trying to get your partner, but someone said he was taking a few days' emergency leave," he said.

Why hadn't David said anything to me about an emergency leave when he'd forwarded the footage? "Can I help you with something?" I asked Pinkerton.

"Your wig hairs and ours are a match," he said.

"Thank you. That's good to know. If you can't get David, maybe this is something you could leave on his voicemail?" I asked. It annoyed me to be taken from what I considered a more relevant conversation.

"Hold your horses." He chuckled. "You New Yorkers are

always in such a hurry. This is news I wanted to deliver in person. Well, so to speak."

"Go on." He had my interest now.

"The hairs also matched a recent murder in Seattle," he said, pausing for a moment. "Do you want me to send you the information for the lead detective on that case?"

I took a moment to comprehend what he'd said. "Wait. Was the first name of the victim in Seattle Dennis?" I asked.

Mary and Lee stopped talking and turned toward me.

"Actually, yes. What are you? Psychic or something?"

"Would you please email me your report, and Seattle's? I'll call them and set up a meeting."

"Sure," he said, and I gave him my email address.

"What was that about?" Lee asked when I hung up.

"The hairs that were at the New York and Boston crime scenes also matched a scene in Seattle. Care to venture a guess on which crime scene?"

"No freakin' way. How did they discover that?" Lee asked.

"As soon as I get the reports from them, we can look at all the details together. Looks like I'll be flying up to Seattle with you after all," I said and waggled my eyebrows.

Lee smiled broadly and laughed.

My phone dinged, notifying me I had an email. It was the reports. I forwarded it to Mary and Lee so we could discuss the findings. It seemed clear we were probably following a multi-state serial killer.

"Man, this is wild," Lee said after reading the report. "This might be your next best-selling novel, Belle."

"Something worth considering," I said. And it was a thought worth more than just a consideration.

"Thoughts?" I asked when Mary finished reading.

"Someone is trying to set Fiona up, or Fiona is leaving a trail of reasonable doubt," Mary replied.

"My thoughts exactly," I said. "I can understand the motive behind Mahir and Chuck's murders. But Dennis's murder...are we missing something? Did something bad happen between them?"

Lee sat and threw his head back against the chair's pillow top. "This means we need to ask Hightower if there was bad blood between Fiona and Dennis. Kill. Me. Now."

I put my hand in the air to stop any further ranting. "It's my case. I'll be talking to him."

I asked Lee for Hightower's number. He answered on the first ring.

"Detective Hughes, have you changed your mind?" he asked in a tone that bordered on flirtatious.

"I've had a development in the murder cases, and I need to ask you a question," I said keeping the tone professional.

"Shoot," he replied with almost a smile in his voice.

"Did Fiona and Dennis share any history that might indicate bad blood between them?"

"Define 'bad blood,'" he said after a minute.

"Did she report him for inappropriate behavior, or make any accusations against him?" I asked.

"Why?" he asked, seemingly hesitant to answer.

"It's part of the ongoing investigation, so I can't tell you specifics. But it is relevant to my case," I replied.

"Yes, there was a problem, and we reprimanded Dennis," he said.

"Did it cause her embarrassment?" I asked.

"Well, she complained about it and wanted him fired. So yes, I would say so, but nothing further came of it," he replied.

"Thank you."

After I hung up, I turned to Lee and gave the response as I interpreted it. "Motive to kill? Not in my opinion."

"God, this is making me crazy," he said, stretching his arms above his head. "What if Hightower is the killer's next target? I really don't think Hightower should go to this thing tonight."

"He may not have been Fiona's target initially. If they were in cahoots, though, and she needed him, he was safe. Now the game has changed, so maybe she no longer needs him," Mary said.

"When you say it like that, and as the layers of Hightower are revealed little by little then it really isn't so farfetched. Can we believe anything the man has said?" I asked.

I looked to Lee for an answer, but his eyes were closed, and it looked like he was deep in thought.

"God, I need a break and a nap before dinner. I slept like shit last night. I just need to recharge," he said, and I nodded. "Belle, if you want to catch a nap with me, let's hit the bed. I'm crashing."

Mary smiled, threw her hands up, and left.

I got up before Lee and tried David's number, which went to voicemail. I'd typically leave a message, but if he were in the middle of a crisis, the last thing he'd care about was the case.

I scribbled a note and left it on my pillow for Lee to find, and I left to get ready for the dinner. Thank God for high-end boutiques in hotels, or I'd have nothing to wear tonight. The white halter dress with a sleek fit was perfect for the evening. It showed enough skin to be tempting yet pulled off a look of mystery. I was about to call Mary to check to see if she and

Lee were ready to head down to the restaurant when I heard a knock at my door. *Good, they're here.* One last spritz of subtle perfume, and I was ready. I picked up my purse and door key and opened the door with my best smile. The smile disappeared when I saw who stood on the other side.

"What the hell are you doing here?" I demanded.

"I might ask the same because you sure as hell aren't dressed like that to run out for a burger," he said, raking his eyes up and down me. "Are you going to invite me in?"

"She most certainly is not," I heard Lee say before I saw him walk right up to David, crowding him. Trying to intimidate him.

I watched the men size each other up, and David was the first to speak.

"I see how it is," he said in a sarcastic tone that was meant to demean me.

I'm sure David expected an explanation from me, but I was so appalled and angry it was more my wrath he was likely to receive.

"You're David, her partner. We met in passing in New York when we came to the station." Mary stepped forward, extending her hand. He ignored it.

"I remember," he said, not taking his eyes from Lee but directing a question to me. "And why are you here?"

"Working the case," I replied.

"Looks more like you're socializing, not working," he said, now turning to me.

Lee stiffened, but this was my argument to handle. "We are, in fact, in the middle of something that necessitates a work dinner. I'm working the case, but I'm here on my own time. So, do I need to answer to you? No. Now I'll meet you for breakfast in the morning and bring you up to speed on the new developments. But right now, we have an engagement we're late for, so I need to leave."

David turned to Lee and asked, "Can you give us a moment?"

"Sorry, man, we're in the middle of something and need to go. I suggest you do as Belle asked and talk in the morning."

David looked between Lee and me and back to me again. "Belle?"

"Look, David, I need to go; people are waiting." I closed the door and wedged my way past him and walked away. "Meet me at nine a.m. in the dining room."

He didn't reply. He stood there with his hands in his pockets, watching us until we got into the elevator.

The elevator ride was silent until Mary spoke. "He seems kind of bossy."

Lee gave her the side-eye and mumbled, "You're one to talk."

"OK, everyone, put David out of your thoughts, and let's get our heads in the game," I said as the elevator doors opened.

When we reached the lobby and entered the dining room, we waited to be escorted to the table where Benjamin Hightower appeared to be engaged in a serious conversation with a woman who left no doubt she was an escort. Her dress covered only enough to keep her from being arrested for indecent exposure. *Hope he gets his money's worth.*

Introductions were made between Ingrid, Benjamin's date, and the rest of us. Once seated, we ordered and got down to business. I had just taken a sip of wine when I sensed something was wrong. The tension coiled Lee's body, and Mary's mouth formed an O. I turned to see what they were looking at. My brain disengaged as I watched David walk up to the table and take a moment to assess the situation. *What in the hell is wrong with this man? Oh my God, is he going to pick a fight? Is he going to embarrass me? Could he be drunk?*

"Evening, folks; I'm Belle's partner, and I thought I'd drop by and introduce myself. David Rizolli. And you are?" he said as he looked at Benjamin and Ingrid.

Benjamin had the good sense to remain quiet and say nothing, giving Lee the opportunity to stop this tsunami of a disaster heading our way.

Lee stood and whispered something in David's ear that moved them away from the table.

"Your partner seems the controlling, jealous type, Belle. I'm surprised to see that," Benjamin said, breaking the awkward silence.

"I apologize for David's behavior. To be honest, I have no idea what he's doing here. He showed up uninvited," I said, placing my napkin on my lap.

"I see. Well, would you care to ask David to join us?" Benjamin asked.

"No, but thank you," I said.

Lee rejoined the table, and I watched David stalk from the lobby. *Oh man, what the hell is going on here?*

"Excuse the interruption; he's a bit of a hothead," Lee said. "Let's get this show on the road so we can make sure you're prepared."

"Ingrid," Benjamin said, turning to his date. "Would you share your wealth of information about how these parties are conducted with these fine people, and I'll follow up with questions."

After Ingrid "educated" us about the philosophy and rules

203

of conduct, she explained the equipment. She was clearly an expert. She would play the dominatrix to Benjamin's submissive, which was a role Ingrid said she preferred.

"I assure you no one gets hurt unless they want to, and most of these parties are well regulated," she said.

"We have a reason to be cautious," Lee said.

"I can assure you I've been to enough of these types of parties to know the signals to watch for if things are about to turn ugly," Ingrid said.

As I monitored the conversation, my eyes swept the room before focusing on the lobby just outside the restaurant area. I couldn't believe it. David was sitting in the lobby.

"Will you excuse me for one minute," I said. I tried my best to make it appear as if I was heading to the bathroom, but I was sure Lee picked up something was going on.

As I approached, David stood, and I motioned him to sit. Before I said anything, he started.

"Are you fucking him?"

It startled me, and I refused to play this game.

"David, these past few months your behavior has become increasingly erratic. Have I done anything to indicate to you that I'm interested in you romantically?"

He remained silent.

"You coming out here is way over the top. If you'd answered your phone when Boston called you'd know my being here is part of the case. They matched a strand of the wig to another murder in Seattle, and I've got the lieutenant's approval to head up there tomorrow. Now, we have to have a serious talk and decide how we will ask to be reassigned. Because I can't get past this type of behavior."

"Are you fucking him?" he asked again, only with a little

more force.

"I'm in the middle of a dinner, which has one hundred percent to do with this case. You need to go back to your hotel and leave tomorrow," I said.

"I've got a room here, which I'd hoped we'd be using later," he said.

Shock must have registered on my face because I actually felt my jaw drop. I felt a tap on my arm.

"Belle, dear, I'm feeling off-balance. Do you think you could help me to the restroom?" Mary asked.

"Certainly, Mary. David and I are finished here," I said and stood to take her arm.

"You clean up good," he said under his breath.

"Come on, Mary. Let's go before they wonder where we are," I said.

When we were out of hearing range, I said, "Not a word to Lee about this; I've got it under control."

She looked at me and nodded her cautious acceptance.

By the time we returned, the entrees had been served. Lee glanced my way with a raised eyebrow, and I smiled.

When dinner was finished, we let Benjamin and Ingrid believe they were on their own while we proceeded to our rooms and changed. We were at our positions to stake out the party within a half hour, and the place was active but quiet.

"Did you put the tracker on her dress?" I asked.

"Of course," he replied.

All we could do was wait.

CHAPTER TWENTY-TWO

Fiona

CAN'T TRUST CLAIRE. I HAVE TO FIND A PLACE TO LIE LOW UNTIL IT'S *time to leave.* Looking around the dressing area in the house they were using for tonight's festivities, I realized Fire and Ice has plenty of living quarters, and they owe me.

As I placed my leather handbag on the table, I noticed a thin plastic strip attached itself to the side. *God, how could I be so careless as to let some piece of trash anchor itself to my bag? I hope it didn't damage the leather.* I examined the strip, threw it away, and retrieved my phone.

Who should I call, Steven or Ray to ask about staying at one of the houses Fire and Ice used, and what should I give as a reason? Steve was my drug contact, and I was sure he wouldn't turn me down. But I needed more than an overnight stay. Ray picked up on the first ring.

"Ray, it's Fiona," I said in my most sultry voice.

"Fi, what can I do for you?" he said; I could hear a smile in his voice.

"It's what I can do for you," I said with an air of mystery.

"And that is?" he asked; I knew I had his full attention.

"Questionable people are nosing around your place,"

I replied.

There was a brief silence, and I heard him close the door to his office.

"Go on," he said.

"My former boss and I had a thing for a while," I said without any guilt. Ray wasn't one to judge. "And when I decided to split, he wasn't happy. He sent some people after me to find me and convince me to come back. I spoke to them today. They mentioned they'd been to Fire looking for me, and I'm concerned they may have tricked someone into offering them an invite."

He was silent for a moment, and then I heard the clicking of his computer keys.

"A man and a woman with an older woman?" he asked.

"Yes," I said.

"I see in the notes they showed up today. The guy's info checked out, so we gave them a code for tonight," he said. "They going to be trouble, Fi?"

"I think they might be, Ray. My ex-boss is relentless," I said.

Based on my relationship with Ray, I knew he was a man who protected his business first and foremost.

"Consider them taken care of," he said. "Are you coming tonight?"

"Wouldn't miss it." I smiled. "And, Ray? One more thing. I need a place to hang for a few days. This whole thing has me on edge and not feeling safe. Can you put me up while things die down?"

"I'm leaving town tomorrow for two weeks. You can crash at my place if you need to," he said. "The code is 0980. Fi, I've got to go. I've got a situation." And he hung up.

I sighed with relief. *Good,* I thought. *Hopefully, this will kill two birds with one stone. If I know Ray, those two will get a beat-down, and that will get their attention and get them to leave me alone. Let that snotty detective try to explain to her boss what she was doing at a sex club under an alias. I'll make sure to keep an eye on them when they arrive. In fact, I have a plan.* I texted Ray a brief message with my plan: Give them some rope.

He texted back: OK.

Fire and Ice is billed as a club designed to meet the social and entertainment needs of the elite. Tonight's entertainment would be a live threesome providing a tasteful performance to get the party started followed by a sexy fire-eating show. The fact women weren't required to pay for membership or pay to attend the parties always worked in my favor. I'd met many generous members willing to indulge my many needs. The parties were not only entertaining but an excellent networking opportunity for me.

Ray took his business seriously. There had never been a problem with law enforcement. Maybe it was because he kept changing locations, but I like to think it was because he was well organized. The etiquette was clearly spelled out; touching before asking gets you banned. That was strictly enforced, and it had earned Jeremy a ban for life.

Public sex was encouraged. Those who preferred to do more than just watch could spend $75.00 for tokens for an interactive experience with the performers who roamed the party. The more adventurous members moved to open bedrooms, stairwells, and padded surfaces to engage in sex in front of eagerly prying eyes. Fire and Ice catered to a particular class of members, kinky, not tawdry or posers. It didn't cater to people looking for hardcore dungeon play, nor those interested in a traditional swingers' party. But, if you had the interest and the money, it was the place to be.

I arrived early to speak to Lawler, who'd be at the door tonight.

"Good evening, Fiona," Lawler said, as he opened the back door for me. Law, a handsome man about thirty, was perfect for the part of greeter. A man who clearly knew his way around a gym, his shirt barely contained his chest, and his muscular legs hardly fit in his custom-made pants. He put everyone on notice the club had muscle when needed. Women wanted him, and men were subtly alerted not to even think about breaking the rules of etiquette.

"Law." I nodded at him in greeting. "Did Ray speak with you about the problem we're working out?"

"He did. How about we step in here, and you can give me some specifics about how you want this to go," he said, opening a heavy wood door that led to a well-appointed room.

Once seated, he offered me a drink, and I declined. At these affairs I, unlike other guests, wanted to keep a clear head. Especially tonight with so much at stake. The fact cell phones would be collected, powered down, and placed in a container gave me peace of mind that Lee wouldn't be in contact with anyone outside.

"The man I'm having a problem with has now become a problem for Ray too. The man was hired by my former boss to stalk me. Ben, my boss, and I, had a brief fling, and he wouldn't let it end gracefully, so I had to leave. I've accepted a new job overseas, and left without notice. Apparently, he didn't like that. Now, he's hired this man and woman team to find me and bring me back. Ben is relentless. This team has a newcomers' invitation for tonight. I'd like you and Jordy to help me persuade these people to stop stalking me."

"You have a plan?" Law asked, raising a cut-glass tumbler to his lips.

"I do," I said. I explained my plan that would end up with Lee and the detective in a room in the basement. They'd be threatened, beaten enough to get their attention, and then put out with the garbage.

Should I tell Ray and Law the woman is an NYPD detective? Probably. But if I do, I don't think Ray and Law would help me. Well, they probably would, but not without some type of remuneration. So, the detective part would be my secret. By the time Lee and Detective Hughes woke up after being drugged, they'd be gagged, and the fun would begin.

"You want a ringside seat? Or do you want to participate?" Law asked.

"I could go for a few whacks with a cane, just to express my displeasure for the inconvenience they've caused, but I think I'll just be a voyeur."

Lee was more than an annoyance, and he needed a lesson. "No broken bones but some split flesh is fine," I said.

"Got it," he said. "I've got to be on the door in ten minutes. I'll find you when we have them restrained and ready to start. I figure we'll give them about a half hour to roam around. Just long enough to start being curious but not long enough to start participating."

"Sounds like a plan, Law," I said, giving him a mischievous smile.

If Ray liked you, the world opened up to so many possibilities. I was wearing a beautiful white gown adorned with hundreds of pearls, courtesy of Ray. It fit every curve and dip as if the dress had been tailored exclusively for me. And staying at his house was like staying on an island where no one could find you. The 10,000-square-foot home sat on acres of land that provided privacy and protection. Let Lee and Detective Hughes try to find me, much less get past the security. That is if they could even walk tomorrow.

Since Lee and the detective knew I'd be at the party tonight, there was no need to hide from them. So I chose a tasteful white mask that covered my eyes and a bit of my cheek, nothing more. I had no reason to cover my face. Identifying the new members wasn't usually tricky. Their masks were generally what I call Casanova masks, elaborate Venetian-style masks that covered their faces from the top of the head to the chin. And that's what I expected Lee and the detective to wear tonight, elaborate full-face masks to hide behind.

I've had this strange sense ever since I left New York that someone is following me, not Lee and his group, but someone else. Someone in the shadows. I was probably just twitchy, but I've learned, over the years, to trust my intuition. I had that feeling again tonight, even though I knew getting into the building uninvited was nearly impossible. I felt like someone was so close that if I turned around suddenly I'd see someone right there, waiting to pounce. I had to shake this feeling, or I'd be off my game tonight.

One last check in the mirror, and I was ready to leave for the main event. I felt the best place to position myself to watch for Lee and the detective was in the greeting area on the large red sofa diagonal to the door. When they arrived as newcomers, Lawler would point them toward the first room containing refreshments, and I'd pick them up and follow them from there.

Ah, and there they are.

Lee looked handsome in a tux, and for a man who wasn't part of the affluent world; tonight he presented himself with ease as he blended in with the crowd. Had he behaved like this when we'd first met I might not have been so suspicious of him. Though his mask covered most of his face, I thought I detected an easy smile right below the ridge of the mask. His posture was relaxed; the opposite of what I'd expected. And the detective, she seemed a bit of a wild card as well. Her form-fitting fire-engine-red dress barely covered her generous breasts. And when she walked, the slit up the side went up her leg to her hip; it was clear she wasn't wearing panties. Quite a conundrum. Both of them appeared as if they'd been part of this scene forever and blended smoothly. I had to give it to them, they took their undercover roles seriously.

As I watched Lee, I could see him subtly sweep the room looking for me, while the detective was more focused on the performers. The party had yet to start, but the people hired for entertainment had already begun their performances. *I'll give them an opportunity to explore before I execute my plan and use my limited time for my own fun.* I'd had my eye on a guy who just reeked of money. I could tell by the way he watched the performers in the drawing room he was into the same kink as me. I think we could spend some time together while I waited for Lawler to let me know he'd restrained my serial stalkers.

About to approach my catch of the evening, I saw Lee turn in an almost slow-motion manner and stare straight into my soul. Was this man taunting me? I disengaged and walked toward the man who would keep me occupied for the next hour or until Law came to get me.

Although this was one of Ray's best parties between the performers and the attendees, I was ready for the finale. I hadn't meant to spend so much time indulging my erotic fantasies; I'd just gotten carried away. Three hours into the party, I got the nod from Jordy, Law's assistant, that they were ready for me to instill my own mark of justice. Jordy escorted me to an elevator two floors down to a soundproof room.

"Fi, something went wrong," he said as we walked closer to the door. "We just got here ourselves a few minutes ago, and we need to do some damage control. Brace yourself; it's a disaster."

He opened the door, and the carnage that flashed in front of my eyes nearly had me bolting for the toilet. How could something like this happen? The guests at the party were highly vetted. Anyone with even a small criminal infraction was turned away. Who could have done this? Neither Ray nor anyone associated with him would ever take things this far. The vision in front of me was nothing short of a massacre.

The woman lay crumpled on the floor, naked in a pool of sticky red-brown blood. Small slash marks marred her body; she'd been tortured with a knife. Some punctures were still bleeding, and others were crusted with drying blood. The way her shoulder protruded, I was sure it was dislocated. But it was what was left of her face that drew my attention. Her face had been so severely beaten it was impossible to identify her. Bruises had started to cover her body, and her breathing was irregular. When she breathed through her nose, small red blood bubbles rose and fell.

My eyes then went to the wall to my left. The poorly lit room revealed a man with a black cloth hood over his head. His body was pressed spread eagle up against the stone wall and restrained with heavy metal chains. Almost in the same position he would have been if a St. Andrew's Cross had been used. From the grunts, he was making I could tell he likely still had a ball gag in his mouth. The noise he made was a combination of crying and attempts at screaming, his words indistinguishable. Marks on his back and legs indicated he too had been a victim of slash knife play. But someone had taken a cane to him as well and beaten him in a way that the wounds would never fully heal. Blood oozed from the red areas where the skin was split open.

The smell in the room was an overwhelmingly nauseating mix of blood and urine. I felt my gag reflex start to take over and immediately started breathing through my mouth to lessen the stench reaching my nostrils.

I felt like my mind had detached from my body and was floating freely, trying to find a place to land. I had never seen anything this violent before. *This must be what it feels like when you die*, I thought, *a total disconnect between body and mind.*

Law and Jordy stood next to me, looking at the spectacle in front of us. But they had gotten past the initial shock and were trying to figure out how to handle the situation.

"Let's step back outside," Law said, and we backed out of the room. "I think I'm going to have to call Ray."

God, Ray must have found out they had ties to law enforcement. He was going to kill me. But I hadn't asked for this type of treatment. These people were almost dead.

"Law, what the hell?" I asked. "What happened?"

Shaking his head, he looked at his shiny black shoes, then back up at me. "I had Jordy put them in here about two hours ago. We came looking for you, but you were busy having a good time, and we didn't want to interrupt. So, we tied them up, left them gagged, and figured we'd wait for you to surface. When I came in to check a few minutes ago, this is what I found."

"So you guys didn't do this?" I asked without thinking it through.

He looked at me as if I had lost my mind. "No!" he exclaimed.

"How bad is Lee's face?" I asked. "Who could have done this; who has access except for members?"

"No one. No one at the party has access to this area," he said. "Jordy and I circulated to see if anyone had bloody knuckles before we came to get you."

"Let me see Lee's face," I said.

We moved back into the room, and Jordy took off the hood. I almost fell to the ground as Ben's beaten face turned to me with an accusatory look. The way he hung from the chains, unable to hold his body erect, I felt he was at a dangerous point between life and death. His breathing was more regular than the woman's, but it wouldn't surprise me if one of his lungs was bruised or worse.

My mind disengaged, and things tumbled out unfiltered from my mouth. "Oh my God. Oh my God! That's Ben Hightower, my old boss. What the fuck is he doing here?"

"What? What do you mean? These aren't the stalkers?" Law asked, pulling Ben's head back by his hair to get a better look at his face. As I shook my head "no" in horror, he let Ben's head flop back down.

Law stepped away and tilted his head to the side to indicate we needed to step out.

"We've got to call Ray. This is too big. These people could die. That bitch is barely alive. Stay here; I'll be right back."

I wanted to go back in. But what good would it do? This was such a mess. Who had done this and why? Was someone after me too?

Before I could think through anything, Ray stormed through the door with Law. "What the fuck? Tell me this wasn't you, Fi," he demanded.

"Oh my God, Ray, no! Why would I do this; how could I do this? Look at these people; someone way bigger and stronger than me beat the ever-loving shit out of them. How would I be able to string Ben up like that? How?"

He evaluated the situation. Then it hit him. "Wait, 'Ben,' as in your ex-boss Ben Hightower?"

"Yes."

"Then who's she?" he demanded, pointing at the crumpled woman on the floor.

"I have no idea, Ray." I felt as desperate as I sounded.

He told Jordy to unchain Ben and put him in a chair. Jordy did as he was told. Ray took Ben's chin between his fingers and examined his face. "Not so bad. It might need a few stitches. But his back and legs will need serious treatment."

I stood there, unsure of what I should do or say.

"I know you can hear me, Hightower," Ray said to Ben who raised his eyes to him.

"Law, go get me a piece," he said to Law who nodded and quickly returned with a .22.

Ray looked down at Ben and said, "You made a serious mistake coming here, Mr. Hightower. Now, if you want to live, this is what's going to happen. I can have a doctor here in minutes to take a look at you and patch you up. He's a qualified emergency room doctor. If he says you need further care, we'll take you to a hospital. If that happens, you tell them you were mugged by MS-13, and you don't know what happened to your companion; she left earlier. I don't care what you say. Am I making myself clear?" he asked.

Ben didn't answer.

I inwardly cringed. That wasn't the way to stay alive in Ray's world. You said yes, thank you, and never showed your face again.

"Law, give me your gloves," Ray said, snapping his fingers. He put the thin leather gloves on and held his hand out for the gun. Then, in what can only be described as surreal-fast motion, Ray fired two rounds into the woman's head. Gunpowder now added to the stink of urine and blood. As blood leaked from the gunshot wounds and started to spread around the woman's head, I heard Ben start to gag.

"Pick him up." Ray then put the gun in Ben's hand, told him to hold the weapon, and pull the trigger. Jordy pulled his phone out and took pictures as Ben fired the gun into her body.

Ray retrieved the gun, placed it in a bag, and handed it to Law who left with it.

"Now, Mr. Hightower, I'm going to let you live, and I'm going to make sure you get home safely. Why you may ask? Because if you went missing, there would be questions. Right now, it appears you killed your companion. Maybe you took bad drugs; maybe you just went nuts. Go home, and live your life. You'll never see me again unless you become a problem for Fi or me. Understand? I have friends everywhere; there's no escape."

A half hour later the doctor had finished his examination;

there were no broken bones. His wounds were cleaned, and some of the edges were closed with super glue. The deeper slash wounds needed stiches. The doctor gave him a shot of antibiotics and some pain meds before he left. Then, Ray made arrangements for Ben to be transported to a safe house where a nurse would monitor him for the night. Once Ben was stabilized, his companion was rolled into a blanket and packed into the trunk of a car for quick disposal.

CHAPTER TWENTY-THREE

Annabelle

"**H**OW MUCH LONGER ARE WE GOING TO WAIT? IT'S THREE A.M., and I've had it. We can't see a thing from this road to the house," I said. Sitting here, waiting for everyone to leave the party, was just like being on a stakeout.

"Alright, come on, let's walk up there, but stay in the shadows," Lee said.

"Is the tracker still on?" I asked.

"No, but if she took off her dress it would disengage. And we have no way to track their phones," he said.

"Shit. Wait, there's a black SUV coming out," I said. Once it passed, we got out of the car and made our way toward the house. We could see the place was dimly lit, and it appeared the guests had left. There were only a few cars outside.

"Maybe we missed them, and they left early," I said, knowing that wasn't probable.

"Then why didn't Hightower call?" Lee asked.

"So, what's the plan, Sherlock? We're now trespassing on private property, and—"

Suddenly floodlights came on, bathing the area, and a man came out front and called, "Can I help you, folks?"

Shit, there must be cameras on the property.

"Sorry to bother," Lee yelled back. "A friend of mine called and said he needed a ride home; he'd had too much to drink. But he hasn't come out."

The large man in a tuxedo walked toward us, and it was evident he had a gun under his jacket.

"Everyone's left the party. The owner of the establishment is careful not to let anyone drink and drive, so he probably put your friend in an Uber. Or if he was too drunk and at the passing-out stage, he'll get him to a place to sleep it off."

"Thanks, I guess it was a wasted trip," Lee said. The man started walking away, and Lee asked, "Mind if we see if his car is still here?"

"Follow me," the man said. We followed him to the back area of the house where several cars still remained. Hightower's wasn't among them.

"Thanks," Lee said, and we left.

"OK, so Hightower gave us the slip. He might have left early with his 'date' and wanted to finish out the evening with her," I said.

"Why not call us? Something's definitely wrong," Lee said.

"Well, there's nothing to be done right now. We can't call the local police, and we can't comb the city. Let's pack it in and call it a night. I'm exhausted, and I need a bathroom," I said.

The drive back to the hotel was quiet. It was evident from the way Lee gripped the wheel that he was anxious and deep in thought. It wasn't that Benjamin was our responsibility; he chose to go, in spite of our warnings. However, he was in deep over his head, and we were helpless to fix whatever mistakes he might have made.

I reached for Lee's hand, and he looked over at me with a

smile. "So tomorrow we still leave for Seattle? If not, I need to call Seattle and let them know I need to push the meeting off."

"I'd say we head up. The drive is still in play for the auction, and that's our main focus," he said.

We parked the car, entered the empty lobby, and took the elevator up. As soon as the doors closed, he turned and lightly kissed my mouth, which by floor eleven, had turned into a passionate kiss that brought a tingle to my skin.

The doors opened, and we stepped from the elevator as the kiss traveled from my lips to my neck and back.

"My room or yours?" he asked as the hot breath of his whisper tickled my ear.

"Mine," I replied, eager to return to the promise of a night filled with exploration.

He looped his arm around my waist and mine around his. He touched his nose to mine and gave a light kiss to the tip. Was my heart practically beating out of my chest, or was that his I could hear? I smiled up at him, and we started the walk to my room, quiet in our thoughts.

As we turned the corner, I reached into my bag for my card key.

"Well isn't this cozy?" a voice asked from ten feet in front of me.

Lee and I both looked up at the same time and froze.

David.

"Oh, you have got to be kidding me," Lee said, letting go of my waist. He stepped toward David who was sitting in the hall. "Get up."

The anger in David's eyes when they met mine would frighten most people. And to be honest, they scared me a little.

"I don't want to have an argument in the hall; everyone

inside," I said and slipped my key card into the slot.

"Let me start," I said, once we were all inside. "David, Lee, how about you both take a seat."

"You come all the way out here," David said, still standing, "putting your job in jeopardy, and chasing after this washed-out ex-cop. The lieutenant will lose his shit when he finds out you're out here fucking some lowlife PI's brains out instead of doing your job," he spat out, taking a step forward.

"That's enough," I said before Lee could weigh in. "I'm out here working the case on my days off. And you have no right to say anything about my personal life. I know we're both flying to Seattle, because the lieutenant called me earlier and said that's what he wants. However, as soon as we get back, I'm putting in a request for a new partner. This has gotten way out of hand."

"You're damn right it has," he said. "If I put one call into the lieutenant, you'll be riding a desk for a month. That is if he doesn't fire you on the spot for sharing information with civilians."

"Is that a threat?" Lee asked, stepping toward him. They were now no more than a foot apart.

David shook his head and snorted. "Take it whatever way you want," he said. "I'm saying if she asks for a reassignment, it's going to look bad on me. The captain will want to know why. And trust me, I'm not going down without a fight."

"David, I really have no words. I think it's best you return to your room, and I'll meet you for breakfast tomorrow morning at seven thirty instead of nine," I said, opening the door for him to leave.

As he left, he turned his head and said over his shoulder, "Screw some sense into her. Detective jobs for women aren't easy to come by. Her transfer might just involve a demotion."

Before Lee could reach the door, I slammed it shut and braced the full weight of my body against it. "Stop. I can't let this get any worse. This is my problem to deal with, so give me some space."

He studied my face, deciding how to answer, and he turned his head away, obviously struggling to gain control of his emotions. After a few moments, he nodded. He reached for me and enveloped me in a hug that said, "I've got you."

A kiss on the top of my head signaled we were done for the night. Damn that David.

"Go ahead and have breakfast with the shithead; get it out of the way. If he's still coming with us tomorrow, let's check out by ten, get to the airport, and get ready to meet with the detective and Ryan. Sound like a plan?"

I was about to answer when his phone rang, and the name Hightower flashed on the screen.

"Quick, answer it," I said.

He put the phone on speaker and answered, "Stone."

"Lee, it's Benjamin," Hightower said in an awkward tone. It was calm yet clipped.

"Where are you?" Lee asked.

"Well, I had a bit of an accident. I fell down some stairs, and well I guess the jig is up. The host was generous enough to call a doctor and put me up in a place for the night. Once the doctor checks me out tomorrow, I should be good to go," he said, sounding like he was reading from a script.

"What happened?" Lee pressed.

"I had too much to drink, made a wrong turn, and rolled down some stone stairs. Nothing too bad, but I'm in no position to move tonight with the drugs I got for the pain and all. So, I'm spending the night, and I'll meet you at the jet ready for takeoff at eleven a.m.," he said. He was breathing hard.

"You want us to push the time out to one p.m.?" I asked.

"No, we're on a tight schedule. I'll see you then. You just show up at the plane," he said.

It was apparent he didn't want to discuss Fiona. Was that because he was in too much discomfort or because someone was listening? Either way, he was ready to disconnect.

"OK then, tomorrow," Lee said, hanging up the phone. "I call bullshit," he said.

"I agree. But why lie?" I asked.

"He's alive and ready to meet tomorrow. I'm too exhausted to think this through. Let's go to bed, get some sleep, and if he calls again, we'll talk to him together. Maybe someone was standing over him, and he wasn't able to talk freely. Plus, I'm concerned David might be waiting for me to leave so he can come back again."

"That works. I'll shower so you can get one in the morning while I meet David. Go to bed, and I'll wake you in the morning." I had hoped for much more tonight but sleeping next to Lee would do it for me. A quick yet lingering kiss was all I had to hold onto for the night.

When I returned from the shower, he was dead to the world, and fifteen minutes later I was as well.

I was the first to wake in the morning, giving myself time to get ready and pack. As I was about ready to leave to meet David for breakfast, I turned and saw Lee watching me finish up my morning dressing routine.

"You're a smart and beautiful woman, Annabelle Hughes, and I feel lucky to have found you. Come here," he said, crooking his finger toward him.

I walked over, leaned down, and planted my lips on his. It wasn't a quick kiss, or a goodbye kiss. It was more like, "I've known you forever, and this is what we do" kiss.

I arrived at the hotel restaurant about five minutes early, and since David wasn't already seated, I asked for a table where I could watch for him. The server brought a pot of coffee, and I noticed Mary across the room, looking at me. When she saw I'd noticed her, she walked over.

"How long have you been here, and how much coffee did you already drink?" I asked.

"A little over an hour. May I sit?" Mary asked, avoiding the question about the coffee.

"If you think you want to be here when David arrives, sure. He should be here any minute," I said, gesturing for her to sit.

"David won't be joining you," she said.

"You can't know that." But from what I knew of Mary, maybe she did know something.

"He checked out forty-five minutes ago."

I heard her say it, but it didn't compute.

"Belle," she said, "I saw him go to that counter, pay his bill, and wheel his luggage out those doors. A van picked him up, and he left."

I couldn't believe what she'd just said. "Hold on a moment."

I walked over to the counter, and told the clerk we were waiting for David, and she said we had just missed him.

I returned, poured myself a cup of coffee, and began to fume.

"Well, he'll have to face me on the plane," I said.

Mary said, "Belle, what he did was uncalled for and

disrespectful. I don't know what has transpired since I saw you yesterday. Decisions will have to be made."

"I'm calling Lee," I said.

Lee picked up on the first ring.

"David stood me up. Mary and I are here; do you want me to order breakfast for you? You could join us down here after you finish your shower."

"No, just get me a toasted bagel with cream cheese and a large coffee, and bring it up, please."

"Will do," I said. After I hung up, I turned my attention back to Mary. "About David. I don't know what to think. He got into it with me last night. And we're not going to be able to work together when we return to New York. I just need to get through the next few days; then I can make a decision about what to do."

"So how did things go last night with Hightower?" Mary asked.

"Long story short, he called and said he fell down some stairs and spent the night at someone's home. He'll be meeting us at the plane," I said.

"Are you buying that?" Mary asked.

"I don't know yet. Maybe he actually participated in the night's events," I suggested.

"I hope so." She chuckled.

We finished breakfast and brought Lee's food up to him in my room. By the time we arrived, he was showered, dressed, and had his luggage next to mine.

"I've already checked out using the app for the hotel, so when you ladies are ready, we can be on our way."

We returned the rental car and were taken to the private jet that was waiting for us. I couldn't help myself; I gasped when I saw Benjamin. He was nearly unrecognizable.

"Benjamin, this is far worse than you let on. Is your nose broken?" I asked.

"My God, man, you look like somebody used you like a piñata. I hope you have some decent drugs running through your bloodstream," Mary said, shaking her head.

He ignored her and watched and waited as Lee made his way down the aisle. Their eyes met, and Lee kept on moving and took a seat next to me.

After we were served a beverage and some fruit, the pilot made his final announcement, telling us to buckle up and saying they were closing the door.

"Wait," I yelled, "David's not here."

Benjamin looked at me and then over his shoulder toward the cockpit. He moved his hand in a circular motion over his head and said, "Wheels up."

Ten minutes later, we were heading toward Seattle.

CHAPTER TWENTY-FOUR

Lee

HIGHTOWER POPPED WHATEVER PILLS THE DOCTOR HAD GIVEN HIM like Tic Tacs, and they barely seemed to help him. Every few minutes he repositioned his body to try to get comfortable without much success. He winced with each move, and his breathing seemed restricted. The bruising on his face was a deep purple color, and the ice he must have used had barely stopped the swelling.

"May I sit?" I asked, more out of habit than a question.

He didn't welcome me. But didn't reject me either.

We sat in silence, and I visually catalogued his wounds. Those injuries weren't from a fall. I'd seen more than my share of domestic violence beatings and bar fights to know Benjamin's injuries had been inflicted by fists, fists with rage behind them.

"I can tell you're really hurting, but we need to talk," I said. Hightower just looked at me. "Obviously, someone hit you. And not just a smack but someone used you like a punching bag."

He turned away and looked out the airplane window.

"How bad is the rest of your body?" I asked.

No response.

"We can play twenty questions, and you can refuse to answer, but it will only lead me to jump to the worst conclusion," I told him.

He still remained silent. I wasn't letting him off the hook. It had been his decision to attend the party in our place, and we needed information, so he could just suck it up.

"Obviously, you got into the building for the party," I said, and he nodded. "Did you get the impression that someone made you?" I asked.

"Not initially. But then about an hour in I sensed someone following us," he said.

"Someone associated with the party, like the people hosting the party, or someone else?" I asked.

"Actually, as crazy as this sounds, both. But at different times," he said. "I felt like when we arrived, the person taking our information took a little too much interest in us and tipped off someone to keep an eye on us."

"What made you feel that way?"

"He held us at the door a little longer than the others and then made it a point to call someone over to introduce us to. A man named Paul was our guide in case we had any questions as newcomers. It just seemed off. I thought the whole purpose of the party was to roam free and remain anonymous," Hightower said.

"Did he ask any pressing questions? Did you feel like they were vetting you further? Or that maybe they suspected something wasn't right?" I asked.

"Who the hell knows what goes on at these things or what is 'normal'? For all I know, that place could be a cult of people involved in devil worship. From the minute I left that guide's side, I felt like I was being tracked by someone. They allowed us to move freely and participate in the activities if we wanted," he said, wincing as he moved his leg.

"Did you participate?" I asked. "I mean did anything happen that could have made someone angry?"

His eyes shifted as he replayed clips of the party in his mind.

"No. Well, I don't think so. The guys there didn't appear to be jealous of the women they brought. I mean, isn't that why they brought them? And I barely spoke to anyone. I mainly watched," he said.

"OK, then it probably wasn't someone that took offense. Did you participate at all?" I pressed.

"No, not really. We watched some performers—"

"Performers? Like jugglers?"

"No, like people having sex," he said sarcastically. "I got the impression these were people paid to perform various sex acts to entertain the guests and get people interested in exploring more. At one point, Ingrid left to explore the upstairs rooms, and I went out on the deck. I decided to take a walk to get some air. A few minutes later, I started to feel a little woozy."

Now we were getting somewhere. "Did someone offer you a drink? Maybe slipped you something like a roofie?" I asked.

"Come to think of it, someone did come out on the deck and offered me a drink from a tray. But the tray only had two glasses on it. So if I was drugged that's probably how they did it," he said. "The next thing I remember I woke up, tied to a chair and unable to focus."

"Was anyone there when you woke up?"

"No, just me in a dark room. Alone," he said.

I sensed he didn't want to give any more information, but this was critical. Fiona couldn't have maneuvered him to the room. It had to have been a man. "And?"

"I have no idea how long I sat in there before someone came in the room. You lose all sense of time in the dark. But it was a man. I was able to make out the shadow of a man's body. And well…"

I waited for him to gather himself. His breathing became more rapid and shallow as he remembered the events. Beads of sweat had collected on his upper lip, and his fingers involuntarily tapped.

"Take your time," I said. I saw Belle looking our way, and I gave her a subtle sign to remain in her seat.

"He ripped my mask off and seemed surprised."

"Surprised?"

"Yeah, he froze for a second, and it seemed just seeing me set him off into a frenzy. I heard him yell something, then I felt him pummeling my face. Punch after punch landed on my face and then my body. At some point, I must have passed out. All I remember is when I regained consciousness I was chained to a wall, and I was naked. I mean the man must have had some super strength to do that all by himself. I don't know if maybe the drugs and shock sent me into an unconscious state that made it easier for him. That's a stupid remark; of course it did, and I just don't want to relive it. I don't want to talk about it," Hightower said.

God forgive me, but at this point, I thought, *thank God it wasn't me that had gone to the party and that I'd had enough good sense to have drawn the line at the risk.*

"What about Ingrid?" I asked.

He looked at me and then averted his eyes. His Adam's apple bobbed as he swallowed back what I'm sure was vomit.

"I don't know. I assume she left the party without me," Hightower said.

"You don't think she came looking for you?"

"Why would she? It was a party, and she probably got caught up in the atmosphere."

What a piece of shit. The man had no idea if she'd been taken too and kept somewhere else. He hadn't even tried to find her.

"OK, so once you were restrained against the wall, what happened next?" I asked.

"The abuse continued," Hightower replied, not giving any more specifics. "He left me barely conscious. By the time he finished, he had unchained me. I lay on the floor, barely able to breathe. I finally came to, got dressed, and found my way back upstairs."

I sensed he was holding something back. Had the people who'd hosted the party drugged and beaten him, or had a guest been involved? One thing was clear, Fiona hadn't done this.

"When I stumbled into the area where the wait staff was gathered, they took one look at me and called one of the hosts. He took me to the doctor."

"So why the subterfuge last night with the false story? Why didn't someone call the police?" I asked.

"I didn't want any trouble with those people. What could I say without stepping into a mess? In actuality, I'd been trespassing. I wasn't an invited guest. For all the host knew, I'd gone to whatever room I'd been in and had asked to be beaten. And the police? No way. So all I wanted to do was get out. Now here we are, and I want to forget this ever happened," he said and turned away from me.

"Did you see Fiona?" I asked, even though I wasn't sure I would receive an honest answer.

"No. And I think you are right about what you said earlier.

Fiona probably has nothing to do with the missing drive. We need to look elsewhere," he said with such resolution in his voice it bordered on anger.

It took me some time to process the enormity of that statement. "OK. Belle is heading to talk to the police, and I'll pay Ryan a visit," I said. I was about to continue, but a call came through from Jackson. "It's Jax. I've got to take this."

He nodded, and I moved toward the rear of the plane next to Mary.

"Jax, what's up?" I asked.

"How do things stand right now? Have you talked to Hightower?" he asked.

"I'll fill you in when we land," I said, not wanting to have this discussion where Hightower might hear.

"OK, tell Mary her contact called, and he couldn't get ahold of her, so he asked me to reach out," he said.

"I'm on it," I said. "We're not too far out now, so I'll call you when we land."

I tapped my phone on my leg and looked over at Mary who I'm sure wanted a play-by-play of my conversation with Hightower.

"Mary, call your contact," I said. "He called Jax."

Surprised, she pulled her phone out. "For the love of God, I didn't power it on; sorry about that."

Mary dialed a number, and although the person answered, there was no conversation on her side. The one-sided conversation lasted barely a minute before she disconnected.

"The IP address is from somewhere around Seattle, and it's bouncing through proxy servers all over the world," she said, placing her phone back in her bag.

"You think it's Ryan?" I asked.

"Or, it could be someone associated with Dennis or Benjamin," she shot back. "Or anyone who works at the lab."

"Can your person trace the transfer of funds if the drive is actually claimed at auction?" I asked.

"Yes and no. It probably will go offshore. So, I'm talking out of my hat right now, but Tyler, can probably track it to a bank but not to the account. Or maybe he can. Honestly, I don't know. He's a cyber wizard."

"Wonderful," I said, knowing if we didn't find the drive before the auction we'd be out of luck. "Let's visit Ryan without giving him any notice."

"Agreed. I can use my little-old-lady ruse to get him to open the door."

I nodded.

In this new cyber frontier, I was out of my depth. "What's so frustrating is, in the end, how do we stop the data transfer? It's not like someone doing a corner drug deal," I said. On the streets you could physically stop a car or person.

"Well that's the easy part," she said with a smug smile.

"How so?" *Please tell me this woman is not also some cyber security expert.*

"Tyler has drilled down to the actual website that's going to be used. Once it's activated, he can hack it and stop the transaction from even occurring. I don't know all the technical stuff, but it sounds like he has already planted a bug or Trojan virus. However, he said he'd rather let the bidding occur, and once the transaction is complete, then jam the transfer," she said.

"I don't understand."

"When the seller comes online and enters the site, Tyler can track him through whatever magic he performs. The information is going to be transmitted over wires, not sold as the actual drive. So once he locks in on the seller, he'll divert and route the information to us," Mary said.

I felt like I'd just been whacked over the head. "What the hell are we doing? My God, you're right. It will all be done digitally. Maybe the drive still exists, but more than likely the information is already uploaded somewhere," I said.

"Not so fast. Whoever has the information is still in possession of it. That person can sell the information again and again. What's the buyer going to do when they find out they've been duped, sue him for breach of contract? Until the person who has it is arrested, this could go on indefinitely," she said.

My head started to hurt. "This is messed up. Hightower should have gone to the FBI and had them set up a sting. I don't hold much hope this will end well for anyone," I said.

"Au contraire. Tyler's a brilliant young man who worked for an elite government intelligence force before going into business himself. You heard about those boys who fly around in jets capturing data from thin air. The ones who stopped the terrorist attack from occurring on that Australian plane? He was part of that group. He's got a plan, and everything will be fine."

"Shouldn't we tell Hightower?" I asked.

"Are you sure he isn't part of the theft?" she asked.

I leaned back and sighed. In truth, I was not. "So what's your plan? We still reach out to Ryan?"

"Of course. We still don't know who the players are. But we go in under the guise of finding out if Fiona was with them that night of the crime and let him think we're on Fiona's trail."

I nodded my agreement. I patted her hand and walked toward Belle. I sat as she listened to a voicemail.

"Give me a second," she said.

I waited for her to finish.

"That was Seattle. Apparently, David tried to take the meeting without me since he got there early, but they said no. They've lined up people to meet with us and will have Boston on the speaker as well. I can see where this is going. When I get back, there's going to be trouble facing me. David's mad, and he's going to spread rumors."

"I'm sorry, Belle. Is there anything I can do?" I asked. I wanted to kiss her or reach for her hand, but it wasn't the time or place.

"Plan B, Lee, is always just a step away. Now what did Hightower say?" she asked.

I gave her the abbreviated version. I left out what Mary and I'd discussed as Mary's contribution was too hard to explain, and I wasn't sure how many laws both national and international her contact, Tyler, broke.

"So, when we arrive, you and Mary are headed to see Ryan. Where's Benjamin going?" she asked.

"No idea. But I hope a doctor's visit is on his agenda," I said.

She was about to say something more when the captain gave us instructions to buckle up as we approached Sea-Tac. Ten minutes later, we landed.

Mary and I approached the address Hightower had given us for Ryan. The place was a lovely tidy townhouse in a comfortable neighborhood. We pulled into the driveway, and as we did, I noticed the curtains move aside.

As we walked to the door, a middle-aged woman opened the door. "Can I help you?"

"Hi, I'm Lee Stone, and this is Mary Collier. We work for

Benjamin Hightower. We're looking for Ryan."

"I'm his mother; please come in," she said. "He's still not back to normal yet. Let me see if he can have visitors. Have a seat in the living room. Can I get you anything?"

We declined and made ourselves comfortable.

A well-dressed young man came down the stairs and gave us a suspicious once-over.

"I'm Ryan, and you are?" he asked, extending his hand in greeting.

"Lee and Mary. We're here on behalf of Benjamin Hightower," I said.

He turned to his mother and asked for some privacy, and she left the room.

"I've already been thoroughly investigated by the police," he started, and I put my hand up to stop him. He was getting defensive, and we didn't want that to go any further.

"We're not here about the murder. We're here about a gene-editing tool you, Fiona, and Dennis had been working on which has gone missing. We're trying to determine if you have any recollection of when you had access to it last," I said. Once it was out, it sounded accusatory, and I hope I hadn't blown our chance. "Mr. Hightower feels Fiona may have information about it, and we've been hired to track her and the data down."

"To be honest, that ketamine wiped my mind of a lot of information. So I have no specific recollection of when I had contact with it. However, based on our routine I'd say I was probably working on it the day I slipped into a coma," he said in an even manner.

"Do you have any recollection if Fiona was with you guys the night Dennis was killed?" I asked.

"Again I don't have a clear recollection. But I wouldn't have met Dennis there without her or some other woman. I'm pretty sure we were there for sex. The three of us had met there before, so I'd say it was likely she was there," he said.

"Well, that's a surprise. Hightower gave me the impression Fiona had a problem with Dennis at work and had tried to have him fired," I said.

That produced a startled look from him. Mary caught my eye and moved her hand, motioning for me to slow down.

"Well, that's news to me. She'd flirt and tease, but she never put out—" Ryan started.

"Did you socialize with her?" I interrupted, getting confused. Was it sex or flirting, or was she a voyeur at the motel?

"Yeah, dancing, drugs, and dungeons," he said.

"Dungeons?" I asked.

"S&M, man. We clubbed together. But it got intense at one of them," he said.

"How so?"

"Some guy she knew from LA showed up and wrecked the whole mood, made Dennis and me on edge. So we stopped going with her. The dude was really intense."

"Can you describe him?" Mary asked.

He gave us a description that sounded like Jeremy Stamos. Mary showed him a picture, and he identified Jeremy as the guy who'd been hassling them.

"I see. So Fiona and Dennis had no issues?" I asked.

"Well, not at work. But one time at a club Dennis dropped some acid, and he called her some names that were pretty raw and tried to force her to have sex. But he was out of his mind and so wasted he couldn't get it up. That was the only time, and it was like three months ago," he said.

He certainly had a selective memory.

"If someone wanted to sell the gene tool information, how would someone do it?" Mary asked.

"Ma'am, I have no idea. I'm in research and development, not sales and acquisitions," he said.

He had an answer for everything. It was evident if he had the drive we weren't going to get anywhere with him.

Before I left, I needed one more answer. "You think Fiona and Hightower had a thing?"

"Is that a trick question? Like if I say yes I get fired?" he asked.

"No, it's just a random question," I said.

"Then it's too random to answer, and I need my job," he said.

The message was clear. Yes.

We thanked him, and his mother walked us to the door.

Once we left, I asked Mary, "Jesus, is everyone lying to us? We haven't had one story match with another. This guy seemed like he was hiding something with his 'I don't remember' routine."

"No need to break your brain. Tyler will get us the answers," she said. "Now find a place to eat; I'm starved. Belle should be done soon, so text her where we'll be."

"A bit bossy, aren't you?" I asked with a smile.

"I'm not getting any younger," she said.

I was about to answer with a snide remark when I got a text from Belle: Meet me at Crepe de France at Pike Place Market.

I showed Mary the text so she could plug in the GPS coordinates, and she punched the air.

Great, a sugar high was on the agenda.

CHAPTER
TWENTY-FIVE

Annabelle

HAVING FINISHED THE MEETING WITH THE SEATTLE POLICE, I SAT A moment longer confirming my plans with Mary and Lee. I finished my text and was putting my phone in my bag when I sensed someone sidle up next to me.

"Can we talk?"

"I'm on my way to meet Lee and Mary for lunch, so make it quick," I said.

"Take a seat for a minute," David said as the last person left the room. "What you did, coming out here without notifying me, was both reckless and hurtful. I've been your partner for three years now. We're supposed to watch each other's backs and share everything. What did you think you were doing, taking off like that without telling me or asking me what I thought?"

I shouldn't have been shocked, but I was. Little by little David had invaded my personal life over the last year to the point where he called me his work wife, and people just accepted it. At first, it sounded playful and protective. Now it was just plain creepy. As I thought about it, I realized he had no steady relationships and had spent increasingly more off-duty time with me. Rather than confront the problem, I'd allowed it to continue. I'd been afraid to address what was going on, because if I raised my voice or snapped at him it would escalate the issue.

"What I hear, is you want to control what I do," I said, looking him straight in the eyes to challenge him.

"No, what I said was I was concerned for you," he replied.

"A concerned person doesn't use police resources to trace someone's whereabouts and then jump on a plane to track down the person. I had four days off, and how I use my time is my business. If you can't see how wrong what you've done is, then there's no amount of talking that will help the situation. I'm not your work wife; I'm your colleague at work and not your partner outside of work. I like you, David, as a friend, and only as a friend. I'm not interested in a romantic relationship with you," I said, proud of keeping my cool and being mindful of his feelings.

His eyes remained focused on me. Laser focused, to the point it was uncomfortable. He stood and looked smugly down upon me. No, it was an expression of malice that crossed his face. "Well, then enough said."

"So are we good?" I questioned.

"Belle, we are so not good that there's a black hole of not good between us," David sneered. "I'll make the lieutenant aware of what has transpired. You run along and enjoy your lunch." He grabbed his keys from the table and left. No good-bye, no looking back.

My exciting news to share with Lee and Mary had been entirely deflated. I'd witnessed David in action when he'd bullied fragile people into doing what he wanted. He'd used physical force without care or consequence. Now he was turning on me because I'd rejected his feelings for me. My mind whirled at the possibilities of what he could do to me, and I realized he was playing a game with me. His game was to make him the focus of my life, wondering what he would do and worrying about when it would happen. David wanted me entirely focused on him and thinking about him every moment of the day. He didn't care if how I felt about him was negative or positive, as long as my world revolved around him.

The door opened, and one detective who'd been at the meeting entered. "Belle, I've got some further information. Can you stay for a moment?"

He sat in the chair next to me and opened a folder.

"You just came from LA. Did you come across a woman named Claire Redson?"

My body stiffened, and my heart rate kicked up a notch. "Yes, we did. She was Fiona's roommate. Why?"

"Someone stabbed her an hour ago. The assailant's description was the same MO as the others. So it narrows his location down, and LA is taking the lead on this," he said.

"Is she dead?" I whispered. Had we caused this? Should we have seen it coming? My gut clenched with guilt. Was there anything we could have done to have prevented it?

"She's in critical condition and on her way into surgery," he said.

"If you give me the LA detective's contact, I'll follow up," I said.

"Here's the file so far; take it with you. I have a copy."

I shook his hand and left. Should I call David with the new information? Probably. Would I? Unlikely.

Lee texted me to confirm they had arrived and where they were seated, and I made my way to them. Mary had already ordered coffee and what could only be described as a pastry buffet of samples, which took up the center of the table.

"Sorry I'm late," I apologized. I was out of breath and could feel my cheeks were heated and flushed.

Lee looked at me in an assessing manner. "Take a minute; we've got all day."

I was about to answer him when Mary's phone buzzed, and she put it to her ear. Someone was speaking to her, and once the person stopped, she disconnected. "Our hot point has now changed to the LA vicinity. Tyler's working on an exact location."

It would do no one any good to discuss what had transpired between David and me. David was my problem to deal with, and I needed a plan. But not one hastily put together. So I kept the focus on the murders.

"Because of the fluid nature of the murders, the departments have kept an open channel and assigned a person from each state to be the point person. Each city tapped into their CCTV cameras, and after sifting through the footage, isolated a frame with the full face of the assailant. It's Jeremy Stamos. He was wearing a wig and trench coat, and posed as a woman. And trust me, his disguise was amazing. He looked like a woman, despite his size and build."

"I knew it!" Mary exclaimed, banging her hand on the table.

"You did not," Lee said, rolling his eyes. "He was on your short list of suspects, but so were ten other people."

Before she could argue, I put up my hand to stop any further discussion. "Stop. There's more."

Just then the server came and took my order, a welcome break so I could get Mary to refocus.

"Claire has been stabbed and is on her way to surgery," I said, and waited for the explosion. They did not disappoint me. "We're working under the theory it was Stamos, and I'm on my way back to LA after we finish here," I said, taking a sip of my coffee.

"Then so are we," Mary responded. "Since Tyler said to go to LA, that's where we're going."

Lee looked at his watch and said, "We have less than twenty-four hours until the auction goes live. Mary, how sure are you that Tyler can pinpoint the exact location of the person controlling the auction?"

"Lee, Tyler's a magician. There's no doubt once this goes live, and the lines are open and unimpeded he'll have a location. The fact he already has it narrowed down to a five-mile radius is huge. We can position ourselves within that radius. When it's time to move, it won't take us too long to reach the place where this is occurring," Mary said.

"People, I'm struggling here trying to decide if we should pull the plug on this and alert law enforcement," Lee said.

I raised my hand. "Law enforcement, sitting right here."

"Yes, but will your authority carry over to another state?" he asked.

"Lee, don't insult yourself or me. Now you're making excuses to dump the case because it has become a clusterfuck. You know even a private citizen can make an arrest, so don't go there. Now, if you want to get Jackson's approval, so be it. But I'm heading south on the murder case, and I'd be happy to do a stakeout on yours," I said.

He was about to say something, but our crepes and

pancakes were served. We waited for the server to leave.

"Leave Jackson out of this," Mary said with a raised eyebrow for emphasis. "I'm a partner and lead on the case. I've just Googled the California statute Belle is probably referring to, and she's correct. So you can come on the stakeout with Belle and me or sit in a café waiting for the auction to go down. Your choice," Mary said, forking her crepe and I smiled. God love Google.

She had him. Even without Mary's confirmation Lee knew we were covered under federal and state law. Once I'd arrested the person selling the information, it would eventually become a federal issue. The feds played by looser rules than the state, so I knew we wouldn't have trouble with them. Now Hightower, he might have some explaining to do. I might have some as well as to why I didn't report this ongoing investigation. I'd deal with that later.

"OK. I'd like to err on the side of caution, but obviously, we can't get law enforcement involved at this point, and we need to take some action. Mary, can't your contact get in trouble for this?" Lee asked.

"Considering the man is over seven thousand miles away, I don't think he's worried," she said.

Lee and I both swung our heads her way, but before we could ask a question, she put her hand up.

"Don't ask; don't tell. That way everyone maintains plausible deniability."

"Should we ask Hightower to use his jet?" Lee asked.

"Since we haven't cleared him, I say no," Mary said. "We don't want him warning anyone we're coming."

"Oh, I forgot to ask. How did your interview go with Ryan?"

"Well, it seems he's still in bad enough shape that his mom is taking care of him. Or maybe he lives with her. We didn't ask. Anyway, I didn't get the impression he was involved. He didn't have the balls to answer our question whether he thought Fiona and Hightower were having an affair. So I don't think he's the mastermind behind a theft and international auction of this magnitude. So again, until we catch someone red-handed, we're still wide open on the suspect list," Lee said, pushing his uneaten plate of food forward.

"And you, Mary, what's your opinion of Ryan?" I asked.

"A follower and not a leader. More like a kid looking for a good time, and I agree, not a mastermind of a heist of this magnitude," she said.

Lee chuckled.

"What are you laughing at?" Mary asked with a tone that showed she was offended.

"'Heist.' Who uses the word 'heist'?" he said, shaking his head.

I rolled my eyes. I needed to get this back on track. "OK, let's finish up. I have permission from the lieutenant to buy a plane ticket to LA for myself. Let's make the arrangements right now. It should only take us an hour to get to the airport. Check to see what flights leave in two hours," I said.

Once Lee had booked the flight reservations, we paid our bill and left for the airport. Mary rode with me.

I knew the ride would not be a silent one, so I braced for Mary's inquisition.

"David?" she asked as she raised both her eyebrows.

"What about him?" I asked knowing where she was headed but trying to use diversionary tactics.

"What did he do when he saw you?"

I searched for the best way to answer and decided on the truth. "He's going to be trouble. Just how much I don't know. He's hurt and angry, but there isn't much I can do about it. He tends to act out when he's mad. I thought about calling my boss and getting ahead of it. But what if part of this is a bluff or a mind game? Then I would have made a mistake telling my lieutenant for no reason."

"So you'll wait to see if he calms down?" she asked.

"Yes, but I always have a plan B," I said.

"Does that plan B involve Lee?" she asked.

Without even thinking, I answered, "Yes."

Mary smiled, and the rest of the trip to the airport was silent.

CHAPTER TWENTY-SIX

Fiona

THE ADRENALINE RUSH FROM LAST NIGHT'S ACTIVITIES MADE IT impossible to sleep or even rest. What the hell was Ben doing there, and where were Lee and Detective Hughes?

I kept remembering that dead woman's battered body. The image kept floating in front of me, a ghost that would haunt me for life. Who did that to her and why? Ray swore it wasn't one of his men, and I believed him. Jordy and Law seemed genuinely surprised by the state of Ben and the woman.

This whole project had turned into such a nightmare.

I found my phone in my bag and dialed the number I'd called countless times.

"Hello," the male voice said from the other end. I couldn't tell if the slurring was from sleep or drugs, but I needed him fully engaged.

"I need your full attention. Are you on drugs?" I asked.

"Just a few," he slurred back at me.

"Then I need you to get up, take a cold shower, and call me back in ten minutes with a coffee cup in hand and caffeine infusing your body," I said. "I need you on your toes and your brain engaged."

He disconnected without saying if he was going to follow my instructions or if he planned to go back to sleep.

I walked to the window to admire the view. A magnificent burst of flowers lined the walkway, and as far as the eye could see bushes with bright flowers covered the area. A large pool was tucked in the corner, and when the auction was finished, I might just take a dip.

The computer screen glared back at me, taunting me to take a peek and see if bidders were lining up like shoppers do on Black Friday, waiting to be the first to enter. One quick peek wouldn't hurt. I woke the computer up with a tap to the space bar, and the neon green digits flashed in front of me.

The beauty of the dark web was it allowed you to operate under the cloak of anonymity and set up your operation as you wished. Everything was ready for the auction to start in four hours. Each participant had logged on earlier and placed an opening bid. At exactly noon the bidders would have precisely eight minutes to compete for their prize, and the last bid at the eight-minute mark would automatically win. The three final bidders who remained were required to place $110,000,000 in an account as an escrow. If they weren't in the final bid, the bank had instructions to release the funds.

I decided not to transfer the data to the cloud; recent events had indicated it was too unstable and not secure enough to depend on for my purpose. All the encrypted information resided on a server outside the United States. Once the computer automatically accepted the final bid at the eight-minute mark and the transfer of funds was complete, then the information would be released. I laughed, remembering the look on his face when I'd told him I had transferred the data so there was no way he could screw me over. He'd gone for my throat; I suppose out of anger. But, didn't he understand when his fingers squeezed my neck I enjoyed the tenuous hold I had hanging between life and death? Couldn't he tell I fed off the rage in his eyes knowing I bested him? He'd played my games before, and he should have known my pleasures and fears. I suppose I could have done this all by myself, and he would never have seen me again. However, looking over my shoulder for life, waiting for his mercenaries to hunt me down, isn't the way I chose to live. No, sharing the spoils, but maintaining control over how the sale played out proved satisfactory. He'd get his share but under my terms.

I wondered if Ray had cameras in the house. Probably. The man's a security nut, so I'd need to be careful of my actions and how loud I spoke. Because of last night's fiasco, things had escalated to the uncomfortable point where I needed to accelerate my plans to leave the US. If anyone wanted to follow me, it would prove difficult. I had four travel itineraries in place, and at the last minute I'd choose one to follow and leave the other three as false leads.

The phone jolted me out of my thoughts. I walked over to the sink, turned the water on, and leaned in toward the fast stream to drown out the camera's ability to pick up the conversation.

"Hello," I answered.

Silence at the other end and a hang up. No number registered.

I decided that enough time lapsed and called him back. He answered on the first ring.

"What the ever-loving fuck were you thinking?" I asked.

Dead silence. Dead air.

"I thought we had a deal? We both agreed on a plan, and I followed it to the letter." My voice escalated with my anger.

Dead silence. Dead air.

"Why would you draw attention to us? What was your thought process? Have you tipped over the edge toward crazy town? Do we need the world breathing down our necks when we're so close?"

Dead silence. Dead air.

"The auction starts at noon. Once we receive our funds, I never want to hear from you again, or I swear to God I will have someone hunt you down and kill you," I threatened, and he knew me well enough to believe me.

Ben disconnected.

There was nothing else to do until I pressed the start button for the bidding to commence. My head started to twinge with the beginning of a migraine, and I felt the pain and pressure behind my eyes begin to build. Stress brought on headaches. My mind needed calm, and I couldn't indulge in a bout of anger, which could cause a misstep. If I didn't stay focused, even a small mistake could ruin this operation.

My plan to steal the data had been flawless. If only Dennis hadn't stumbled on my plan.

But that fiasco last night. That was why I didn't work with others; you never knew when they would go off script. But I still held all the cards. The server and the auction were under my control. Without me, years of work would disappear, and I was willing to do whatever it took to maintain control of that.

I needed to clear my head. I slipped on my tennis shoes and grabbed a bottle of water, took my phone, engaged the alarm, and headed out toward the trail.

What a lovely place. Ray had added landscape touches that made you feel like you were walking through a natural forest. As I finished what must have been about a mile walk, a lake and wood benches came into view. It was the perfect place to sit, decompress, and let my mind wander. As I came closer to the area, I saw a dock with a small motorboat attached. I wondered if the keys were in it, and if Ray would mind if I borrowed it for a spin. I'd come back after the auction and check it out, but all I wanted now was to sit on the bench and listen to some music. I pulled my phone from my pocket, put my earbuds in, and sat with my face to the morning sun. I could get used to this life. Not here, but maybe Lake Garda or Lake Como in Italy.

Closing my eyes, I immersed myself in the music, letting my mind dump the negativity and absorb the surrounding quiet, making myself forget all the distractions of the day.

Suddenly, I felt someone removing my right earbud. A man so close I could feel his hot breath against my skin. I froze.

"Good morning, Fiona," he whispered, placing his left hand on my left shoulder and giving it a gentle squeeze. "Mrs. Abajian has sent me to have a conversation with you."

As I moved to stand, I felt something small and sharp push against the skin of my neck. Sharp enough and with enough pressure to make me realize if I moved there would undoubtedly be a problem.

Mahir's mother. That woman had been a thorn in my side from the start. Initially, Mahir had proved an easy target. Quiet, docile Mahir, always so polite. What was $100,000 to them to sweep an embarrassing event under the carpet and settle my claim?

How did this man get in here and how long had he been following me? Was he the one who'd gone through my hotel room?

"Well, you've got me at a disadvantage. Say what you came to say and go," I said with confidence.

His breathing against my neck was even, and the instrument stayed in place.

He chuckled and said, "You're a feisty little thing, aren't you? Full of bravado for sure. Tell me, Fiona, with all the men who would do anything for your attention why Mahir?" he asked.

He had an accent similar to Mahir's, Armenian. Was he a relative? I hoped he was, because he was about to be played. And I'd enjoy playing with him.

"Mahir liked to fly his freak flag. At first, he was a bit shy. But when I opened the wild world up to him, he totally immersed himself in it. He had some ideas about pain and pleasure that even pushed my safe boundaries," I said with an air of confidence. That should embarrass him and shut him up.

And for several minutes it did.

"So—" he started.

"So I'm saying you can tell *Mom* that her little boy was a high-octane fetish freak. He lost his shit one night in a frenzy, which led him to beat and sodomize me while he yelled her name."

These people were unbelievable. Why couldn't they leave me alone? But maybe this was an ordained event for me to get the final word for messing with my settlement plans.

"And did you kill him for any particular reason? Or were you cleaning up loose ends before you left the country?" he asked, grabbing my hair to stabilize my head.

Well, that got my attention.

"How do you know about my plans?" I asked, trying to stand, but the hold he had on my hair made it impossible.

"Sit down, or I will slit your throat," he insisted and used that opportunity to jab the sharp object in a little more.

"I didn't kill him," I said. But the quiver in my voice even left me doubting that statement.

"You or someone you sent as your emissary, no difference," he said with a calm that was unsettling.

These people really think I killed him. Well, that changes this whole scenario. I had to think. If I argued, it would undoubtedly show guilt.

"I've got things to do, so finish what you came to say," I said, starting to squirm.

"As you wish." I could almost hear a smile in his voice.

Shit.

"Do you see that boat over at the dock?" he asked.

"Yes," I said and swung my eyes that way, but the way he maintained control of my head I couldn't turn to look at it.

"We're going to walk over there, and you're going to get in the boat," he said as he yanked my hair, forcing me to stand.

I tried pulling away, but the hold he had made it impossible. *Had I played this all wrong? Jesus, I'd allowed him to take control.* "You're kidnapping me?" I asked more angry than frightened. Fear hadn't yet entered my mind.

He walked and pushed me toward the boat. As isolated as this place was, no one would hear me scream. With everything that should have gone through my mind, the only thing I could think of was if I wasn't manning the computer for the auction, the information would reside on some obscure server until it was finally purged. No one would ever find it.

I heard our shoes echo against the old dock floor. *Should I break free and try to run? Or try to jump into the lake and swim away? Or maybe, when we start to head out, hit him with the hope of knocking him overboard?*

As if my body had unconsciously signaled my thoughts, he

reached into his pocket, pulled out a plastic zip tie, and secured my hands together at the wrists behind my back.

Standing behind me, he ordered, "Get in," as he guided me. "Sit there."

The boat was just a small motorboat and not much room for maneuvering.

OK, I would bargain with him. "Money? You want money?" I asked.

He remained silent.

"Sex?"

He sneered.

While I sat there contemplating my escape, he moved the motorboat away from the dock, but not so far I couldn't swim back. *Good, he probably is going to scare the shit out of me and then let me swim back. What an idiot. What made him think I wouldn't hunt him down and kill him?*

Suddenly he cut the engine and sat looking at me. Studying me.

"So, do you still say Mahir brutalized you and raped you?" he asked, leaning forward with his forearms on his thighs and hands clasped between his legs. The man had a dangerous look about him, and I came to believe, at this point, he was probably not a family member. He was too detached.

I raised my head and said, "I know he did."

He nodded, taking in my statement. Thinking about it.

"Let me tell you a story about a young man who lived in Armenia. Two countries, Armenia and Azerbaijan, had been immersed in conflict since 1994. In 2008, the brutality in the region escalated, and hatred between the two countries led to unimaginable bloodshed. A young Armenian man was caught in the company of a young Azerbaijan woman. A woman he loved and respected. And for the brief moment they'd indulged in their chance at love and happiness, that man was dealt multiple blows that left him physically incapable of ever performing sexual intercourse in a normal fashion for the rest of his life. His family was intimidated and fled Armenia, then settled in New York where they became productive citizens. Are you following me?" he asked.

I nodded.

"So I'm telling you it was impossible for Mahir to do what you accused him of," he said, his black eyes holding mine. There was a calm about his speech that was so unsettling I wanted to scream.

"That can't be true. Why wouldn't he reveal that when he was arrested?" I challenged. "Why go through the investigation?"

"Because it would have humiliated him as a man and made him a laughing stock at the school. What woman would want him? If the legal action had gone further, it would have been revealed."

As I processed what he said, I remained silent. Check and mate.

"You're probably wondering what will happen next," he said reaching into a box next to him.

He took out a small glass vial and a syringe. He removed the metal cap from the vial and pulled the plastic cap from the syringe. He then pierced the orange rubber top with the needle and pulled back the plunger to fill the chamber with fluid. Once that was done, he put the vial back in the box.

He suddenly jabbed the needle into my thigh and pushed the plunger to empty the syringe contents into my body.

"I'm administering a drug called Anectine into your thigh. This drug will immediately start shutting down the ability of your nervous system to send impulses to your muscles. You might wonder what that means. That means you'll be paralyzed, and then you won't be able to breathe, and then your heart will stop."

I stared at him as panic flooded my body. My hands were restrained, and I had nowhere to go. I knew what Anectine was and could do. You suffocated to death as your brain recognized everything going on. Already my body was shutting down.

"Your brain will continue to function, but you won't be able to move your lips to beg for your life. All you can do is embrace the panic of what's happening. I'll walk you through it, so you'll know what to expect. Your muscles will twitch. When I'm sure your lungs aren't able to take in any air because your diaphragm is paralyzed, I'll top the dose off, just a tiny bit. I want you conscious, but unable to respond to your brain's commands. Then I'll cut the ties, drop you in the lake, and motor away."

"Why?" was all I asked as I felt my ability to move my lips become difficult.

"Because the lie you just told me is the last lie you will ever tell."

CHAPTER TWENTY-SEVEN

Annabelle

"**P**EOPLE, CAN WE ALL AGREE SOMETHING'S WRONG HERE?" LEE asked as we waited for instructions from Mary's contact on where to go. The area just outside LA proper gave us the ability to sit and wait without worrying about being asked to move.

As soon as he asked that question we heard the booming whirl of helicopter blades overhead. The thump thump thump drowned out all other noise as it circled three times, hovered, and left.

As we watched the helicopter leave, Mary's phone rang. Once again there was no conversation on her end; she just listened to the person speaking.

After she disconnected Mary told us, "Tyler said he hasn't been able to pick up any activity from the auction site, and his people did an area sweep just now. Nothing is being transmitted from this area."

"Well, it's only fifteen minutes late," Lee said. "What if someone's trying to build up the tension?"

"The way Tyler explained it to me these things are strictly regulated. The bidders have already placed their opening bid funds into a reserve escrow account to show good faith. Once the bidding is over, the money is released by an automatic trigger. The question is, if the bidding doesn't occur, what happens to that money? Does it get released after a specific time, or does it stay there forever?" Mary asked.

"So what you're saying is that it's likely something has happened to prevent this auction," I said.

"Who knows? I'm flying blind here as well," Mary said.

My phone rang. "Hughes."

What I heard caught me by surprise. I gave the detective who'd called my location so a squad car could pick me up.

"LAPD picked up Jeremy Stamos and offered me a ringside seat at his interrogation."

Shock reverberated through the car. Mary was the first to ask the how and when questions, but I had limited information to give her.

"Don't forget; all we have right now is circumstantial evidence. He's only a person of interest, and we can't put the murder weapon in his hands."

Lee shot me a "really?" expression.

"A cruiser is picking me up. How long are you going to stay here?"

"I'd say another hour. Tyler can continuously monitor the auction from his location," Mary said.

"What if the person found some way to divert the funds in all the escrow accounts and made off with it?" I asked.

"Why would the person running the auction take such a loss? The data is worth millions, so why just take the money from the opening bids? Unless of course there was no data or it was incomplete, and all this was a ruse. Let me call Jax and see what he says. He's probably waiting by the phone. He might want to confer with Hightower about when we should pull the plug."

I listened as Lee and Jax discussed the issue and then disconnected. Within five minutes or so Lee's phone rang.

When he answered his phone, he opened his door and stepped outside. Mary and I watched as Lee paced, and the longer he paced, the more animated his movements became. His expression grew more and more angry. Finally, he disconnected and remained outside the car. His breathing was rapid, and he looked off into nowhere.

Mary and I stepped outside the car and cautiously moved toward him.

"What happened?" I asked trying to decide whether or not to touch him.

"Hightower has lost his mind. He wants us to hack the website and cancel the auction," he said.

"That's impossible. We don't have those skills. You'd need someone like an advanced black hat hacker or some government nerd to do something like that," I said.

Mary was silent, and I sensed she was formulating a plan.

"Do you want my theory?" Mary asked.

Simultaneously, I said yes, and Lee said no.

"The yeses have it," she said. "I think Fiona and Benjamin are in this together—"

"Wait, I thought we'd discounted Fiona," Lee said, leaning against the car.

"Well, we never totally discounted her. We never considered that the two of them might be partners," she said.

"But if they're partners, why did Hightower send us after her? Why call attention to her?" Lee asked.

"Are you going to keep interrupting me or let me

hypothesize?" Mary asked.

He gestured for her to continue.

"I think they were in cahoots. I think they planned the whole thing together from removing the data to setting up the auction. I've said from the beginning, I thought it was difficult to believe a server could be totally wiped with no backup anywhere. My theory is they did it together, figuring they could get more money selling the information illegally than legally. And as an extra bonus, they could sell it privately over and over. Only one person I can see being able to truly wipe the server clean is Hightower. He pins it on her for plausible deniability, if the investigation goes south, and sends us off on a wild goose chase for two reasons. First, if the shareholders want a scapegoat, he's got one ready to serve up and can say, 'Look, I tried my best.' That's where we come in. And second, it puts her on notice that we're watching, if she gets any ideas about going this alone," Mary said.

We saw the squad car coming toward us. As much as I wanted to stay, right now I had an obligation to attend Jeremy Stamos's interrogation. We decided to meet back at the hotel café in three hours.

As I waited for Mary and Lee to arrive at the restaurant, I replayed in my mind the brief conversation I'd had with David not a half hour earlier. Things were going to get ugly when I went home.

I was lost in thought and heard Mary before I saw her.

"So what happened?" Mary said as she pulled back a chair. Lee was right behind her.

"It was very anticlimactic," I said, shaking my head.

"Oh, I was hoping for a dramatic build up and then a ta-da moment," Mary said as her shoulders slouched in disappointment.

"It was anything but exciting once he lawyered up. And now the jurisdiction fight begins. They really have nothing to hold him on here in California, and so Washington, Massachusetts, and New York are going to battle out who gets extradition first—"

"Washington? When did Washington come in?" Mary asked.

"This is so fluid and evolving that my head's about to explode. The working theory is Stamos was so obsessed with Fiona that he decided to dispense his own brand of justice to those he perceived had wronged or betrayed her—"

"Wait, am I missing something?" Lee asked. "This has never been discussed. I thought from the way it was going that Jeremy was trying to implicate Fiona. You know dressing up like her and leaving the wig hair evidence."

I slapped my palm to my head. "Right, I'm ten steps ahead of you. They told me at the station that apparently, before Claire went into surgery, she said, 'He said this is for betraying Fiona. Rot in hell. You didn't deserve to breathe the same air as her.' Claire was pretty incoherent and loaded up with pain meds, so that's all they got. We're making a leap that the 'he' was Jeremy. But really all we have is his presence in LA. So that's the working theory."

Lee sat back as a server placed our water glasses in front of us and took our order. "Look, it's an excellent theory, but the evidence is, well, let's say slippery. If Claire can identify him when she recovers as the 'he' she was referring to, then you've got motive for the murders and her attack. We already know you have the opportunity, because he was picked up on cameras. So that's a bridge to the crimes. But there's no direct evidence. Yes, his behavior is bizarre, but there's no murder weapon tied to him. You didn't say they found his clothes, which may have some blood spray to analyze, or the wig to make a definite match. What do you actually have to tie him to the crimes? The circumstantial evidence is good. But is it enough?"

"Right now, that's not my problem. I'm leaving it to the people with higher paygrades. Because in the end, we'll be hearing he's pleading the insanity defense, blah, blah, blah," I said.

"Not if it was premeditated," Mary piped in. "But I understand what you're saying. The one thing that I don't understand is why now? Why right when all this is going on with the drive does he decide to go on an avenger spree? Has Fiona got something to do with this? Was this her last hurrah?"

"Legal discussion over," I said. "The LAPD has him in custody, so there shouldn't be more murders. Wherever he's extradited first they'll probably do some type of forensic psychological evaluation. And let's not forget the man does have a history of violent crimes. He fits as someone having a predisposition for it, and he has a motive and opportunity. But was he working alone? The big question is, why did he go on this killing spree right now? So, what's going on with the auction?"

"Nothing. There hasn't been any activity at all," Mary said.

"Has anyone seen Fiona?" I asked.

"No," Mary said in a lowered voice. "Let's just say I may have information that she made four different plans to leave, and she's in the wind," Mary said, touching the side of her nose.

I knew better than to ask how she'd gotten this

information. "So, thoughts? Where do you go from here?" I asked.

"We were hired to find Fiona and the drive. We found her and couldn't prove she had the drive. We all believed she wasn't a part of the theft, until Mary's theory. Which, I might add is truly just a theory and has no basis in fact. The woman has a right to find a new job and leave. The fact she had four exit strategies just says she didn't want to be found. There's nothing to tie her to the murders. We found the auction site, in effect finding the data; therefore, my work is done," Lee said.

"So should I tell Tyler to stop looking?" Mary asked.

Lee's phone rang. "It's Jax," Lee said, answering. "Stone." He was very quiet, and there was minimal conversation before he said, "I'll tell them."

He disconnected and turned toward us.

"There was a shooting at Hightower's office," Lee said. "They don't have all the details. But apparently, Ryan came into the office with a weapon and shot Hightower point blank. Hightower's alive, but they're rushing him to the hospital."

"My God! What? Why? What was Ryan's motive?" I asked, as I pulled my phone out to call the Seattle detective assigned to the case. He answered immediately.

Lee and Mary waited while I gathered what information was available.

"Right now Ryan's back in the hospital and under arrest," I told them. "But apparently, everyone thought he was going in to talk to Hightower about returning to work, and then they heard a lot of arguing. He was yelling he wanted his cut and then a gunshot. No one else was hurt."

Lee stared at the table, but I could see his eyes moving back and forth deep in thought. "Well, there, you have all the pieces as far as I'm concerned," he said.

"What?" I asked.

I saw Mary open her mouth to offer an opinion and shook my head no at her. "I don't want to go into a 'what if' Ryan and Fiona were in it together. Or a 'what if' Fiona, Ryan, and Hightower were in it together," I said. "We could spend days on what-ifs and continue going down a rabbit hole of possibilities."

"This has been a horrible mess," Lee said, picking up his spoon and tapping the table with it. "Belle, it's pretty clear to me all three of them were in on it. Here's what I think. Ryan had access to the drive and stole it. Hightower wiped the servers, and Fiona was in charge of putting the drive up for auction. The auction never took place, and we don't know where Fiona is right now. Maybe she took off, and now the other two are left with nothing, wondering if the other is in cahoots with her. Hightower will probably be fired. Ryan will go to jail, and Fiona is probably sitting on some island sipping some fruity drink."

Lee was just hypothesizing, but it sure sounded plausible. Once a forensic computer team was in place I believed they would find Lee was right. We sat in silence; no one wanted to admit we all felt defeated. Everyone wants things tied up in a bow at the end. But maybe this wasn't the end. Maybe it was the start of peeling back the layers. Like how Hightower really came into possession of the editing tool and how Ryan so easily stole it.

Lee raised his eyes to Mary and said, "I'm done. This isn't for me. Everyone has lied to us. There has been total misdirection at every turn, and the body count keeps mounting. It's bad enough when the bad guys lie to you, but when the people you think are the good guys lie, then there really is no hope. I believe our client is guilty, and I'm hoping to God he gets caught. So maybe it's time to take another path where life isn't all about lies and misdirection. You and Jax will have my resignation tomorrow. I'm going to start my own wood sculpting business where, at the end, everyone will get something they like and be happy."

"That's what I wanted to hear." Mary smiled.

CHAPTER
TWENTY-EIGHT

Annabelle

THE MORNING LIGHT HADN'T EVEN PEEKED THROUGH MY SMALL apartment's curtains, and I was already dreading the day. I looked around the pitch-dark room and cataloged my life here in New York. It was dull and minimalist. There was no longer even a flicker of a flame to brighten the room or my life. My stomach clenched thinking about returning to work, even for a minute. There was no doubt in my mind David was going to be a problem. By now, he'd probably recruited some of his friends to give me a hard time. Just who he'd recruited would dictate how hard of a time I'd have making it through the day.

I let myself run the scenarios of what-ifs as my anger built and swirled around me. Faces flashed before me as I decided who would be my friend or foe. The sides lined up pretty evenly, despite the fact most people realized David's jokes weren't really jokes but ploys for power. Once he found your weak spot, you either played for his team or became a punching bag for him. I decided to pull myself out of it with a shower and coffee. If I was going to run the gamut of bad things that could happen, I should multitask while doing it. I passed my laptop on the way to the bathroom and realized I hadn't written anything in a week. Well, who could blame me? I was two chapters from the finish, and that would be my priority tonight. This was going to be a best seller. I felt it so strongly I wrote it on a sticky note and stuck it on the top of the loose pages of the manuscript. A call to the universe I was positive would be answered in my favor.

I pushed open the heavy door to the precinct and felt like I was entering a place I no longer belonged. What normally felt comforting, today seemed foreign. I received the usual hellos from the staff up front as I braced for a cold front from my colleagues in the back. The people who were supposed to be my people. Yet when I walked back, there was almost a festive air about the place. No one appeared to have been tainted by David, if he'd told them anything.

The first thing that caught my attention was a small murder board propped up on an easel. It had pictures of Jeremy Stamos and Mahir with some notes scribbled on it. The word "closed" was written across it in bold red letters. Surely they hadn't given up on this? Or was there an update I wasn't aware of?

I walked through the squad room past my desk and went to the back area where the lockers lined a wall. I retrieved a manila envelope from the small shelf of my well-used and dinged-up beige locker. My locker, just like my apartment, reflected my ability to leave without a trace. No roots and no commitment to a physical place.

"Lansing, what's with the closed notice on the Abajian case?" I asked.

"Didn't you hear? Last night that girl who'd been stabbed in LA came around after surgery. The first thing she did was ask the police for her phone. We got real lucky on this one. When she'd seen Stamos coming toward her, she'd hit record on her phone so she could catch him saying something she could use to get an order of protection. Well, she got a lot more than she bargained for. The sick fuck wanted to terrorize her before he killed her, so he went into great detail telling her how he'd killed the others and how he planned to kill her. And as a bonus he admitted to killing the guy in Seattle. Win-win for everyone. LA recovered her phone from evidence, and by God, there it was, a confession," he said, slamming his locker and locking it.

"Did they recover his clothes or any murder weapon?" I asked, excited. I had so many questions but so little time to ask, or we'd be late for the briefing.

"Last I heard they had just got a search warrant for the fleabag he was staying at," he said.

"You think LA would send us a copy of the confession so we can listen to it in full?" It was so surreal. For some reason I needed to hear, in his own words, why he went on a murderous rampage. I needed to listen to the inflection in his voice and try to determine if it was the voice of a deranged man or a psychopath.

"The captain already has a copy," he said with a wink.

Before going into the briefing, I took a moment to text Lee and Mary the good news and promised to call later. Mary responded immediately with a thumbs-up emoji, and Lee texted back "good luck."

After a quick trip to the bathroom to give myself a small pep talk, I entered the briefing area.

I was surprised to see David and the lieutenant engaged in a lively conversation that ended with the lieutenant slapping David on the back. Odd, David remained standing there instead of returning to his seat.

"OK, people, settle down, settle down. We have a lot to cover today, and we need to get rolling," the lieutenant said as he gestured for everyone to sit.

David remained standing in an arrogant pose with his arms across his chest and legs apart in a balanced position. His eyes swept to mine and held my stare.

"The good news is the Abajian case is closed. Last night Jeremy Stamos was charged with aggravated battery in LA after his latest victim identified him as her assailant. I just heard from the lead detective that they executed a search warrant and took a coat and wig into evidence that matches the description of the coat and wig in the footage from our cameras and Boston's. He was stupid keeping those things. But that wig cost a couple of grand, so I guess I can understand keeping it. But a trench coat? That's a pretty cheap purchase. They haven't retrieved the knife yet.

"The latest victim had some instinct to hit record when he approached, and we have him confessing to the murders along with his motive. Everyone needs to get their paperwork in order. At some point, you may need to rely on it when he comes back here for our whack at him. Every T needs to be crossed, and I dotted; there will be absolutely no speculation in your report. I don't want to read that you thought or felt something. I want to see what you did based on an occurrence and what the outcome was. I want that paperwork by the end of the shift," the lieutenant said, tapping his papers on the podium to straighten them.

"Who gets the papers?" Clackker asked.

"I'm coming to that," the lieutenant said, as David stepped toward the podium.

Well if that doesn't beat all. David was going to be the lead name on finalizing the case. I knew a hell of a lot more about the case than him. I had invested a lot of time into the case—triple what David had.

"Now, for some good news. David, step right up here," the lieutenant said as David came closer to the podium. "I'm proud today to announce that David Rizoli has been promoted to the rank of sergeant. He has worked tirelessly for…"

That's all that registered. It was like I'd been stricken deaf. David was going to be my boss and in charge of my future. Every worst-case scenario filtered through my mind, and the more I let the possibilities infect my mind, the more dismal my life looked. The fifteen-minute briefing ended with, "Detective Hughes, a moment in my office."

The long walk down the hall to the lieutenant's office hit me as what a defendant must feel like waiting for the verdict and sentence to be announced. I heard laughter inside his office and waited for it to die down. I gave two quick raps and stepped inside where he and David were waiting.

"Come in, Belle," he said waving me in, no longer laughing. "Take a seat. Now I'm sure you're as surprised as David was at his promotion. There was a lot of competition, but we'll get to that in a moment. I must say I'm disappointed and shocked to find out you were working the Stamos case out of the state without my authority."

David had ratted me out. No surprise.

"Yes, I was on my own time, but I'm not surprised Detective Rizolli told you."

"Normally, this would be placed on a review docket to determine what type of disciplinary action would be appropriate, but since the case is closed, I'm bypassing that procedure. No need for more paperwork to accumulate on my desk. A three-day suspension would be the usual disciplinary action, but I'm bypassing normal protocol. However, this behavior is unacceptable, and the next time something like this occurs, Belle, the consequences will be quick and serious."

David stood there with that smug look on his face. I watched how he bit his lower lip almost to the point of drawing blood to avoid laughing. I took a calming breath in through my nose and out. The adage "He who laughs last laughs best" held little solace for me.

"Yes, sir," I replied looking away from David and back to the lieutenant.

"David, Sergeant Rizolli, will be taking up his new position in a month. As that will leave you without a partner, he has recommended you go into the float pool and float to precincts where extra bodies are needed. Budget cuts prevent us from hiring another detective to replace him, so that leaves you without a partner. What do you think? Is this something you could work with?" the lieutenant asked, sitting back and tossing his glasses on his desk.

David raised an eyebrow, waiting for me to explode. He would be disappointed.

"Well, sir, that would be an excellent idea—" I started and watched David's face reflect a bit of shock, "however, I have something that might preclude that becoming a necessity."

I stood and pulled the paper from the envelope, added a date to it, and handed the paper to the lieutenant.

I watched as he placed his glasses back on his nose and seemed to read it twice. He looked at me and handed it to David. David's jaw tightened, and I thought I saw his hand tremble as he handed the paper back.

"Have you thought this through, Belle? I can hand this back to you and just pretend I didn't read it," the lieutenant said, placing it on his desk.

"Sir, I'm certain; I want you to accept it," I said, knowing I'd done the right thing.

"Why? Why now?" he asked, his face creased with worry.

"Lieutenant, this place has been my life, and it's been a good one. I've thrived working under your command, so I would never want you to think it has anything to do with you. Sometimes things happen that push you in a direction you never saw coming, and this is one of those times," I said, and smiled at him.

"Do you have a plan in place?" he asked with concern.

"Sir, I always have a plan B," I said.

I gave a month's notice that I was leaving, and as David transitioned into his position, the two of us worked well to distribute all our remaining cases. Once David realized he held no power over me, things eased up a bit. However, anger seemed to simmer just below the surface, never quite extinguished.

Within the month, Lee had set up his new wood sculpting business as he transitioned from Jackson's firm. The firm hired a new employee who was a bit of an odd choice. Dalia, the new employee, was an ex-assistant district attorney from the cyber-crimes division. A feisty redhead with a sharp tongue and good sense of humor.

In a plea deal worked out between all the states where Jeremy Stamos had committed his crimes, he gave the district attorneys' offices a confession in exchange for life in prison without parole. He admitted to having been obsessed with

Fiona from the time she was a member of Fire and Ice. He described her as his possession, someone he owned and felt an obligation to take care of. She was, in his eyes, his responsibility. Yet when asked why he dressed like her and left clues implicating her in the crimes, his answer was strange. He wanted her arrested and held somewhere he could visit her. He couldn't convince her not to leave the country, so he'd tried to prevent her from leaving.

Hightower was convicted by an alphabet string of federal agencies on over a dozen charges and would be behind bars for years to come. Ryan, although probably a part of the theft, wasn't indicted on any charges from that incident. However, he would be spending the next eight years in prison for aggravated assault and battery with a deadly weapon.

"Well, how does it feel to be leaving?" Lee asked.

"Freeing," I said, giving him a squeeze as we walked around the empty apartment.

"You're sure it's OK to leave the key under the mat for the landlord?" he asked.

"Absolutely, he'll have the broker showing the apartment in an hour," I said. "So let's pick up my bags and get this show on the road."

"No regrets?" he asked.

"No regrets," I said. "I'm excited to see the warehouse you set up for your work."

"You think Fiona is at her new job?" I asked. "Will we ever find out what happened to her?"

"My gut can't even formulate an answer. We were sent on a wild goose chase that started with her and what happened to her might be the only answer we won't ever have. The best I can do is say its main purpose was to bring us together," he said, gently kissing me.

"Now. I have a surprise, and Mary will kill me if I spill the beans, but I'm going to live wild. Mary had the construction people wall off space in the warehouse for an office for you. If you get tired of being alone, you can write there during the day when you want. It's soundproof, and she really did a great job decorating it. Well, to be honest, it probably was her niece, Emma, and Jax's wife who did the decorating. But we'll give her credit, or she'll be hurt," Lee said.

"God, Lee, I feel like a freeloader. She's letting us use her house and now this?" I said.

"Belle, Mary's thrilled to have moved in with Emma to help her with the twins. I offered her rent for the place, but she said it was paid off, and all she asked was we keep it up and if we wanted to, improve on it. I'm certain she wants us comfortable so we won't want to leave, and so we'll buy her house once we're settled there," Lee said.

I gave the place one last look.

"Are you sure there's nothing else you want to take as a reminder?" he asked.

"Nope. Furniture is with Goodwill and all I want is in my two bags. Letting go is freedom," I said.

We crossed the threshold of my apartment, and I entered my new life.

THE END

OTHER BOOKS

ABOUT THE AUTHOR

Kathleen McGillick is a practicing attorney who sorts through the pieces of people's lives much like a puzzle master. Each piece carefully placed makes up the whole of this unique person. Who is this person? What drives them? What makes them tick? What are their deepest secrets and unspoken fears? No surprise she ended up writing a legal thriller!

Why and how people commit crimes has always held an interest for her and that is reflected in her latest novel.

Kathleen grew up in New York and has lived in Georgia for thirty-three years. She has enjoyed a career in nursing as well as the law. After obtaining a Bachelor of Science degree in Nursing, and a Master of Science degree in Nursing she set out fifteen years later to obtain her Juris Doctorate. This varied education and experience helped mold the eclectic writer she is today.

She considers herself a global citizen and an avid international traveler. With her son in tow as an early travel companion she has visited over eighteen countries in the last twenty years. Some cities like Paris, London and Rome deserving multiple returns. A pilgrimage to London at least every two years is a must to keep her batteries charged and give her the history fix she craves. In her spare time, you can find a book in her hand or wandering through an art museum. Kathleen is a mother and grandmother as well as the food lady to her cats and any wild life that wanders to her porch.

CONNECT WITH K. J. MCGILLICK

www.facebook.com / KJMcGillickauthor

kjmcgillick@gmail.com

www.kjmcgillick.com

twitter.com / KJMcGillickAuth